Magic's Embrace...

Gaining his feet, he offered her his hand.

She hesitated a moment before taking it.

Not that he could blame her after what had just happened. He pulled her gently to her feet.

For a moment, his gaze searched hers.

And then he drew her into his embrace.

And kissed her.

She tasted as sweet as he remembered. She fit into his arms as if she had been made for him and no one else. Her scent—tinged with magic and a hint of lavender—enveloped him.

Seleena pressed her fingertips to her lips, her gaze searching his. Why did he have this power over her? One kiss and she wanted to take him to her bed, to run her hands over his shoulders, explore the corded muscle in his arms, run her fingertips over his ridged belly. No other man had ever affected her so strongly, aroused her so quickly, intrigued her on so many levels.

He cocked his head to the side, a silent question lurking in his dark eyes.

Taking a deep breath, she eased out of his embrace. And immediately felt the loss of his warmth, his strength. His tattoo possessed a small portion of her own magic. Was that what made him so irresistible? But he also possessed a bit of Nardik's power. And Serepta's, as well. It was a potent combination.

He had been her daughter's lover.

She had to remember that.

Quinn's Lady

&

Quinn's Revenge

Amanda Ashley

ISBN: 1-68068-033-1
ISBN-13: 978-1-68068-033-1

QUINN'S LADY

PROLOGUE

Trapped in a prison of stone. How long had it been? One year? Two? How was it even possible that he could still be alive?

Was he alive? Or was this dream-like state really Hel—periods of awareness followed by bizarre dreams and nightmares punctuated by nothingness.

He tried to remember who he was, but he had no memory of himself. No recollection of his past. Only a sense of emptiness. Of loss.

How had he come to be here?

How?

The image of a woman flashed across his mind—a beautiful, treacherous woman with hair the color of cinnamon and eyes as black as the ebony caves of Brynn Tor.

Her name danced along the edges of his memory, always just out of reach.

A relentless hunger clawed at his vitals. All-consuming. Excruciating.

And then the blackness swallowed him up again.

Chapter 1

Seleena sat in her favorite rocking chair, one hand lightly stroking the big black cat sleeping on her lap.

She stared into the flames that danced and crackled in the fireplace while silent tears tracked her cheeks. Her daughter—her only child—was dead, though, in reality, they had lost Serepta years ago.

Guilt nibbled at her conscience. Was it her fault her daughter had chosen to pervert her gift and embrace black magic? Her fault that Serepta had chosen to enhance her magic by becoming a vampire? Seleena dabbed at her tears. Should she have tried harder to redeem Serepta? Had it even been possible?

In her heart, she knew she could have done nothing to help. Serepta had been blessed with a wonderful gift, but it hadn't been enough. She had craved power the way some craved strong drink, chased it relentlessly until she found what she was looking for. In the end, it had destroyed her...

Seleena rose so abruptly, Freyja tumbled from her lap.

Her daughter was dead, but what of the people she had left behind? Had they all fled the castle? Or, unaware of Serepta's demise, were they awaiting her return, unwilling to leave for fear of incurring her wrath?

Chanting a translocation spell, Seleena donned her cloak.

Moments later, she stood in the great hall of Serepta's black castle.

It was eerily silent, as if the very walls were holding their breath. She cocked her head to the side, listening intently, but heard only the faint sound of the wind scratching at the door.

Feeling as though she were walking across her daughter's grave, she made her way through the castle's rooms. All were empty of life. Only bits and pieces left behind by the previous occupants remained—among them a single shoe, a pair of trousers, an apron, a bonnet.

She went down to the dungeons last. It was here where Serepta had imprisoned the shape-shifter, Gryff Donovan. Here where she and Serepta's father, Nardik, had confronted their daughter, intending to deprive her of the magic they had once bestowed upon her. Here where Serepta had died.

Seleena closed her eyes and saw it all again…

Serepta tore free of her father's grasp. Bodies rigid, they stared at each other, a silent duel raging between them. Sparks exploded through the air.

Eyes blazing, Nardik hissed, "Now!" He lunged forward, his cloak folding around his daughter like the wings of a large, black bird until it covered her from head to heel. Seleena rushed forward at the same time, her arms wrapping around Nardik and their daughter.

Power seethed in the room as the three witches struggled.

And then, as if someone turned a switch, the air stilled. Seleena had backed up a few steps. Nardik's cloak fell away. He stood straight and tall, his dark eyes alight.

"What have you done?" Serepta stared at them, her eyes filled with confusion. "What have you done?" She screamed the words.

"Deprived you of your gift," Nardik said, his voice as cold as the stone floor. "You have abused it long enough."

"No! No, that's impossible!"

"I am sorry," Nardik said quietly. "Seleena, let us depart." Taking her hand, he turned to leave.

Serepta stood as though frozen, her expression blank. And then, eyes filled with rage, she lunged at Gryff, her fangs bared, her hands like claws.

With a growl, Gryff had shifted into a large, black wolf and sprang at the vampire's throat…

With a strangled cry, Seleena opened her eyes. A thought took her out of the dungeon and out of the castle. She stood there a moment, breathing in the cool, fresh air.

A twisting path led her into a garden where wildflowers bloomed in colorful profusion, even though the sun had set hours ago. Tall green and yellow ferns shared space with blood-red roses. A variety of trees grew to remarkable heights. Their leafy branches intertwined at one end of the garden, providing a thick canopy capable of blocking both sun and rain.

Curious, she followed one of the footpaths that meandered through the verdant foliage. Stone benches had been placed at intervals. Brilliantly colored peacocks wandered the grounds.

Rounding a bend in the path, she came upon a number of statues—soldiers and peasants, warriors and maidens—all remarkably life-like down to the last detail. The workmanship was truly amazing.

At first glance, they appeared made of stone, but as she drew closer, she realized they weren't statues at all, but flesh and blood rendered inanimate by a spell more horrible than death. She trailed her fingertips down the cheek of the nearest statue. It was a man. He wore no shirt, only a pair of tight-fitting buff-colored trousers and brown boots.

Seleena shook her head, sickened by such cruelty, by the horror reflected in the unblinking eyes of those who had displeased her daughter and paid a terrible price. With Serepta's death, it was unlikely that any still lived, but if there was a chance…

Bowing her head, Seleena called upon her magic, felt the very air around her hum with power as she chanted softly, then unleashed the spell with a wave of her hand.

And nothing happened.

Perhaps it was just as well, she thought. Who knew what manner of men and women were trapped inside the stone?

And then the statue in front of her moved. The cold shell that encased him fell away and he stood there, his dark blue eyes blazing with hatred. For a moment, he pinned her with his gaze, then, in a voice rusty with disuse, he growled, "Where is she?"

"If you're asking about Serepta, she's not here."

"Where is she?"

"Nowhere you can follow," Seleena replied.

"I don't care where in Hel she's gone," he declared. "Just tell me where to find her."

"I'm afraid your need for vengeance must go unfulfilled," Seleena said quietly. "My daughter is dead."

He stared at her. "She was your daughter?" He wondered why he hadn't noticed the resemblance before. Though this woman wasn't as tall as Serepta, their features were similar. They both had waist-length hair the color of cinnamon. But Serepta's eyes had been Hel-black. This woman's were a clear dove gray. "Are you a witch, too?"

Seleena nodded. "I'm sorry for the pain she caused you."

He was a handsome man, tall and broad-shouldered, with shaggy, dark brown hair and the tawny skin common to those from the north country. A faint white scar ran in a jagged line from just under his right ear to his collarbone. He might have been a soldier, she thought. Or perhaps someone in law enforcement. He had that look about him. A black dragon tattoo covered his left arm from his shoulder to his elbow. The creature's forked tail curled around his bicep.

"Pain?" He barked the word. "Pain! Do you know what it's like, to be unable to move or to speak? To be trapped in smothering darkness?"

"No. It must have been horrible. But it's over now."

"Is it? How do I get back the days or years I've lost?"

Seleena shuddered. Could he truly have survived *years* in there? A few days would have been beyond bearing.

He shifted from one foot to the other. Tension poured off him like heat from a stove.

Seleena took a wary step backward as his eyes went red. "Vampire!" She spat the word as she summoned her magic once again. "Another bloody vampire!"

CHAPTER 2

Quinn's gaze moved to the pulse in the witch's throat and felt a faint stirring similar to hunger only much stronger. She had called him a vampire? Was that what he was?

The witch took several steps backward, one hand at her throat. "Don't even think about it," she warned. "My blood will sicken you to the point of death."

"I don't believe you."

"No?" She pushed her hair behind her ear, then cocked her head to the side, a challenge in her eyes. "Come see for yourself."

He took a step forward, then paused. What if she was telling the truth? He was in enough pain. "Why don't I remember being turned?"

She shrugged. "Perhaps she wrought the change just before turning you into a living statue."

He shook his head. You'd think a guy would remember something as life-changing as that.

"How are you called?"

"Quinn."

"I am Seleena. How did you meet my daughter?"

"I was on my way to Bosquetown." He frowned, wondering how

he could remember something as insignificant as that but couldn't recall being turned into a vampire. Or a statue.

"Is that where you live?"

"I don't live anywhere."

She lifted one brow. "Why not?"

"I'm a bounty hunter." The memory came easily. "I don't stay in one place long enough to put down roots."

"A despicable profession," she muttered under her breath.

He shrugged. "It's a living."

"Who do you work for?"

"Jagg." It wasn't his whole memory that was gone, he decided. Just parts of it.

"The owner of the slave auction?"

"He pays well," Quinn said, grinning. "And there are benefits."

Seleena grimaced. She could only imagine what those "benefits" might be. Jagg sold men, women, and children to the highest bidder. Except for Bosquetown, such human trafficking was illegal in all the other regions of Brynn Tor.

Moaning softly, Quinn wrapped his arms around his waist and doubled over.

He needed to feed, Seleena thought. But letting him prey on some poor unfortunate soul was out of the question.

Grabbing his hand, she murmured a quick incantation. A moment later, they were in the timbered hills of Nardinnia.

Quinn shook his head. "How about a little warning next time?" He glanced around. "What are we doing here?"

The witch gestured at a herd of wild cattle.

"Yeah? So?"

"You can survive on animal blood."

He stared at the big, shaggy, brown and black cows. "Are you shittin' me?"

"No," she said, her tone covered in ice. "I am not *shitting* you. If you're thirsty, drink your fill."

"I need blood, witch. Not milk."

"Cows have blood."

Quinn shook his head. "I want human blood." He started walking away, only to be brought up short when she waved her hand. "What the Hel!"

"I will not let you feed on humankind."

"Dammit, woman, you're not my mother, or my sire, or my keeper. Turn me loose!"

"Perhaps you would like to be a statue again?" she asked, ever so sweetly. "You would look quite handsome in my fountain at home."

Eyes red, fangs bared, he glared at her. Try as he might, he couldn't move.

She folded her arms over her chest, one foot tapping impatiently.

Five minutes passed. Ten.

"Fine." He spat the word through clenched teeth. "I'll feed on the damn cows."

She freed him with a wave of her hand. He stalked away, his whole body screaming resentment. She found a log to sit on, then watched curiously as he approached the herd. Most of the cattle moved away, some instinct warning them of danger. A few watched him warily, then they, too, trotted away.

Quinn wasn't deterred. With preternatural speed, he hurled himself at the nearest animal, wrapped his arms around its neck and wrestled the creature to the ground. He glanced at Seleena over his shoulder, his eyes blazing red, and then sank his fangs into the cow's throat.

Gagging, Seleena turned away, her mind filling with ghastly images of her daughter bending over some poor unsuspecting human male, drinking her fill.

She didn't hear Quinn's footsteps but she sensed him coming up behind her.

Vampire.

She spun around to face him, gathering a protective spell around her, but there was no danger. The cow he had fed on had rejoined the herd, grazing now as if nothing had happened.

Quinn grimaced. "I can't survive on that stuff," he remarked as he licked a bit of blood from the corner of his mouth. "Neither did Serepta. I know, because she fed on me before she turned me." He frowned. "She was able to walk in the sunlight. How was that possible?"

"She was a witch. Her magical powers allowed her to walk in daylight and eat and drink mortal food."

"Can you make me a witch?"

"No." She hesitated a moment. "But I can conjure the same spell for you so that you can walk in the sun. And consume mortal food, if you wish."

"Yeah?" His eyes narrowed suspiciously. "What's it gonna cost me?"

"Your promise not to feed on humankind."

He snorted. "I'm a vampire, remember? I can't make a promise like that."

"Then you must swear to me that you won't kill anyone, and you won't prey on children."

He considered a moment, then nodded. "I can do that."

"If you break your word, the spell will also be broken. It won't be pleasant."

"So, do it."

"I can't do it here." She held out her hand. "Come along."

He took her hand in his. It was small and warm. Fragile. One squeeze, he thought, and he could break her fingers.

She looked at him, one brow arched, as if she knew exactly what he was thinking.

She murmured a few words in a language he didn't understand.

Quinn closed his eyes as her magic wrapped around him. It was warm, tingly, but not unpleasant. When he opened his eyes, they were in the great hall in Serepta's castle. He shuddered as he looked around, remembering all too clearly how easily he had succumbed to the allure of the beautiful vampire-witch, and the excruciating pain that had followed.

"Let's go upstairs," Seleena said. "I need a bowl and a little of your blood."

He trailed behind her. Their footsteps echoed off the walls.

"I take it you've been here before," Quinn remarked.

Seleena nodded. "Briefly." She moved slowly down the corridor, checking each room until she found the one she was looking for. It was large and square. The walls were white and bare save for a full-length mirror edged in gold. A long black table held a cauldron, a knife, several bowls in different sizes, some made of wood, some of silver. A shelf held a number of unlabeled jars and containers in various shapes and sizes.

"What is all that stuff?" Quinn asked, moving into the room behind her.

"Tools of the trade. Herbs. A few more exotic things."

"Like what? Eye of newt? Dragon's teeth?"

"Among other things." She picked up the athame and tested the edge of the blade with her thumb. "Give me your left hand."

Quinn held it out and she made a shallow gash in his palm. His blood was thick, dark red, almost black. She held his palm over a small silver bowl. He jerked his arm back, hissing with pain when his hand touched the basin. Few things could hurt him, but silver was one of them.

He bled only a few drops before the cut healed itself. She cut him again, and yet a third time, before she had enough. "What kind of magic is this?"

"It's an advanced form of mind magic and blood magic. I learned it from a wizard some years ago."

"Have you done it before?"

"No."

He looked at her, one brow raised, then shrugged. "Now what?"

"Be quiet." She opened a small blue jar and poured a small amount into the bowl. Then, using her finger, she stirred the bloody mix. Next, she took Quinn's hands in hers, closed her eyes and began to chant softly.

Power filled the room, lifting the hair on Quinn's arms, making it difficult to breathe. The contents of the bowl bubbled and hissed then turned into a dark mist. Unable to help himself, he breathed it in. When he would have backed away, her hands tightened on his. A shock sizzled through him, as if he had been kissed by lightning. It seared his veins like liquid fire. And then it was gone. He glanced at the bowl. It was empty.

Seleena dropped his hands and stepped away, unsettled by what she had felt when she touched him. Had he felt it, too, that sense of inevitability?

"What are you going to do now?" she asked.

Quinn shook his head. He had no idea how to be a vampire, knew little about them other than they were hard to kill, needed human blood to survive, and lived for a very long time. Time, he thought, what was he going to do with the years that stretched ahead of him? He had no home, no family. The only job he'd ever held was being Jagg's assassin. Probably not much call for that outside of Bosquetown.

Seleena shifted from one foot to the other. She couldn't stay in this place any longer. The walls, the floor, the very air itself, were heavy with her daughter's scent. And with the scents of blood and pain and death. It threatened to crush her. "I'm going home." She drew her cloak around her, then paused. "Do you have a place to stay?"

Quinn shook his head. He was still reeling from the force of her magic; but, more than that, he was stunned by the feeling that everything that had happened in his life had inevitably led him to this moment. This woman.

"You're welcome to come home with me, if you wish." She hadn't intended to invite him, but he seemed so lost, so alone.

"Thanks," he said, unable to hide his surprise. "Let me see if I can find a change of clothes."

She waited in the corridor while he searched the rooms. He spent several minutes in the one near the end of the hall. He emerged wearing a black silk shirt, black pants, and knee-high black leather boots.

"Are they yours?" she asked.

He shook his head. "The closet was filled with clothes. I guess whichever lover stayed in it left in an all-fired hurry."

Seleena nodded. Or never left at all.

Wondering if she was making a horrible mistake, she took his hand in hers and magicked the two of them home.

* * *

Quinn shook his head. Witchcraft, he mused. A handy talent. He glanced at his new surroundings. The room was decorated in shades of beige, brown and sage. The furnishings were simple but exquisite—a long couch, a low table, plush carpeting on the floor, a well-used rocking chair. A shelf held a collection of delicate vases made of china and crystal. And, in the far corner, a shrine of some kind.

A large black cat rushed into the room. It took one look at Quinn, hissed, and darted under the sofa.

Seleena removed her cloak and tossed it over the back of a chair. "Some animals, like my Freyja, are very sensitive to predators."

Quinn nodded. Some of the cows had shied away from him, too.

"Make yourself at home," Seleena invited. "I'm going to make a cup of tea. I'm guessing you would like something stronger. A glass of red wine, perhaps?"

"Yeah, that would be great. Thanks."

He watched her leave the room, then strolled toward the shrine. It held a blue stone, a knife with an ebony haft, a small black cauldron, and several white candles.

Serepta had taught him a little about magic. The knife was called an athame. It was a double-bladed, ceremonial dagger often used to direct energy out of the body and into the environment. He was tempted to pick it up, but Seleena's voice stayed his hand.

"Please don't touch anything."

The warning was mild, but he heard the steel beneath the words. He turned to face her. "Afraid I'll contaminate it?"

Nodding, she offered him a glass filled with dark-red liquid; then, in a lithe movement, she lowered herself onto a padded rocking chair. Indicating the sofa across from her, she said, "Please, sit."

He dropped onto the couch, one arm flung across the curved back. What the Hel was he doing here? With a witch!

* * *

She offered him dinner, but he declined. In spite of her assurances that he would be able to keep it down, he wasn't quite ready to give it a try.

She didn't argue. She poured him a second glass of wine, invited him to sleep in her guest room, and went to bed. The cat trailed at her heels.

Quinn stayed on the sofa in front of the fire, his legs stretched out in front of him, his fingers locked behind his head. Seleena. She was a pretty woman. Not as blatantly beautiful as her daughter, but just as lovely in her own way. With Serepta, he had been on edge every minute, always aware of the evil that lurked beneath her beauty, yet unable to extricate himself from her spell. Seleena put him on edge, too, but in an entirely different way.

He wondered how old she was. She didn't look much older than thirty. Thirty-five at the most, which would make her his age, but that seemed unlikely. Of course, he had no idea how old Serepta had been, either. He had asked her once, but she had just laughed and refused to answer. Someone—he couldn't remember who—had told him that witches aged slowly, and that they were capable of altering their appearance to hide the ravages of time. For all he knew, Seleena could be a hundred. But it didn't matter, he thought, because he was a vampire. And they didn't age, either.

Vampire. He stared into the flames....

She reclined on a bed of silk sheets, her hair spread like skeins of silk across the pillow. She wore a long, black gown that did little to hide the voluptuous figure beneath. She smiled invitingly as she beckoned him to join her. Helpless, he stretched out beside her, drew her into his arms, and covered her mouth with his. He had never known a woman like her—insatiable, inventive. Cruel. She had enjoyed causing him pain and yet, foolish man that he was, he had welcomed the ache for the pleasure that followed...

What had he done to incur her wrath? When had she turned him into a vampire? Why had she imprisoned him in a statue? And why couldn't he remember any of it? Some parts of his mind felt like mush.

He glanced at the closed bedroom door. Was the mother as insatiable as the daughter?

He bolted upright.

Mother.

Daughter.

Who—*and where*—was the father?

CHAPTER 3

The question about Serepta's father was the first thing Quinn asked when he woke late the next afternoon.

He found Seleena in the kitchen, stirring something in a large pot. She regarded him for a moment, then said, "I don't see as how that's any of your business."

"It is if he comes busting in here and gets the wrong idea."

"I can assure you that won't happen." She stirred the pot again, then covered it and turned down the heat. "He's quite happily engaged to someone else."

Quinn's gaze moved over her, amazed that any man in his right mind would leave this woman for another.

"Are you hungry?" she asked.

His gaze moved briefly to her throat. "Yeah, I could eat something if it's no trouble."

"Sit down. There's beef stew in the pot, or I can fry you up a steak."

"You're sure I can eat it?"

She nodded.

"Stew sounds fine." Better to start with something mostly liquid, he thought, rather than dive into a hunk of meat. He watched her dish it up. How could he have forgotten being turned into a vampire? Had the witch made him a vampire and encased him in stone the same day? Dammit! Why couldn't he remember?

"You look troubled." She placed a pretty flowered bowl and a spoon in front of him, then took a seat at the table.

"Why can't I remember when she turned me?"

"I'm not sure. Perhaps it was so traumatic, that you've buried it deep in your sub-conscious." She shrugged. "Perhaps she conjured a spell to make you forget."

"Maybe." He regarded the contents in the bowl before taking a bite. It was hot and spicy. "It's good."

"Thank you."

"Do you know a lot of vampires?"

"No. Most of them were destroyed in the last century."

"Did Serepta ever try to turn you?"

"She knew better. My daughter might have been a powerful witch, but she was no match for me. Or for Nardik."

"Nardik? The king's advisor?"

"Yes. Do you know him?"

"I met once, a long time ago. I doubt he'd remember me."

"He's the queen's advisor now. King Leonid is dead."

"What happened to him?"

"It's a long story."

"I've got no place to go and nothing to do when I get there."

Seleena folded her hands on the table and took a deep breath. "Do you know the royal family?"

"I know *of* them. Never met any."

"Leonid's youngest child, Artur, wanted to be king, but he was last in line and couldn't wait. He murdered both of his brothers and then decided to get rid of his sister. Marri vowed she didn't want the throne, but, in his mind, she remained the only obstacle keeping him from his heart's desire. Besides his father, of course. When the king learned the truth of Artur's treachery, Artur killed him. And Nardik killed Artur. And now Marri sits on the throne."

"Hel of a story."

"Indeed."

Quinn finished the last of the stew, declined Seleena's offer of more. Suddenly restless, he pushed away from the table. In spite of the food he'd just eaten, he felt empty inside.

He needed to feed. Something warm and red and liquid.

Seleena recognized the hunger in the pale crimson glow behind his eyes. "Remember your promise," she warned.

He nodded. "You saved my life, literally, and I'm grateful."

"You're leaving?"

"Probably for the best, don't you think? I need to find out what I am, if you know what I mean." He knew vampires had powers. It was time to discover just what they were.

"Take care of yourself." Rising, she held out her hand.

It was swallowed up in his.

His gaze searched hers. She was a powerful witch and even though she wanted him, he couldn't forget that her daughter had beguiled him with her beauty and then encased him in stone. Nor could he forget that the mother claimed to be more powerful than the daughter.

But her hand was still in his and her slightly parted lips were an invitation he couldn't ignore.

Seleena's eyelids fluttered down as his mouth covered hers. It had been years since she had been in a man's arms, and Quinn's were strong and sure, his chest as hard as the stone that had once encased him. His lips moved over hers, intimate, familiar, as if they had kissed many times before. As if they had all the time in the world.

Vampire. The word whispered through her mind but she shoved it aside. What difference did it make? He was leaving. But for this one moment, he was hers.

She went up on her tiptoes, her arms twining around his neck to hold him closer, tighter. He tasted of vegetables and broth and man and she wanted to stay in his arms forever.

When he broke the kiss, she felt as if she had lost a piece of herself.

He stared down at her, his deep blue eyes filled with lust and confusion. And then, to her dismay, he vanished from her sight.

* * *

Quinn came to a stop by the fountain in the middle of the village, his whole body throbbing with need. Once the witch put her arms around his neck, he had wanted nothing more than to sweep her off her feet and carry her to bed. But the last time he had bedded a witch, he'd woke up a vampire. No telling what Seleena might do if she suddenly had second thoughts. Although the way she had caught fire in his arms, it might have been worth the risk to stick around long enough to find out.

Taking a deep breath, he glanced at his surroundings. From where he stood, he could see a number of houses strung out around the village square. Most were built of wood, others of brick. Several open-air stalls surrounded a pretty, bubbling fountain. Vendors hawked a variety of goods - food and drink, hats and scarves and imported trinkets. In the distance, he heard the ring of a blacksmith's hammer, the chiming of a church bell.

As he walked through the square, people eyed him curiously, but that was to be expected. He was a stranger in a small town. Likely everyone knew everyone else. A few of the inhabitants smiled and nodded his way. A scruffy dog ran up to him, growled deep in its throat, then tucked its tail between its legs and darted under a wagon.

Quinn walked from one end of the village to the other. There was nothing to indicate where he was—no street signs, nothing to indicate the name of the place or the population. One thing was for certain, it was Hel and gone away from the more prosperous parts of the country. If there was a spaceport, it was miles away. He saw no vehicles of any kind save one rusty old LandSkiff that had seen better days, and a couple of horse-drawn wagons. Damn, he really was in the backend of the planet.

But then, he was a vampire. He didn't need transportation. He knew from spending time with Serepta that vampires were remarkably strong and fast. They could jump incredibly high. They didn't grow old. They never got sick. They could change shape, dissolve into mist. Wounds healed quickly and left no scar. And, as he had just proved when he left Seleena's house, they were capable of moving faster than the eye could follow.

Maybe being a vampire wouldn't be so bad after all.

* * *

Seleena washed and dried the dishes. Usually, she just magicked them clean and into the cupboard but this afternoon she needed the distraction. She swept the floor, pulled the sheets from the bed Quinn had slept on. She lingered there a moment, the sheets pressed to her face. His scent was there, clean and fresh and masculine. The house felt empty without him.

Freyja twined in and out between her legs, meowing loudly for attention.

With a sigh, Seleena hurried out of the room, dumped the sheets in the washer, and then bent to pick up the cat. "I'm sure you're glad he's gone," she murmured, stroking the cat's ears. "But I miss him already." It was an odd sensation. She had lived alone ever since Serepta left home. Until now, she had never been lonely. "And how odd is that? I don't even know the man. And yet I felt something happen between us the first time we touched." She moved into the living room and settled in the rocker. "Maybe I just imagined it." She shook her head. "No. Whatever it was, it was real. But it doesn't matter now. He's gone."

Freyja hissed softly.

"Yes, I know. I could force him to come back. Compel him to stay with me. But that's not what I want."

* * *

With the setting of the sun, the vendors closed their stalls and headed home. Quinn watched them the way a hawk watched a flock of chickens. Made his choice and followed the woman down a narrow dirt path lined with trees. It led to a solitary house.

Quinn stayed out of sight until she went inside. He circled the place, but detected no other occupants. Satisfied that his prey lived alone, he rang the bell.

* * *

Seleena's heart skipped a beat when she heard a knock at the door. It was him.

She took two deep breaths, smoothed her hand over her hair, and lifted the latch.

"Think I could bed down in your spare room again?" Quinn asked.

"I thought you went off to find yourself."

He shrugged. "Maybe I changed my mind. Or maybe what I'm looking for is right here."

Seleena started to invite him in, then paused when she caught the faint scent of blood.

"She's fine," he said, meeting her gaze. "I only took a little." He cocked his head to the side. "Don't you believe me?"

"Yes," Seleena said, stepping aside so he could enter. "I do."

He followed her into the living room, took a place on the sofa while she settled into the rocker. The cat immediately leaped onto her lap, tail twitching, yellow eyes unblinking as it stared at Quinn.

Seleena stroked the cat's head. "I didn't think I'd see you again."

"You seemed happy enough to find me at your door."

"If I wasn't, you'd still be outside."

His gaze probed hers. "Why *did* you let me in?"

"I don't know."

"Don't know? Or won't admit it?"

She lowered her head to hide the rush of color she felt climbing up her neck into her cheeks. She wanted him. He was the most attractive man she had ever met. But that didn't change the fact that he was a stranger. A vampire. Nor could she forget that he had been Serepta's lover. That bothered her more than anything.

"You want me."

The words hung in the air between them. She imagined she could see them there, in bold black letters, floating just out of reach.

"You don't have to admit it," Quinn said. "I can smell it on you."

Her eyes widened. "No, you can't."

He winked at her. "Yes, I can. Just so you know, I want you, too. That's one of the reasons I came back. To finish what we started this afternoon."

Seleena pressed her hand to her heart to keep it from jumping out of her chest. He wanted her. Unbidden came an image of Quinn and Serepta locked in each other's arms.

Seleena shook her head. There was just no way she could let Quinn make love to her, no way on earth that she could look into his eyes and wonder if he was comparing her to her daughter.

"What's the other reason?"

"I want to get to know you better." He leaned forward, his gaze holding hers. "You can try to fight the attraction between us. You can deny it until you're blue in the face. You can throw me out of your house. But it's gonna happen, Red," he said smugly. "Sooner or later, it's gonna happen."

* * *

Lying alone in bed, listening to the clock chime the hour, Seleena couldn't remember anything else she or Quinn had said. All she could hear was his smug voice echoing in her mind—*You can fight the attraction. You can deny it until you're blue in the face. You can throw me out of your house. But it's gonna happen, Red. Sooner or later, it's gonna happen.*

She tuned onto her stomach and punched her fist into the pillow. Turned onto her side. Onto her back. *It's gonna happen....it's gonna happen.*

She closed her eyes and his image flashed before her—thick dark hair, dark-blue eyes, shoulders as wide as her doorway, tawny skin, a flat belly ridged with muscle. And that tattoo. Her fingers itched to touch it, to follow the tail where it wrapped around his bicep...

"Stop it!" She jackknifed into a sitting position and turned on the light, banishing his image from her mind.

Freyja meowed in protest when Seleena slid out of bed. Pulling on her robe, she went to the window and drew back the curtain. All was quiet outside. The twin moons hung low in the sky, bathing the land in a faint yellow glow.

Too keyed up to sleep, she eased her bedroom door open. She listened a moment before tiptoeing through the dark house into the kitchen. A wave of her hand warmed a cup of water. She dropped a tea bag inside, stood at the counter, arms folded over her chest, while she waited for the tea to steep.

Her thoughts drifted toward Quinn again. She tried to rein them back, but it was no use. Was he asleep? She knew little of vampires except that they slept during the day, had exceptional powers, and drank blood to survive. But she had altered part of that. Would he now sleep nights, like everyone else? Where would he go when he left here? Would he go back to bounty hunting for that despicable man, Jagg?

She turned her thoughts to Marri and Gryff. She had never known a couple more in love. What was it like, to feel that way? She had never been in love, not even with Nardik. When the year of mourning for the king was over, Nardik would wed Marri's mother, Amerris. Another happy-ever-after, she mused, and wondered if she would ever find one of her own.

Aware that she was no longer alone, she whirled around and came face-to-face with Quinn.

"What's the matter?" he asked, a hint of amusement in his voice.

"Can't sleep?"

The darkness suddenly seemed far too intimate. Reaching behind her, she flipped on the light. "I just wanted a cup of tea."

"Uh huh."

She glared at him. "Are you calling me a liar?"

He took a step forward. His nearness seemed to suck all the air out of the room. "I know something that works better than tea." His voice was raw, husky with desire. It moved over her senses like rough velvet.

He wasn't wearing a shirt. Her gaze was drawn to the dragon tattoo on his shoulder. She curled her hands into fists to keep from running her fingers over his arm.

His knowing smile infuriated her.

She didn't know who was more surprised when she slapped him, Quinn or herself.

Shocked, she stared at the bright red print of her hand on his cheek. She had never struck another human being in her life.

He had the audacity to grin. "Feel better now?"

She shook her head, horrified by her loss of control.

"Your tea's getting cold."

Afraid of what she might do next, she dumped the tea into the sink and fled the room.

The sound of amused male laughter followed her.

CHAPTER 4

Quinn stared after her. He couldn't remember ever being so anxious to get to know a woman. Serepta didn't count. He knew now that his feelings for her hadn't been real. She had enchanted him, turned him into a vampire, and trapped him inside a stone prison. He doubted the woman knew the meaning of love. But Seleena…she was sexy. Mysterious. Soft-spoken, but not soft. He wanted to know her in every way a man could know a woman. Explore every inch of her. She would be a generous lover, as eager to give pleasure as receive it.

But he would never get to know her as long as she was afraid. But was she afraid of him—or of her attraction to him?

He took a deep breath as he stepped outside. He felt at home in the darkness. But then, that was probably to be expected, now that he was a vampire. If not for Seleena's spell, which would allow him to walk in the sun's light, he would be alive only at night. He owed her big-time for that. Maybe he should do her a favor and just walk out of her life.

He glanced back at the house. She was in her room, asleep. He could hear the slow, steady beating of her heart. Smell the blood flowing through her veins. Would her life's blood really sicken him to the point of death? Or was that just an empty threat—a way of protecting herself from his bite? For a moment, he considered taking a sip while she slept. And then he shook his head. She had saved his life, given him shelter. He wouldn't break her trust by stealing her blood.

And he wouldn't leave her. Not unless she told him to go.

* * *

Seleena woke before dawn after a restless night. Her dreams had been filled with images of Quinn. In the most bizarre dream, his dragon came to life and chased her through Serepta's garden. In the last, and most pleasant, Quinn had seduced her with sweet words and honeyed kisses. She'd awoken in the middle of the night, a smile on her face, only to spend the rest of the night trying to find her way back into his arms. In the dream, of course.

Rising, she drew on her robe and padded into the corridor. She paused at his door. Was he still asleep? Her hand curled around the latch, then she jerked it back. What was she doing?

Hurrying into the kitchen, she made a cup of hot chocolate and carried it into the living room. Freyja trailed at her heels, meowing softly.

"Yes, he's still here," Seleena said, lowering herself into the rocker. "And no, I haven't decided what to do about it."

Freyja curled up at her feet, a sure sign that she wasn't happy with her indecision.

"I know you don't like him, but it's nice to have company. *Human* company," she added, when the cat hissed at her.

Rocking gently, Seleena sipped her chocolate. It was very dark, very decadent. An old recipe known only to members of her family. Her thoughts turned to the man sleeping in her guest room. What was she to do with him? She liked having someone to talk to, but sooner or later, she was afraid words would lead to something far more intimate. She was all too aware of the sexual attraction that hummed between them, that sense of inevitability. He wanted her. And she most definitely wanted him. Her dreams had proved that beyond doubt! It had been years since she had been close to a man, felt a man's touch, his skin against hers…

A flush warmed her cheeks as she remembered last night's erotic dream. As if on cue, Quinn strolled into the room. He wore the same black trousers. His shirt hung open, revealing a broad expanse of tawny skin. For some reason, the fact that he was barefooted made her cheeks grow hotter. It seemed so intimate somehow.

"Kind of early for you to be awake, isn't it?" His voice was as deep and sultry as the night itself.

She stared up at him, unable to think of a single thing to say.

"Bad dreams?"

Her heart skipped a beat. Quite the contrary! But she couldn't tell him that. And yet he knew. She could see it in the faint glint of amusement in his eyes.

"Maybe not so bad?" he asked.

"I don't keep regular hours," she said, as if that explained everything.

He took a place on the sofa, his long legs stretched out in front of him. "Why do you live in this dreary village? There's a whole world out there filled with fine homes outfitted with all the latest conveniences. Yet you live here, in this tiny house. Why?"

"The people need me. There's no doctor here, no hospital. I heal the sick, deliver their babies, bring rain when it's needed."

"And that's enough for you?"

"Yes." At least it had been. Until she met him. She couldn't stop looking at him—his shaggy brown hair tousled, the faint white scar along his neck. His nose was sharp, his lips full, sensual…unbidden she remembered how he had kissed her in her dream. And how quickly - and willingly - she had responded to his touch.

Quinn lifted one brow as her cheeks bloomed with color. "You're blushing. Why?"

"It's warm in here, that's all." Seleena focused inward and raised the temperature of the room.

He smiled, as if well aware of what she'd done. "Is it?"

"Tell me about yourself."

"I don't think so. You'd probably throw me out on my ear if I did."

"It can't be that bad."

"No?" He regarded her a moment. "My mother worked in one of Jagg's brothels in Bosquetown. I was born there. Never knew who my father was. Neither did she. He could have been one of the hundreds of men who frequented the place. I was nine when she died in childbirth and the baby with her. Jagg raised me from that time on.

He made no pretense of doing it for any reason other than he expected to make money off me later. He taught me to fight dirty and how to cheat at cards and dice, and when I was old enough, he set me to bounty hunting." His expression hardened. "Occasionally, I acted as his assassin."

Seleena stared at him, unable to imagine such a terrible life. She had grown up with loving parents. She had never known poverty or want. Whenever she had seen cruelty or need, she had used her magic to make things better. "Where did you meet my daughter?"

"She came to Bosquetown to buy a slave. She bought me from Jagg instead." How could he have forgotten that?

"She *bought* you?"

"Yeah. For a right hefty price, as I recall. Next time I'm in Bosquetown, I'm going to have a little talk with Jagg." *And then I'm going to kill him.*

Seleena bit down on her lower lip as Quinn's eyes went red. She had a feeling Jagg's days were numbered, and while she didn't approve of murder, she could understand Quinn's anger. "How long were you with Serepta?"

"About a year, I guess, before she turned me into a garden decoration." Except for being her slave, it hadn't been all that bad. He'd had everything he desired, except his freedom…memories stirred in the back of his mind…they were in her bed, wrapped in each other's arms. *I'm going to give you a gift,* she whispered. *A wonderful gift*…But he hadn't thought it was wonderful.

Seleena gazed into the fire. He had spent a year with Serepta. How many times had they made love? Her daughter had embraced Dark Magic, turned people into statues, did any number of despicable things, and yet Seleena suddenly envied Serepta the nights she had spent in Quinn's arms. And how sick and disgusting was that!

"She turned me to stone because I wasn't happy to be a vampire." He muttered a vile oath as the memory returned. "She said she'd given me a wonderful gift and I didn't appreciate it." A muscle ticked in his jaw. "Being trapped in that stone was agony. There were times when I was aware of what was happening. I felt the heat of the sun during the day, a relentless hunger at night."

"I'm so sorry." Tears filled her eyes as she imagined the horror he had described. Rising, she placed her hand on his shoulder. "I can make you forget it," she said. "All of it."

"No." Quinn covered her hand with his own, his fingers wrapping around hers.

"I should think you'd like to forget."

He shook his head. "It's part of my past, part of me."

His gaze, filled with longing, burned into hers. She knew what he wanted. She wanted it, too. The thought of letting him make love to her was tempting. Far too tempting.

He gave her hand a squeeze when he read the indecision in her eyes. "It's going to happen, Red," he promised. "Sooner or later."

He had made the same promise before, Seleena recalled as she bid him goodnight and returned to her room.

But this time, she believed him.

* * *

Quinn remained on the sofa, his thoughts turned inward. Memories assailed him, sweeping through his mind like a flash flood. Serepta standing behind him, the crack of her whip like a pistol shot as she laid his back open. Serepta leaning over him, licking the hot blood from his torn flesh as her hands moved over him, healing him. Serepta, laughing as she tortured one of the servants who had displeased her…

She had been as cruel as she was beautiful, truly the most evil woman he had ever known. Brynn Tor and its inhabitants were well rid of her.

He shut the door on the past and turned his thoughts from the daughter to the mother. He couldn't help grinning as he remembered how flustered she had been earlier, the blush in her cheeks. She might be a powerful witch, but her thoughts were practically transparent. She wanted him. Unless he missed his guess, she had been dreaming about him earlier. Judging by her musky scent, those dreams had been far from innocent.

Sooner or later, she would be his. It was only a matter of time. And now, thanks to Serepta, time was something he had plenty of.

CHAPTER 5

Seleena woke to the sound of someone frantically ringing the bell. Blinking the sleep from her eyes, she donned her robe and ran to answer the door.

"Lonn, what's wrong?" She smiled at Kerry Frazzier's son. Though he was only nine, he was the man of the house.

"It's Lissy! She's been in labor for hours. I think the baby's stuck! Can you come?"

"Of course. Just let me get my shoes." She hurried down the hall, colliding with Quinn as he stepped out of his room.

"I didn't know you were a midwife," he said with a wry grin.

"I am whatever I need to be."

"Mind if I come along?"

"No, you might be useful."

"In childbirth? I doubt it."

She grinned up at him as she stepped aside. "You might be surprised."

* * *

Quinn was, indeed, surprised to learn that the baby Seleena had been called on to deliver wasn't a baby at all, but a calf.

He stood behind her as she examined Lissy the cow, listening in amusement as she spoke softly to the animal, which was obviously in distress judging from the swish of its tail and sweat-sheened flanks.

The boy stood at Quinn's side, wide-eyed as he watched Seleena's forearm disappear inside the cow.

"One of the calf's feet is blocking the birth canal," Seleena said. "I can't get a good grip on it." She looked inquiringly at Quinn.

"You want *me* to do it? Can't you just wave your wand and magic the calf out?"

"Not this time." Rising, she washed her arm in a bucket of soapy water and dried it with a rough piece of cloth.

"Sure, what the Hel." He washed his hands and dried them on a clean length of toweling before stepping behind the cow. She glanced over her shoulder with a baleful stare.

With a sigh of resignation, Quinn rolled up his sleeve and slid his hand inside the animal. It didn't take long to find the problem. "Okay, I've got hold of it," Quinn said as he wrapped his fingers around the calf's leg and slowly straightened it out.

"Can you grab hold of the other leg?" Seleena asked.

"Yeah. Why?"

"Let me know when you've got both of them. Then, when I say the word, I want you to pull on both feet together. Wait…not yet. Now!"

The cow pushed.

Quinn pulled.

And a tiny black-and-white calf slid out in a gush of blood and water.

The boy clapped his hands.

Seleena grinned at Quinn. "Well done!"

"Yeah." He glanced down. His pants were stained with blood. His hand and forearm were covered with who-knew-what. But he couldn't help grinning when Lissy the cow began to lick her baby. It was the first time he had ever seen anything born. It was, he thought as he washed his hands, a Hel of a sight.

They waited around until the calf was on its feet and nursing.

By then, the sun was up. Lonn scooted out of the barn to tell his mother the good news.

Kerry Frazzier arrived a few minutes later. "Bless you and thank you," she said as she offered Seleena two loaves of crusty brown bread still warm from the oven.

"It was really Quinn who did all the work," Seleena said. "I just diagnosed the problem."

The woman clasped one of Quinn's hands in both of hers. "Thank you so much, Mr. Quinn! I don't know what we'd have done if we lost our Lissy."

He muttered, "Glad to help," as he extricated his hand from hers.

Moments later, they took their leave.

Seleena smiled at him as they walked back to her house. "Feels good, doesn't it? Bringing a new life into the world."

"It was just a cow."

"But it's their livelihood. Kerry's husband passed away last year, leaving her with three little ones to care for. She provides for her family by selling butter and cheese at market."

"And all she paid you was two loaves of bread."

"But it's good bread," Seleena remarked as they reached her door. "We'll have a couple of slices for breakfast, with some ham and eggs."

* * *

Later, with the breakfast dishes done and Quinn resting in his room, Seleena went out into her garden. She had planted it in a concentric circle, with healing herbs—fennel, garlic, ginger, jasmine, rosemary, sage, and lavender—on the outer ring and poisonous ones, like pennyroyal, on the inside. Brick paths were laid around the circles.

A wide variety of flowers grew along the fence. Thanks to a bit of earth magic, they bloomed all year round—a riot of color no matter what the season or the weather. A small fountain bubbled in one corner, the sound of the water always a pleasant diversion. She smiled as she recalled threatening to turn Quinn back into a statue and use him for a decoration in her fountain.

She spent an hour pulling weeds and raking leaves, but nothing could divert her thoughts from Quinn. He was the most beautiful, beguiling man she had ever known. He made her feel young again. Feminine. Desirable.

She paused under her favorite tree. Even though she had conjured a spell that allowed Quinn to walk in the light of day, he preferred the darkness. And that bothered her greatly. Serepta had embraced the dark and it had been her downfall.

Feeling suddenly depressed, Seleena set the rake aside and sank down on a wicker chair. It was hard to reconcile her happy, chubby-cheeked daughter with the evil woman Serepta had become. Time and again, Seleena had warned her daughter against dabbling in the Dark Arts, but to no avail. There was an allure to black magic, a horrible fascination that, once tasted, was hard to resist.

She wondered again where the men and women who had been in service to Serepta had gone. Where were all the cooks, the maids, the men she had employed to do her bidding? Had any of them willingly served her? Or had they all been trapped inside the castle, unable to leave, or had they been afraid to incur Serepta's wrath and end up as another stone statue in her garden?

The twin suns were warm on her face and Seleena closed her eyes, felt herself slipping into sleep's abyss…

And Quinn was there, lying beside her on a patch of white sand. Overhead, the light of the twin moons turned the night to day. He rose over her, his eyes blazing with desire.

She stared up at him, her heart pounding with trepidation as she traced the dragon on his shoulder. Her eyes narrowed as she felt a rush of power beneath her fingertips. Had she imagined it? It felt much like her own magical power. The same, yet different.

Quinn's brows drew together. "What's wrong?"

"What's wrong?"

It took her a moment to realize she was no longer dreaming. Opening her eyes, she saw Quinn standing beside her, frowning. "Nothing. Why?"

He shrugged. "You were thrashing around."

"It was just a dream."

He sat on the bench across from her chair. "Must not have been a good one."

Her gaze swept across his shoulder. "How long have you had that tattoo?"

"I'm not sure. Why?"

"May I see it?"

He lifted one brow, then shrugged out of his shirt.

"It looks so life-like." She could almost feel the heat from the flame erupting from the creature's mouth. She wouldn't have been surprised to see the dragon leap off his arm and run across the floor. And then she frowned. Hadn't the head been facing the other way the first time she had seen it? She reached out to touch it, then hesitated. "May I?"

Quinn shrugged. "Sure."

She ran her finger over the dragon's scales, jerked her hand back in surprise. She could feel each individual scale. Sense the same magic she had felt in her dream. "Where did you get it?"

"Your daughter gave it to me."

Seleena stared at him. So, she hadn't imagined that sense of power. Nor was it any wonder she had recognized it. It carried her signature.

"You've got that look again," Quinn remarked. "Want to tell me what's wrong?"

"Did Serepta say why she gave you that tattoo?" "No. All she said was that she liked dragons."

"She didn't say anything else about it?"

Quinn leaned forward, hands braced on his knees. "What are you getting at?"

"I'm not sure, exactly. But that's more than just a tattoo. How did you get it?"

"I told you, from Serepta."

"No. I mean, did she apply it in the usual way, or did she use her magic to put it there?"

"I don't know. I went to sleep one night and when I woke in the morning, it was there. Why?"

"Because it isn't a normal tattoo."

Quinn glanced at the dragon as if he'd never seen if before. "Yeah," he said slowly. "I sort of figured that out the first time it moved."

"You've seen it move?"

"No." He rubbed his hand over the dragon. "But it changes position from time to time. What do you think it means?"

"I'm not sure. I've never seen—or felt—anything like it."

"What do you mean, *felt*?"

"It contains latent magical powers of some kind."

"Magic!"

Seleena nodded. "Serepta's magic. And mine. And Nardik's."

It was, Quinn mused, a Hel of a combo.

* * *

Towards dusk, Seleena went to look in on a sick child. In her absence,

Quinn wandered through the house. Pausing in front of a mirror, he peeled off his shirt and stared at the dragon. He had never given the thing much thought, or spent much time looking at it. Tattoos weren't uncommon, but there was nothing ordinary about this one. He had known the thing changed position from time to time, but he'd figured it was just some trick of the light. There had been times, when he had been half-asleep, when he would have sworn he could feel the thing moving. He knew now that he hadn't imagined it at all.

Did the tattoo really hold some kind of mysterious magic? Or was it merely a clever bit of body art?

Shrugging into his shirt, he left the house. When he reached the edge of the village, he continued south, following the road for a mile or so, until it gradually disappeared. As the trees grew farther apart, patches of green gave way to miles and miles of sand and cactus.

Turning back, he wondered again how Seleena had ever landed in a village with no name, and why she stayed. Sure, she'd said the people needed her. But it didn't seem like much of a life for a beautiful, vibrant woman.

Lost in thought, he was on his way back to the village when the hunger rose up within him, sharp and demanding, triggered by the scent of fresh blood coming from behind a small house at the edge of the town.

The scent led him into the backyard, where it was overwhelming. And no wonder.

A middle-aged man lay sprawled on his back on the grass in a pool of blood, his arms flung out to the side. Blood leaked from two tiny puncture wounds in his neck. A faint, but familiar scent hung in the air, but he dismissed it out of hand. Seleena had assured him Serepta was dead.

He cursed under his breath as he stared at the twin marks on the man's neck. He knew all too well what they meant.

Vampire.

Chapter 6

"A vampire?" Seleena stared at him, her eyes wide. "Are you sure?"

"Takes one to know one."

Pressing a hand to her heart, Seleena lowered herself onto her rocking chair. *Vampire.* Serepta had been one of the undead. Was it possible? No! She refused to consider it. For a moment, she stared, unseeing, into the distance. "I need to see the body."

"Why?"

She stood abruptly. "Just take me to it."

Quinn frowned, confused by her reaction, and then he left the house. She trailed behind him.

"Tinnly's place," she murmured as she followed him down the path to the back of the house. "He lived alone."

Quinn opened the rusty gate.

Seleena hesitated a moment before following him into the yard. Then, as if going to her doom, she walked slowly toward the corpse. For a moment, she stood there in silence. Closing her eyes, she lifted her arms skyward, chanting softly in a language he didn't understand.

It went on for several minutes. When she finished, her face was fish-belly white.

"What is it?"

She stared up at him through haunted eyes. "If I didn't know it was impossible, I would swear Serepta had been here. But I saw her die. Her throat was ripped out…"

"That wouldn't kill her."

"She was dead. It was a killing wound," Seleena insisted. "There was blood everywhere."

"Vampires can recover from almost anything. If you want to make sure they stay dead, you have to drive a stake through their heart, cut off the head, or burn the body. Otherwise, they'll rise again."

At his words, her face paled even more, if that was possible. "I know all that, but I couldn't stay and watch. I just couldn't. Nardik gave instructions to one of the servants and paid him to dispose of the remains for us and then we went to Brynn Castle with Marri and Gryff. I stopped at Serepta's grave on my way back home. Sennix was working on a headstone."

"Did you look inside the coffin?"

Seleena stared at him in horror. "Of course not!"

"So, for all you know, it could have been empty."

"No!" Seleena shook her head vigorously. "I refuse to believe that."

Quinn blew out a sigh "You need to at least consider the possibility," he said quietly. "Because if I'm right, then Serepta is still a threat. Odds are that the man who was supposed to dispose of her remains is buried in that grave."

Seleena's gaze moved to his shoulder. The dragon's tail was visible beneath his rolled-up shirt sleeve. "Serepta imbued you with a part of her magic," she mused, her expression pensive. "She was always a clever girl. Always thinking ahead, planning for every eventuality."

"Why would she come here?"

"Revenge."

Quinn glanced at the corpse. "Against him?"

"No. I think she just wanted us to know she's still here. Let's go. I need to find Waggner and ask him to collect Mr. Tinnly's remains."

Quinn followed her out of the yard, his brow furrowed, one hand rubbing the tattoo. What the Hel did it all mean?

* * *

That was the question he put to Seleena when they returned home.

"I don't know what it means." She sat in the rocker, the cat cradled in her arms. "I hadn't seen my daughter for years before she died. She could have shared her magic with dozens of fledgling witches."

"So, can anybody be a witch?"

"Most are born. A few are blessed with the ability to learn the art, although that is extremely rare." She closed her eyes a moment, her expression thoughtful. "Serepta was born a witch. Her magic was inherited, a part of her. Nardik didn't actually *take* her magic away from her, so much as neutralize it."

Quinn scrubbed a hand across his jaw. He had a bad feeling about what she was trying to say.

"The thing is, another wizard could restore it, although he would not only have to be ancient, but also possess the power to restore magic. Not every wizard has that talent."

"Does such a man exist?"

"To my knowledge, Nardik is the oldest wizard on Brynn Tor. But there are other galaxies. Other covens."

Quinn dragged a hand over his jaw. One more thing to worry about. "The dragon on my shoulder. It feels like it bites me every time you mention Serepta's name. How do you explain that?"

"Like I told you before, it's imbued with a form of magic, some of it dark."

"Yeah, you said yours and hers and Nardik's. How can it be all three?"

"I learned some of my magic from Nardik. Serepta learned some of hers from both of us. It's all entwined, light and dark, good and bad."

He didn't like the sound of that, couldn't figure out why Serepta had branded him with ink in the first place. "The tattoo, can you remove it?"

"I don't know. Take off your shirt and come here."

Ears laid back, the cat hissed at his approach.

"Freyja, quiet." Taking hold of Quinn's arm, she chanted softly as she ran her fingertips over the tattoo. Power coalesced around them, vibrant, palpable.

Seleena gasped as pain shot from the dragon's mouth to her fingers and skittered up her forearm, leaving her hand and arm feeling numb.

The cat howled and bolted out of the room.

Quinn dropped to the floor, his body shaking uncontrollably, curling in on itself as agony splintered through him. Sweat dripped from his brow.

Seleena knelt beside him. "Quinn? Quinn!" She reached toward him, then drew back when the dragon hissed at her.

A minute passed. Two.

Gradually, his body relaxed. The tremors stopped. Struggling to sit up, he grabbed his shirt from the floor and wiped the sweat from his face and chest.

"Are you all right?" Seleena asked, still wary of touching him.

"I'm guessing what just happened means you can't remove the damn thing."

"I'm sorry."

"Well, it's good to know, one way or the other. Are you all right?"

She shook her hand, which still felt a little numb. "I don't think we should try that again."

"Yeah, probably not a good idea." Gaining his feet, he offered her his hand.

She hesitated a moment before taking it.

Not that he could blame her after what had just happened. He pulled her gently to her feet.

For a moment, his gaze searched hers.

And then he drew her into his embrace.

And kissed her.

She tasted as sweet as he remembered. She fit into his arms as if she had been made for him and no one else. Her scent—tinged with magic and a hint of lavender—enveloped him.

Seleena pressed her fingertips to her lips, her gaze searching his. Why did he have this power over her? One kiss and she wanted to take him to her bed, to run her hands over his shoulders, explore the corded muscle in his arms, run her fingertips over his ridged belly. No other man had ever affected her so strongly, aroused her so quickly, intrigued her on so many levels.

He cocked his head to the side, a silent question lurking in his dark eyes.

Taking a deep breath, she eased out of his embrace. And immediately felt the loss of his warmth, his strength. His tattoo possessed a small portion of her own magic. Was that what made him so irresistible? But he also possessed a bit of Nardik's power. And Serepta's, as well. It was a potent combination.

He had been her daughter's lover. She had to remember that. Wanting to take him to her bed seemed like…like incest, somehow, even though the two of them weren't related.

"Can't blame a guy for trying." He kissed her lightly on the forehead, grabbed his shirt, and left the house.

Seleena stared after him. And then she sank down in front of the fireplace and wept for all she had lost.

And for all she wanted that she could never have.

CHAPTER 7

With no particular destination in mind, Quinn strolled through the village. Passing Tinnly's house, he noted signs had been posted warning neighbors and other curious folk to keep out.

The faint scent of blood still lingered at the scene, arousing his hunger, but there were few people on the roads to choose from, mostly old men that he didn't find appealing. But he needed to feed, and it didn't seem like a good idea to keep hunting for prey where he lived. Better to hunt elsewhere. The next village, perhaps…

Vampire, he thought. Maybe it was time to try out some of his own preternatural powers. Like Seleena, Serepta had been able to rapidly transport herself from one place to another. Could he do the same?

He had no idea how vampires managed it, only knew it was possible. Griggstown was the next village. He pictured the place in his mind, pictured himself there. Power surged within him. The next thing he knew, he was on the outskirts of the city.

He had been in Griggstown once before, searching for one of Jagg's runaways. He was suddenly inundated with sensory overload as what seemed like a thousand different scents assailed his nostrils, while a cacophony of sound pummeled his ears. What the Hel! He looked at the world around him as if seeing it for the first time. Colors were brighter, sharper. He noticed details before unseen. And blood…the scent of it tantalized him. The sound of a hundred beating hearts thundered in his ears.

This was what it was like to be a vampire. Power hummed through him. It took every ounce of willpower he possessed to keep from attacking a middle-aged woman hurried by.

Hands shoved deep into his pockets, he ambled down the street. Several blocks later he found himself in a less upscale part of the city. The houses were ill-kept - fences sagging, windows broken, paint peeling. The air smelled of drugs and alcohol.

He was about to turn back when a woman staggered toward him. She was young, no more than twenty. But her skin was dry and wrinkled, her eyes older than her years.

"Hey, mister, I've got what you want if you've got the credits."

Quinn smiled faintly. Ordinarily, he would have been offended by the stink of her unwashed body, but the lure of her blood was stronger. Folding his hands over her shoulders, he pulled her body against his. "You've got exactly what I want," he growled.

And buried his fangs in her throat.

* * *

When Quinn returned to the house, he found Seleena sitting in her rocking chair, the cat on her lap. Freyja hissed at him but didn't leave the room. He took that to mean the furry beast was finally getting used to him.

Refusing to meet Seleena's eyes, Quinn dropped down on the sofa.

"Where have you been?" she asked.

He lifted one shoulder and let it fall. "Just out."

"You went hunting, didn't you?"

He nodded, suddenly ashamed. And how stupid was that? He hadn't wanted to be a vampire, but the deed was done and he had to endure the consequences of Serepta's treachery as best he could. "I didn't hurt anybody."

"I know."

Quinn frowned. "How could you know what I was doing?"

"Maybe it's because you carry a little of my magic in that dragon."

"Swell." That was all he needed, someone able to monitor his every move 24/7. Could she read his thoughts, too? Probably not. Because if she had been able to read his thoughts when he was kissing her, she would have thrown him out on his ear. And bolted the door behind him.

He risked a glance in her direction.

She was watching him, one hand idly stroking Freyja's head. The cat was watching him, too.

"At Tinnly's, you said you thought Serepta wanted you to know she's here," he remarked, deciding to change the subject of where he'd been and what he'd been doing. "Why warn you?"

"I think she always planned to destroy her father and me, eventually. But we took her magic from her before Gryff....before Gryff did what he did. Like I said, she always planned ahead. I'm sure that's why she imbued you with a part of her magic. And now she wants it back."

"You don't seem very worried about her coming after you."

"I've been around a long time. Not much scares me anymore." *Except my feelings for you.*

"Just how long have you been around?"

"A gentleman *never* asks a lady her age."

"I'm a bounty hunter, remember? Not a gentleman."

"Can't you be both?"

He shook his head. "I don't think so."

"Pity."

He grinned at her, his dark eyes filled with amusement. "Yeah? Why's that?"

"I prefer gentlemen."

"Really?" Rising, he crossed the distance between them and pulled her gently to her feet.

Freyja hissed irritably as she tumbled to the floor.

Muttering, "Damn cat," he pulled Seleena into his arms. There was nothing gentle about his kiss. His mouth covered hers, his tongue demanding entrance.

At first, she was too stunned to resist. And then all thought of resistance fled.

He kissed her until she clung to him, breathless, mindless, her whole body on fire for his touch.

When she thought she might faint dead away, he lifted his head.

"Still think you want a gentleman?"

She stared up at him. Then, drawing his head down, she whispered, "Shut up and kiss me again."

He had no sooner claimed her lips than there was an urgent knock on the door.

Murmuring, "Save my place," she slipped out of his arms.

Quinn swore softly. Talk about lousy timing. He heard the door open, Seleena's gasp of surprise, the rumble of a deep male voice.

Quinn frowned. He had met Nardik only once, but his was a voice not to be forgotten.

Seleena and Nardik whispered together for a moment.

With his preternatural senses, Quinn had little trouble overhearing their conversation as Seleena explained why he was staying at her home.

"Quinn." The wizard's voice and expression were neutral as he stepped into the room.

"Nardik." The wizard looked as Quinn remembered, tall and thin but solid as oak. A narrow face framed by long gray hair. Flat cheeks, an aquiline nose, eyes the color of honey. Power radiated from him.

The wizard didn't offer to shake hands.

Neither did Quinn.

"Please, both of you," Seleena said, "be seated."

Quinn sat at one end of the sofa, Nardik the other.

Ever the good hostess, Seleena asked, "Can I get either of you anything?"

"I'd like a glass of wine," Quinn said. "Thanks."

Nardik smiled at her. "A cup of your green tea would be wonderful."

Obviously ill at ease at the idea of leaving the two of them alone, Seleena glanced from one man to the other before hurrying into the kitchen.

"So," Quinn said, "what brings you here?"

"I am sure you know."

"The dead man."

"Yes. I fear Seleena is in danger."

"I can look after her."

"I am afraid she is in equal danger from you."

"She's got nothing to fear from me," Quinn said sharply.

"No? How long do you think you can keep your lust for blood under control?"

"As long as I need to."

Nardik lifted his head, nostrils flaring. "Serepta's magic is all around you."

"I'm handling it," Quinn snapped.

Nardik looked doubtful but said nothing.

When his temper was under control, Quinn said, "You know the man, Tinnly, was killed by your daughter, don't you?"

"I have my suspicions."

Stepping into the room, Seleena asked, "Suspicions about what?" She handed a china cup to Nardik, a crystal goblet to Quinn. Her skin tingled pleasantly when his fingers brushed her. Smiling inwardly, she resumed her seat in the rocker.

"I visited the dead man's house," Nardik said. "Like Quinn, I suspect our daughter is behind the killing."

Seleena's face paled.

"Her scent is there," Nardik said.

Quinn nodded. "It's the same, yet different than I remember."

"Yes," Nardik said. "The signature of her magic is gone."

"You need to visit her grave and see who's inside that coffin," Quinn said. "It's the only way to know for sure."

"I think you are right. We will leave in the morning. If Serepta is indeed alive, I do not wish to confront her after dark." Nardik glanced at Quinn, his expression thoughtful. "How long do you intend to stay here?"

"Nardik!" Seleena glared at him. "That's hardly any business of yours."

"Considering our past, and what he is, I have every right to be concerned."

Quinn put his glass aside, then turned toward the wizard, his hands clenched into tight fists. "Just what am I?"

"You are a young vampire with much to learn. My daughter's evil magic resides somewhere within you. Dormant, at the moment. I have no idea what, if anything, will restore that magic. Or if it is even possible. There is no way to know for sure."

"Nardik," Seleena said quietly, "I can take care of myself. I've been doing it for years. It's nice of you to be concerned, but you needn't worry about me. Or about Quinn."

Nardik regarded her a moment, then glanced at Quinn. "You carry a mark of some kind. I would like to see it."

"Why?"

"Please." The word was more demand than request.

Quinn hesitated a moment, then peeled off his shirt.

Nardik put his cup aside. Leaning forward, his brow furrowed, he studied the tattoo. When he reached toward it, a small streak of white-hot flame shot from the dragon's mouth. The wizard recoiled, an oath escaping his lips. Looking at Seleena, he asked, "Have you attempted to remove it?"

Seleena nodded.

"It's not something I'm willing to try again," Quinn remarked.

"Nor I," Seleena said.

"Probably not a good idea, at any rate." Putting his cup aside, Nardik stared at the tattoo. "Does it move?"

"Yeah. So, what now?" he asked.

"I sense the dragon is imbued not only with remnants of Serepta's magic, but with a bit of her very essence. I am not sure what that means, especially for you. But she has obviously come here to retrieve whatever magic the dragon holds."

"She's welcome to it if it will rid me of the damn thing."

"I am afraid you do not understand," Nardik said. "She cannot recover it while you live."

CHAPTER 8

Eyes narrowed, Quinn stared at Nardik. "Are you saying she has to kill me before she can use it?"

"Yes."

"What happens if I kill her first?"

"I cannot say for sure. In many instances, when a witch dies, whatever spells she has cast die with her. But the dragon is obviously not dead." Rising, he added, "Until we know one way or the other if it is Serepta we are dealing with, I would caution both of you to be vigilant when you leave the house."

"Where are you going?" Seleena asked.

"It grows late," Nardik said. "I will find lodging nearby."

"You're welcome to stay here," she said.

Nardik glanced pointedly at Quinn. "I think it will be best if I go elsewhere."

Nodding, Seleena walked him to the door. "You need to be careful, too."

"Do not worry about me."

"How are things at Brynn Castle?"

"Very well. Though Marri has been Queen only a few weeks, she has already settled into the role. The people adore her. She is a remarkably astute woman for one so young."

"And Gryff? How is he doing?"

"Surprisingly well for a man of his background."

"I had no doubt that he would. They complement each other perfectly." She glanced away before asking, "Does Amerris make you happy?"

"As much as anyone can." Leaning down, he brushed a kiss across her cheek.

"Take care, Seleena. Vampires cannot be trusted."

* * *

Seleena watched Nardik until, with a wave of his hand, he vanished from her sight. And still she stood there, gazing into the darkness. Was it possible their daughter still lived? She had never stopped loving Serepta, but she had long ago known, as had Nardik, that their daughter was no longer the promising young woman she had once been. She had immersed herself so deeply in Dark Magic that the girl they had loved so dearly no longer existed in the woman she had become.

Her thoughts turned to Quinn and the kisses they had shared.

A pleasant tingling warned Seleena that he had come up behind her.

"Are you all right?" he asked quietly.

"I'm fine." There was a faint tremor in her voice. Had he heard it? Did he know she was thinking about what they had been doing before Nardik arrived? She shivered as his hands slid over her shoulders.

"Come inside," he said. "It's cold out here."

"Is it?" His breath fanned her cheek, warming her in a way no fire could.

"You're worrying about what you'll find tomorrow."

She nodded.

"Come inside," he said again, taking her hand in his. "And I'll make you forget all about it."

"Forget about what?" Seleena murmured as they moved into the living room.

Quinn's gaze searched hers as he sat on the sofa and drew her down beside him.

He could feel her trembling, smell the heady musk of her skin.

And beneath the musk, a faint scent of fear, no doubt planted by Nardik's parting words. *Vampires cannot be trusted.*

Quinn lowered his gaze to the pulse throbbing in the hollow of Seleena's throat. Maybe the old wizard was right. He could smell the blood flowing through her veins, feel the brush of his fangs against his tongue as his hunger roared to life, knew his eyes had gone red with need.

"Quinn…"

Bolting to his feet, he turned his back, hands clenched at his sides. What was happening to him? He had never known a need like this before, never felt so helpless to resist it.

Afraid to spend another minute in her presence, he fled the house.

* * *

Wrapping her arms around her waist, Seleena rocked back and forth, her mind in turmoil, her body aching for Quinn's touch. And all the while, she heard Nardik's unwanted warning—*vampires cannot be trusted.*

Perhaps he was right. The sudden red glow in Quinn's eyes certainly made it seem so. Where had he gone? Was he coming back? Should she let him in if he did?

Rising, she moved through the house, placing new wards on the chimney, the doors and the windows. When that was done, she contemplated withdrawing Quinn's invitation to enter. Should she? Was it foolish of her to welcome a vampire into her home? If he intended to do her harm, wouldn't he have done so by now? Better safe than sorry, she mused. But she couldn't do it. As far as she knew, he had no friends, nowhere else to go. But it was knowing that Serepta had turned him against his will that determined Seleena's final decision. She couldn't deny Quinn the hospitality of her house, not after what her daughter had done to him.

Returning to the living room, she collected the cup and wineglass, carried them down to the kitchen and placed them in the sink. As she brewed a fresh pot of tea, she wondered where Quinn had gone and if—and when—he would return.

* * *

Shrouded in a cloak of invisibility, the vampire prowled the darkness outside the house, her heart filled with thoughts of vengeance. Those who had plotted her demise were inside. They had failed before. They would again.

Once she retrieved the power that resided within the dragon, she would be immortal. Indestructible.

She smiled into the darkness as she returned to her lair. If there was one thing her mother had taught her, it was the value of patience.

* * *

Quinn left the village with no destination in mind except to get away from Seleena. He had told Nardik his hunger was under control and when he'd said it, he was certain it was true. But now…now he wasn't so sure. Holding Seleena in his arms, he had wanted nothing more than to carry her to bed, to make love to her all night long. To taste the very sweet essence flowing through her veins even though she had warned him it would be painful. Perhaps fatal. At that moment, he hadn't cared.

He stalked the darkness in search of prey, finally ending up in front of a run-down spaceport on a lonely stretch of road. Several LandSkiffs were parked near the entrance.

He paused inside the doorway. Two pilots were hunched over a table, a bottle between them. An old man sat at a corner table, snoring softly. A middle-aged woman with frowsy black hair regarded him speculatively as he stepped up to the bar and ordered a glass of red wine.

Quinn slid a glance in her direction. She looked to be well-used and smelled bad. No doubt her blood was tainted with drugs and alcohol, but at the moment, all he cared about was easing his hunger. Summoning his preternatural power, he called her to him, took her by the hand, and led her outside into the shadows.

As he had suspected, the woman's blood tasted foul. A blessing, perhaps. Otherwise, he might have broken his promise to Seleena and drained her dry.

After wiping the memory from the woman's mind—another handy vampire talent - he strolled through the darkness. Serepta had been able to turn into mist. Could he actually do that?

Even as he considered it, it happened. One minute he was a solid physical mass. The next, he was little more than ethereal pale gray vapor hovering above the ground. He could see and hear and move, but had no sense of touch. No sense of himself. It was scary as Hel. What if he couldn't return to his own form again? His first two tries failed. Fighting the urge to panic, he calmed his thoughts and tried again.

Relief swept through him when he again felt the earth beneath his feet. He ran his hands along his arms, over his chest and face. He looked down at his legs, wiggled his toes. Everything seemed to be in the right place and in working order. Dissolving into mist might be a handy talent, but he wasn't sure he ever wanted to do it again.

Vampires were also able to change shape. Any shape, he wondered?

He spent the next twenty minutes experimenting—a bull, a horse, a wolf. Changing into a wolf came the easiest and satisfied some deep feral need he didn't quite understand. Perhaps it was because both vampires and wolves were predators.

It was near dawn when he returned to the house with the blue door.

Seleena had left a light burning in the window for him. He stood in the yard for several minutes, just staring at the faint welcoming glow. As he strode up the walk, that beckoning light made him feel like he was coming home.

An unexpected warmth flooded his heart as he stepped inside and closed the door behind him. A small fire burned in the hearth.

He stood in the center of the small living room, surrounded by Seleena's scent. He had never had a home of his own. Never had anyone—man or woman—who gave a damn whether he lived or died.

But Seleena cared. It was a sobering thought, and a little frightening. The last thing he wanted to do was hurt her.

Nardik's words echoed through the corridors of his mind. *How long do you think you can keep your lust for blood under control?*

It was a question that haunted him throughout the night.

* * *

Nardik arrived at Seleena's front door early the next morning. He glanced at Quinn, obviously displeased to see him again.

"Are you ready to go, Seleena?" the wizard asked.

"Yes." She donned a long, dark blue cloak. "I've asked Quinn to go with us."

Displeasure flashed across the wizard's face. "If you wish." Closing his eyes, he murmured an incantation that carried the three of them out of Seleena's house and into the great hall of Serepta's castle.

The room was eerily silent. Dust motes danced in a slim ray of sunshine. A rat scurried across the floor and disappeared behind a credenza.

"Do you feel it?" Nardik asked.

Seleena nodded.

Quinn didn't have to ask what he meant. Serepta's scent fouled the air. She had been in the room not long ago.

Quinn and Seleena followed the wizard through the kitchen and into the back yard. A narrow gravel pathway led to a tall wrought-iron gate. A small cemetery lay behind it.

Seleena reached for Quinn's hand as they followed Nardik through the gate toward a fresh grave located near the far wall.

A wave of the wizard's hand removed the earth, revealing a wooden coffin, the top intricately carved with runes and symbols.

Seleena took a deep breath as Nardik's magic lifted the lid.

The body inside was male. Two puncture wounds, smeared with dried blood, told the tale of his death.

With a cry of denial, Seleena buried her face against Quinn's chest.

Quinn didn't miss the sharp look of censure in Nardik's eyes. The wizard might be engaged to another woman, but it was obvious the man was jealous as Hel. Unable to resist the urge to poke the bear, Quinn smiled faintly as he slid his arm around Seleena's waist.

With a look of disgust, the wizard replaced the lid on the coffin. A wave of his hand filled in the grave.

"Where do you think she's holed up?" Quinn's question wasn't directed at anyone in particular.

"I am sure her lair is nearby," the wizard said, his voice cool. "Perhaps even in some hidden room within the castle itself."

"She's helpless during the day," Quinn remarked, thinking out loud. "This would be a good time to hunt her down…" He shut his mouth abruptly at the look of horror on Seleena's face.

"I fear he is right," Nardik said. "Without her magical powers, she is helpless until the sun sets."

"Perhaps we can help her now," Seleena said, stepping out of Quinn's embrace. The wizard snorted. "Painful as the truth is, we must face it. With or without her magic, Serepta is beyond redemption."

"I refuse to believe that." Seleena glared at Nardik. "I simply cannot."

"She must be stopped. She has taken two lives that we know of in the last few days, and who knows how many others? Do you want more innocent blood on your hands?"

Seleena flinched at his words.

"I am going to search for her," he said. "You can join me, or not, as you wish."

Quinn laid his hand on Seleena's arm. "You're in danger as long as she's alive," he said quietly.

"I am not afraid of her."

Quinn shook his head ruefully. "Maybe you should be."

"No one is safe as long as she is alive," Nardik said. "I intend to destroy her. And this time, I intend to make sure nothing is left to chance."

CHAPTER 9

"I'm going home," Seleena declared. "Quinn, are you coming?"

He hesitated. Daylight was when Serepta would be at her most vulnerable. If she was here, if they could find her and destroy her, Seleena would no longer be in danger. On the other hand, if he destroyed Serepta while she was helpless, Seleena might never forgive him. And that was a risk he wasn't willing to take.

"Quinn?"

He nodded. "I'll go with you."

Smiling, she reached for his hand.

Being transported magically was similar, and yet different, from when he did it as a vampire. Both were fast, but they didn't affect him the same way. When he transported from place to place, he had no real sense of movement. He thought of where he wanted to go and he was there. When Seleena did it, he was aware of moving through time and space.

But both methods got you where you wanted to go.

As soon as they reached home, Seleena went into the kitchen and brewed a pot of tea. He could see she was still badly shaken at knowing that the daughter she had thought dead these past weeks was still alive.

Thinking she probably needed a few minutes alone, Quinn went to his room and stretched out on the bed. While he appreciated being able to be awake during the day, he was sometimes overcome with the urge to crawl into a dark place and rest.

Eyes closed, he followed her progress in the kitchen by sound alone – her footsteps as she crossed from the stove to the cupboard. The clink of china as she placed cup and saucer on the counter. A hiss of hot water as she filled her cup. Her footsteps again as she moved into the living room. The creak of the rocker as she sat down. Freyja's purr as the cat settled on her lap.

The near-silent whisper of tears slipping down her cheeks.

He stayed on the bed, eyes closed, for several moments and then, unable to help himself, he went into the living room. Took the cup from her hand, placed it on table next to the rocking chair, and pulled her to her feet.

And into his arms.

Her eyes were red and puffy, her hair mussed, and she had never looked more desirable. Murmuring her name, he covered her mouth with his.

She leaned into him, her eyelids fluttering down as she clasped her hands behind his neck. Every thought fled her mind as his tongue swept over her lower lip, stealing the breath from her lungs, the strength from her legs. She clung to him, her whole body aching for his touch.

Until she remembered that he had been her daughter's lover. She tried to tell herself it didn't matter, but she couldn't get past it, especially now, knowing that Serepta was still alive. That she might still have power over him.

With a choked cry, she placed her palms flat against Quinn's chest and pushed. It was like trying to move a mountain.

For a moment, she thought he wouldn't release her.

For a moment, she hoped he wouldn't. But only a moment. So why did she feel bereft when he stepped away?

His knowing gaze met hers. She could almost hear his voice, slightly taunting, assuring her that sooner or later, it was going to happen.

Hands clenched, she lifted her chin. Maybe he was right, she thought defiantly. But it wouldn't be today.

* * *

Too restless to sit still, Seleena went out to work in her garden. She had been afraid that Quinn would follow her, but he had sent her one last smug look and returned to his room.

Angry with him, annoyed with herself, she pulled weeds with a vengeance, turned the soil, gathered a variety of herbs. And all the while she relived his kiss, the way his arms felt around her—sure and strong and, yes, even comforting. The way she felt so at home in his embrace. How was that possible when she had known him such a short time? When they had nothing in common? He was a bounty hunter, a rootless wanderer. A vampire. Even though she had conjured a spell to allow him to walk in the sunlight and to consume mortal food, he was no longer mortal. Nardik was certain that, sooner or later, Quinn would lose control and succumb to his vampire nature. That fear, however much she tried to ignore it, was a very real possibility.

She looked down when Freyja rubbed against her leg. "What is it?"

The cat meowed loudly, her bright yellow eyes glinting in the sun's light.

With a nod, Seleena left the basket of herbs on the kitchen table on her way to open the door for Nardik.

She knew by the look on his face that he hadn't found Serepta.

"There was no sign of her," he said as he followed her into the living room. "I searched every inch of that castle, from the dungeon to the turrets. If she was there, she is well-hidden."

Indicating Nardik should have a seat, Seleena lowered herself into the rocker. Freyja curled up on the floor at her feet. "What do we do now?"

"I believe we only have two options. We can send Quinn to the castle to wait for her. Or we can wait for her to come to him."

"You want to use him as bait?"

"They are going to meet eventually. It is only a matter of where and when."

Seleena didn't have to look over her shoulder to know Quinn stood in the doorway. The very air in the room felt charged with his presence.

He strode across the floor and stood in front of the fireplace, his arms crossed over his chest, his eyes like flint. "Maybe the two of you ought to consult me before making any plans that include pitting me against Serepta."

"Quinn…"

"We were merely discussing possibilities," Nardik said curtly.

"Uh-huh. And what do you think the possibilities are of me surviving such an encounter?"

Nardik lifted one shoulder and let it fall. "I have no idea. I do not know how powerful either one of you are. I know she was once a witch to be reckoned with, but I have no knowledge as to what her abilities as a vampire might be. Just as I have no idea of yours."

"That makes two of us. I didn't want to be a vampire and my lack of enthusiasm made her angry. She trapped me in that damn statue a couple of days later. I never had a chance to explore what being a vampire really means. I'm just now learning what powers are mine."

"That is unfortunate," Nardik said, his voice totally lacking any hint of concern, "as she has been a vampire for several decades."

Quinn's brows rose. "That long. Then I guess the power's on her side."

"Perhaps not," Seleena said. "If you could learn to wield the magic in that tattoo…"

"Wield it how?"

She shrugged. "I don't really know. I've never seen anything like it." She paused, her expression thoughtful. "I have an old grimoire that my mother left me. Maybe there's something in there that could enlighten us."

"It's worth a try, I guess," Quinn remarked.

"I shall leave you to it," Nardik said, rising. "I must return to Brynn Castle to advise the queen on a matter of state business. Let me know if you discover anything."

Nodding, Seleena stood and walked him to the door. "I'm glad you didn't find her," she said. "I know you think she is past redemption, and maybe she is, but I still have hope that we can save her."

"It springs eternal, they say." He touched her cheek lightly. "Good day."

Seleena closed the door, then stood with her back pressed against it. Not long ago, her life had been quiet, peaceful. She had tended her garden, helped the villagers, taken long walks. Grieved for her daughter.

Now there was a man in her living room who tied her emotions in knots, who, by merely looking at her, made her whole body ache with longing. And Serepta was alive. Or as alive as a vampire could be.

Sighing, she pushed away from the door and went to face the man who had turned her life upside down.

* * *

When she returned to the living room, she found Quinn standing with his back to the fireplace, hands shoved into his pants pockets. For a moment, they simply stood there, facing each other, while the air between them crackled with sexual tension.

Finally, clearing her throat, Seleena said, "I'll just go look for that grimoire."

Quinn nodded, though magic—at least book magic—was the last thing on his mind.

Her scent filled his nostrils and teased his hunger as she hurried passed him on the way to her room.

A good twenty minutes ticked by before she returned, a large book cradled in her arms. When she put it down, the coffee table groaned beneath its weight. Dust motes drifted up from the cover.

Sitting on the edge of the sofa, she used her athame to make a tiny cut in her thumb. Murmuring an incantation, she held her hand over the grimoire. A small drop of blood fell onto the cover, sizzled a moment, then disappeared. A faint puff of what looked like white smoke rose from the book when she lifted the cover.

Quinn moved in behind the sofa and peered over her shoulder. The page she was studying looked like an ancient work of art. Colorful flowers and intricate vines, faded by time, decorated the border. A small drawing depicted a witch bent over a cauldron. The text below the picture was in some fancy, foreign script.

"What's it say?" he asked.

"It's a spell to summon a lover."

Quinn rubbed his hand over his jaw as he considered and rejected several ribald remarks.

She turned another few pages, each as beautiful and ornate as the one before.

He was thinking they were wasting their time when she turned one more page, and even though he couldn't read the words, the pen and ink drawing in the center of the page spoke volumes.

Seleena looked up at him, then back at the drawing, which depicted a man tattooed with a dragon similar to Quinn's, save that the dragon was yellow instead of black.

"What does it say?"

"As we suspected, your dragon is a receptacle for black magic. There is no way to remove it, no way to undo it except by killing the host. However, it indicates that the magic can be transferred to the host, but it doesn't say how."

"So we're back to square one."

"Not exactly. At least we know it's possible for you to unleash the dragon's power."

"That's something, I guess. Is there anything in there about a vampire becoming mortal again?"

"I don't know. I'll look for that, too."

He watched her for several minutes, then started to pace the floor in front of the hearth. What if she found a way to make him human again? Did he really want that? He kind of liked his new strength and powers. And then there was the tattoo. What if she discovered the secret to controlling whatever magic the dragon held? If he could combine the power of the dragon and his vampire strength, maybe he would be able to defeat Serepta.

Quinn grunted softly. Power or not, he wanted the dragon gone before Serepta got hold of him again.

He glanced at Seleena. How was it possible she had given birth to such a cruel, vindictive woman? No doubt about it, he thought, the daughter must surely take after her father.

And he didn't trust either one.

Chapter 10

It was near midnight when Seleena closed the grimoire. "I'm going to bed." Rising, she stretched her arms over her head. "Will I see you tomorrow?"

Quinn nodded. "Do you really think you'll find the answer we're looking for in that book?" She had gone through half of it in the last couple of hours with no real results.

"I hope so. Good night."

He watched her glide out of the room. And then, unable to resist, he called, "Sweet dreams."

Her answer was the slamming of her bedroom door.

Grinning, he left the house.

The village lay quiet under a cloudy sky, the silence broken only by the serenade of crickets, tree frogs, and night birds. All the houses were dark, curtains drawn against the night.

A large gray owl swooped down out of a nearby tree, talons extended as it descended on some luckless rodent.

His mother had once told him a story about a boy who turned into an owl. He remembered little of the tale, except that when the boy's journey as an owl was over, he discovered he would rather be a little boy.

His mother…she had been young and beautiful with silky black hair and bright blue eyes before life on the streets took its toll.

She had died too young, Quinn thought. As a child, he had vowed to avenge her death, but time and Jagg and Serepta had got in the way. But there was nothing to stop him now.

Power surged within him as thoughts of vengeance filled his mind. He ran his tongue over his fangs.

It was time for Jagg to pay the piper.

* * *

Bosquetown was a Hel-hole without equal. The smelly armpit of Brynn Tor, Quinn mused as he stalked the back alleys toward Jagg's place. Nothing had changed since he'd last been here. The brothels were ablaze with light, the streets crowded with drunken men, and women willing to do anything for a few credits. Fat brown rats scurried from building to building. Feral cats scavenged the trash cans, eyes shining in the dark. The air reeked with the stink of sweat and stale perfume, of lust and blood and death.

Jagg's place was at the end of a narrow lane. The doors stood open. Two men—each one built like an ox— guarded the entrance. Quinn didn't recognize either one of them, but then, Jagg had a hair-trigger temper and his henchmen rarely lasted long.

They eyed him suspiciously as he stepped inside. Something in his demeanor must have warned them to tread carefully because they nodded and looked quickly away as he passed by.

The interior was dark, thick with the stink of whiskey and drugs and stale sweat. A heavy layer of smoke hung in the air. There were perhaps two dozen people inside - most of them men. None of them sober.

He found Jagg in his usual place—slouched at a back table with a pretty girl at his side, another one massaging his bull-like neck, while a third knelt at his feet. Jagg looked the same as always—sallow skin, close-set eyes, a nose that had been broken several times. He was easily the ugliest man Quinn had ever seen.

Jagg's attention stayed on the girl at his side until Quinn said, "Some things never change."

The big man looked up, eyes narrowing and then widening with surprised recognition. "Quinn! Glad I am to see ya again!"

"Uh-huh. We need to talk."

Jagg grinned, exposing a set of badly-stained teeth. "I can't be leaving these three beauties now, can I? Have a drink. We'll talk later."

Quinn glanced from one girl to the other. The youngest—the one at his feet—was no more than fourteen. The oldest might have been sixteen. They all looked scared to death. "I don't think they'll miss you."

Jagg's eyes narrowed again. "I take it this isn't a social call."

"You got that right."

"What happened to that witch? She get tired of you already?"

Quinn tensed as he heard movement behind him. He felt his eyes go red, felt his fangs descend as he whirled around to find the thugs who had been guarding the front door lumbering toward him.

With preternatural speed, Quinn lunged forward and broke the neck of the first one and tossed him aside. He landed on a nearby table. Men scattered. The table splintered.

The second man hesitated.

"What are you waiting for?" Jagg screamed. "Kill him!"

Quinn grinned as he beckoned the man toward him. Either the guy had found his courage or he was just plain stupid, but he lunged forward, his ham-like hands reaching for Quinn. Quinn danced out of his way, then clipped him a good one on the jaw. The thug went down like a felled tree.

The snick of a gun being cocked echoed loudly in the suddenly-silent room.

Fangs bared, Quinn turned to face Jagg. "You gonna shoot me? Really?"

For a moment, Jagg stared at him. And then he fired the gun. Six quick shots.

His face paled when Quinn remained standing.

"Get out of here," Quinn told the girls. "And don't look back."

The three of them bolted out of the place as if their feet were on fire.

"You're through trafficking in human flesh," Quinn said.

Jagg grunted. "Selling you to the witch was nothing personal, my boy. It was just good business." Before the last word was out of his mouth, he pulled a knife and scrambled over the table.

He was remarkably quick for such a big man. But not quick

enough, Quinn thought as he jerked the knife out of Jagg's hand and buried it to the hilt in his heart. "As of tonight," he said, giving the blade a savage twist, "you're out of business."

He backed away as the body sprawled face down on the floor. Turning, Quinn confronted the crowd.

A few of the men from nearby tables lumbered to their feet. They glanced at Jagg's body, then at Quinn, weighing their chances.

"Anybody else?" he challenged.

Nobody moved.

Nobody spoke.

And nobody tried to stop him when he walked out the door.

Outside, Quinn took several deep breaths. *It's done, Ma,* he thought. *I hope he burns in Hel.*

A thought took him back to the small white house with the blue door.

* * *

Seleena paced the living room floor, Freyja at her heels. It had been hours since she had gone to bed, and it was still hours until dawn.

Where had Quinn gone? And why hadn't he told her he was leaving, or at least left a note? Was he coming back? Did she want him to?

She stopped so abruptly, Freyja bumped into her, then let out a yowl of protest.

Murmuring, "Sorry," Seleena cradled Freyja in her arms, then sat in the rocker, and gently stroked the cat's head. "I just don't know what to do. Maybe, if I just take him to my bed, it would solve everything. What do you think?"

Freyja's hiss left no doubt as to what she thought.

"Yes, I know you still don't like him. But…" Seleena shook her head. "I can't help thinking that once he adjusts to being a vampire and puts his anger at that horrible man, Jagg, behind him, you'll discover he's really a very nice man."

With a twitch of her tail, Freyja jumped out of her arms and ran from the room.

A moment later, the bell announced a visitor.

Seleena's heart skipped a beat when she opened the door and saw Quinn standing there.

"Okay if I come in?" he asked.

"Of course," she said. And then frowned. "Why wouldn't it be?"

"I killed a couple of men tonight."

"But…if you had broken your promise, I would have known."

"I didn't kill them like that….by draining their blood. Hel, I would rather die than take a sip of Jagg's blood."

"Jagg," she murmured. "You killed Jagg."

Quinn nodded. "And one of his men."

"Come in." She closed the door behind him, then followed him into the living room. "I rarely say this about anyone, but I think that, after what Jagg did, he had it coming."

"It didn't bring my mother back."

"Then you have learned an important lesson."

"Yeah? What might that be?"

"Just what you said. Revenge doesn't restore what you've lost. And rarely eases the pain."

"You're a wise and beautiful woman." And she was beautiful, he thought as he stared at her in the flickering firelight. She wore a long white nightgown under a dark blue robe. White slippers peeked beneath the hem. Her hair fell in soft waves over her shoulders.

She smiled, pleased by the compliment. "Would you care for a glass of wine?"

"Sure." He followed her into the kitchen, stood with his back to the counter while she filled two goblets with dark-red liquid.

"What shall we drink to?" she asked, handing him one of the glasses.

His gaze met hers. "How about new beginnings, Red?"

* * *

Standing in the shadows, Serepta's heart swelled with anger as she listened to the byplay between her mother and Quinn. When had the two of them become such intimate friends? And how dare they?

She called upon her power, but it was weak, so weak. She missed her magic, missed the spell that had allowed her to walk in the daylight, to eat mortal food. Vampires were supposed to love the taste of blood, but she loathed it. It was thick and warm and always the same. She wanted bread and meat and cake.

And Quinn's head, on a platter.

Dissolving into mist, she drifted up to the kitchen window, her anger turning to rage when Quinn drew her mother into his arms. He would pay for his disloyalty, she vowed. In blood!

***

Quinn gazed into Seleena's eyes. He had never known anyone with such beautiful eyes—deep and gray and peaceful. Lowering his head, he whispered, "Are you going to tell me no again?" while he rained kisses along the side of her neck.

Seleena clung to him as he covered her mouth with his. Why was she fighting this? Why not surrender to the desire thrumming through her? Who would know? Who would care? "Quinn…"

He released her abruptly. Eyes narrowed, nostrils flared, he glanced around the room, then stared at the window.

"What is it?" Seleena asked, her gaze following his. "What's wrong?"

"She's out there."

Chapter 11

Seleena stared at Quinn, her expression stricken. "She's here? Now? Are you sure?"

"I can smell her." The scent was faint but one he would never forget. It sparked memories best forgotten.

"There's nothing to worry about," Seleena said, her voice trembling. "She can't come in. I revoked her invitation after the last time I saw her."

He nodded. And yet he couldn't help wondering which of them would prevail in a fight. Serepta no longer had magic on her side. Physically, he was sure to be the more powerful of the two. But a vampire's preternatural abilities grew stronger with age. Nardik had mentioned that Serepta had been a vampire for "several decades." How many decades was that, exactly? Five? Ten? More?

"What are you thinking about?" Seleena asked.

"It's said that vampires grow stronger as they age."

"Yes. So?"

"So, she's been a vampire longer than I have. But what if I inherited her strength when she turned me? What if we're equally matched?"

"What if you're not?"

"Only one way to find out."

Seleena placed a staying hand on his arm. "You're not thinking of going out to confront her, are you?"

"It's tempting."

"Are you out of your mind? That's the craziest thing I've ever heard!"

"Maybe," Quinn allowed. "But how else are we ever going to defeat her?"

Seleena pulled a chair from the table and sat down. "I don't know. I can't help thinking there might still be a chance to save her."

"I think that ship sailed long ago."

Seleena slumped in the chair. "Is she still out there?"

"Yeah."

"What's she doing?"

"Watching us."

She looked up, her gaze fixed on the window. "I don't see her."

"Do you see that faint, shadowy mist hovering near the top corner?"

Seleena nodded.

"That's her."

"Can you do that?"

"Yeah. It's kind of creepy, though. The first time I did it…Wait. She's gone."

"I don't know whether to be sorry or relieved."

"I don't know how you can be sorry. She wants to kill you, remember? There's not a doubt in my mind that she'd do it without a qualm."

Rising, Seleena blinked away her tears. "I'm going back to bed. I'll see you tomorrow."

Quinn muttered an oath as he watched her go. Why the devil had he said anything? She was already hurting. All he'd done was make it worse.

Minutes passed.

And then he followed her.

* * *

Serepta floated away from the window, eased down to the ground, and resumed her mortal form. So, Quinn had murdered Jagg. That was an interesting piece of news. And she knew just what to do with it.

* * *

Seleena had barely settled into bed when there was a soft tap on her bedroom door.

"Seleena?"

Sitting up, she used the edge of the sheet to wipe the tears from her eyes before inviting him in. "Is something wrong?" She felt her heart skip a beat as he walked toward her, a tall, dark shape gliding silently across the floor.

From the foot of the bed, Freyja hissed at him.

Ignoring the cat, he sat on the edge of the mattress. "You tell me."

"I'm fine. Just…" She wiped her eyes again. "You know."

Nodding, he cradled her in his arms. "I'm here for you," he said quietly.

She looked into his eyes, thinking she had never felt so safe. For the first time in her life, she had someone to turn to, someone she could trust. She closed her eyes as his hand lightly stroked her hair, let herself relax in his embrace.

The slow, steady sound of her breathing told Quinn she'd fallen asleep. Holding her close, knowing she trusted him enough to fall asleep in his arms, filled him with a surge of protectiveness he had never known before. She was a strong woman, a powerful witch, but still vulnerable to pain and heartache.

He had never worried about anyone else in his entire life. Never gave a damn about what people thought of him. He had lived his life with only one thought in mind—survival. But now, for the first time, he cared more for someone else's welfare than his own. And he wasn't sure what to do about it.

He eased Seleena under the covers, removed his boots and shirt, and slid into bed beside her, his arm around her shoulders, the silk of her hair soft against his cheek.

Surprisingly, it turned out to be the best night's sleep he had ever known.

* * *

Seleena woke slowly, her eyes widening when she realized she wasn't alone in bed. Quinn lay to her right, sleeping soundly. Freyja lay on the other side, staring at her with disapproving yellow eyes.

Turning onto her side, Seleena studied Quinn. His expression was less harsh in repose. For a moment, she simply admired the sheer, masculine beauty of the man. The sheet was pooled at his waist, revealing the broad expanse of his chest. She was intrigued by the fact that the dragon on his shoulder seemed to be asleep, as well.

After dislodging Freyja, Seleena eased out of bed, drew on her robe, stepped into her slippers, and went into the kitchen. While waiting for a pot of tea to steep, something compelled her to turn on the news channel, something she rarely did.

There were the usual reports of thefts in outlying areas, a photo of Queen Marri welcoming a dignitary from a nearby star system. Seleena spied Gryff and Nardik in the background.

She was about to shut down the receiver when the onscreen reporter mentioned a killing in Bosquetown. Seleena pressed a hand to her heart as the murdered man was identified as Jagg Corwinn, a local businessman. The killing had taken place in Corwinn's tavern in front of two dozen witnesses, who had provided the culprit's description to local law enforcement. Seleena gasped as a police sketch of the killer appeared onscreen. The resemblance to Quinn was unmistakable. A large reward was being offered for any information regarding his identity or whereabouts.

Behind her, a familiar male voice muttered, "Well, damn."

Seleena glanced over her shoulder at his soft-spoken expletive. "At least they don't know your name or where you live."

"Yeah." He dropped into the chair across from hers.

Her gaze slid away from his.

He didn't have to read her mind to know she was embarrassed about letting him spend the night in her bed, even though nothing had happened between them. She had an old-fashioned sense of morality which he found faintly amusing and endearing at the same time.

"I was just about to fix breakfast," she said, pushing away from the table. "Eggs and sausage. Would you like some?"

"Sure. Thanks." Sitting back, he watched her move around the kitchen, gathering the things she needed. She didn't drink coffee, and he couldn't help smiling when she made a pot, knowing it was just for him.

His mother was the only other woman who had ever prepared a

meal especially for him. Since his mother's passing, he had eaten in taverns or café's when he could afford it. When he'd been with Serepta, the maids had done the work.

Serepta. He would gladly give a year of his life to know where she holed up during the day.

Minutes later, Seleena put breakfast on the table. Still not meeting his eyes, she took her seat.

He stabbed a forkful of egg, then put it down. "You gonna look at me any time today, Red?"

"Quinn…"

"Hey, I get it. It makes you uncomfortable, having a man in your house. Having a vampire in your house. If you want me gone, just say the word."

"No!" She looked up. "This is just all so new to me."

"New?"

"I have never felt this way about anyone."

"Never? What about Serepta's father?"

"He taught me much of what I know. We shared a very brief relationship. It burned hot and quick and then it was over."

"But you kept in touch."

"How could we not?" she asked. "We had a child together." She had been fond of Nardik. Untouched and curious. Flattered by his attention. But he had never touched her heart. Never made her feel the excitement, the anticipation, that Quinn stirred within her. Was it love? Or merely a stronger, deeper passion than what she had felt for Nardik? And how was she to know?

"So," Quinn said, leaning across the table. "What now?"

"I guess that's up to you. The village is my home, my life. It's enough for me. Is it enough for you?"

Quinn leaned back in his chair, arms folded over his chest. *Was* it enough for him? He had never had a home of his own. Never stayed in one place long enough to put down roots of any kind. Working for Jagg didn't count. The year he had spent with Serepta was the longest he had lived in one place, but he hadn't been there willingly.

"Quinn?"

"I don't know, Red," he admitted. "But I'm ready to try."

* * *

Seleena thought about his words off and on the rest of the day, whether picking herbs to prepare a poultice for Nannie Bednar, or shopping for a roast for dinner. That night, sitting across from him at the table, she couldn't help wondering what it would be like to have Quinn stay with her indefinitely. To go to bed at night, knowing he was in the next room? How long before she surrendered to the desire in his eyes? To the yearning of her own heart?

How long would it take before he grew bored with her quiet life, before he grew restless and moved on? Did she want to enjoy his company for however long he stayed, knowing it would break her heart when he left?

"There are no guarantees in life," she told the cat as she got ready for bed that night. "Better to snatch what happiness I can instead of worrying about what might never happen, don't you think?"

Pleased with her decision, she crawled into bed and closed her eyes with Freyja's disapproving hiss rumbling in her ears.

Chapter 12

The sound of breaking glass, grunts of pain, and Freyja's urgent meows woke Seleena. Sitting up, she glanced around the room. The cat was nowhere to be seen, but her frantic cries grew louder.

Slipping out of bed, Seleena padded barefooted into the living room, only to come to an abrupt halt at the sight that met her eyes. Freyja, spitting and hissing, was trapped in a net. Bits of broken crockery littered the floor. Three Enforcers, all with long, bloody claw marks on his cheeks, were dragging three of their downed companions through the doorway. A half-dozen others, heavily armed, were in the act of restraining Quinn. His chest, neck, and hands were bound with thick silver restraints. She caught a quick glance of his bloodied face before they hustled him out the door.

"Here, now!" she exclaimed, hurrying after them. "What's going on?"

One of the Enforcers turned to face her. "We received an anonymous report that a fugitive was staying here."

"You had no right to barge into my house without my permission," Seleena declared, arms akimbo. "Or a warrant, or something."

The man reached into his pocket and withdrew a sheet of paper.

"Got it right here," he said, waving it in front of her face. "You're lucky we don't haul you in as an accomplice."

For a brief moment, Seleena considered using her magic, but before she could conjure a spell that would effectively incapacitate almost a dozen men without the danger of doing any permanent harm, they were already out the door and speeding away.

She stared after them. There were times when having a conscience was a terrible inconvenience. Had she practiced Black Magic, she could simply have killed them all.

But that kind of violence was abhorrent.

As soon as they were gone, Seleena released Freyja. Meowing her thanks, the cat rubbed against her ankles.

"Not now," Seleena said. "I need to get dressed and go after Quinn. I know, you think it's dangerous. But I'll be fine."

In her room, she threw off her nightgown, pulled on a long black skirt and blouse, stepped into a pair of boots.

Going into Quinn's room, she found one of his shirts, which she carried into the living room. After placing it in her cauldron, she lit a candle, picked up her wand, and invoked a location spell.

* * *

Quinn didn't struggle as they hustled him into a LandSkiff, chained him to a bolt in the floor, and slammed the door behind him. The silver burned where it touched his skin. Worse, it weakened him, as he discovered when he tried to yank the bolt from the floor, something that should have been ridiculously easy. He tried dissolving into mist, but with no success.

Cursing softly, he sank down on his haunches, wondering where they were taking him. What would happen when they reached their destination. And why Seleena hadn't worked a little magic and turned his captors into hop toads.

He leaned his head against the sidewall and closed his eyes. How had they found him? And how had they known he was a vampire and that silver would weaken him and render him incapable of dissolving into mist? "Serepta," he muttered. Of course. She had been prowling around Seleena's place last night. No doubt she had overheard the news of Jagg's death. Seen the sketch of his face.

He ground his teeth in anger.

Damn her black soul to Hel.

His only consolation was in knowing he had taken three of the Enforcers out of action before the others overpowered him.

He scrambled to his feet as the LandSkiff slowed to a stop. Hands clenched, he watched the door open. Three of the Enforcers waited outside. Big guys. Over six feet tall. Two-hundred-and-fifty pounds easy. One of them stepped inside. The other two covered him with their weapons.

Knowing that struggling would only get him shot, Quinn let himself be led outside, docile as a newborn colt.

He had never been inside the Bosquetown prison. It was a large, rectangular building made of solid gray stone. Armed guards patrolled the walls. His captors marched him into the precinct, demanded his personal information - name, date of birth, residence, employment.

The first two were easy. He had no residence. "And no employment at the moment," he added with a wry grin.

The Enforcer taking his information snorted. "You should have thought of that before you killed your employer."

"Who accused me of killing him?"

"I'm not at liberty to say."

Serepta, again, Quinn thought. A short time later, he found himself inside a small, square cell, his hands and feet shackled with thick silver chains that blistered his flesh. Biting back a groan, he sank down on the stone floor, preferring it to the narrow, bug-infested cot against the wall.

Too bad he hadn't killed Jagg in Brynn City, he thought ruefully. He had heard the jail there was something to see. Double beds with clean sheets. Hot and cold running water. Three good meals a day. Movies every night. Even a little female entertainment if you had the money to bribe the right people.

He looked up when one of the guards strolled by. "Hey!"

The man stopped, his expression surly. "What do you want?"

"How about some breakfast?"

The guard, whose name tag identified him as Ryann, snorted. "Sorry, we're all out of blood."

"How about some ham and eggs?"

Ryann's brows rose to his hairline. "I thought you were a vampire."

Quinn jerked a thumb at the narrow, silver-barred window above his head. "The sun's up. How can I be awake if I'm a vampire?"

"I don't know. I don't care."

"What about that breakfast?"

With a shake of his head, Ryann continued on his way.

Quinn had resigned himself to going hungry when Ryann came back, a wooden plate in his hand. He slid it under a slot in the door, stood there, watching with ill-disguised curiosity, while Quinn ate.

"Well, I'll be damned," the guard muttered. "Why'd they think you were a filthy bloodsucker?"

"Bad information, I guess."

"Yeah?" Ryann asked skeptically. "What about those burns on your wrists and ankles? Doesn't happen to normal folk."

"I'm allergic to silver, that's all." Quinn groaned softly. "Any chance you could get rid of these shackles?"

The guard met Quinn's gaze for the first time. "I don't have the authority to do that."

It was the opportunity Quinn had been waiting for. He captured the man's gaze with his own. "I need you to come in here and remove these chains."

"Yes," the guard said, his voice wooden. "Remove them." He unlocked the cell door, stooped down to unlock the restraints.

"Now you will put them on," Quinn said, gaining his feet. "When I'm gone, you won't call for help. And you won't remember me or this conversation."

"I won't call," Ryann said as he locked the shackles in place. "I won't remember."

With a growing sense of urgency, Quinn dissolved into mist and fled the prison.

* * *

Seleena was about to step out the door when Quinn suddenly materialized in front of her. She let out a little cry of surprise, then threw her arms around his neck.

Not one to pass up an opportunity when it presented itself, Quinn pulled her closer. After the foul stench of his jail cell, she smelled good enough to eat. The thought made him grin.

"I was just coming after you!" She leaned into him. "How did you get out?"

"A little magic of my own," he said, smiling down at her. "Vampire style."

She caressed his cheek. "I was so worried."

He closed his eyes, savoring her nearness, her concern. She was the only woman, besides his mother, who had ever given a damn whether he lived or died.

Seleena drew back to get a good look at him, gasped when she saw the horrible burns on his wrists and ankles. Grabbing his hand, she led him into the kitchen. "Sit."

She quickly filled a basin with water, warmed it with a word, then gently bathed his burned flesh. Unlike most wounds, those caused by silver didn't heal immediately. When she was done, she opened a jar of pink ointment and then, chanting softly, she spread a thick coat over his wrists and ankles.

And the pain was gone.

Quinn blew out a sigh. "Thanks, Red."

"I don't think you should stay here anymore," she said, taking the chair next to him. "Not now, when they know where to find you."

"Yeah. I guess you're right. You probably don't want them barging in here again after the mess they made."

"It's not that. I'm just afraid that next time someone might get killed. And it might be you."

"Hey, I understand. I appreciate all you've done for me." He was going to miss her, he thought. More than he had ever missed anyone. He raked his fingers through his hair, then stood. There was nothing else to say. He didn't have anything to pack. Once he was gone, there would be nothing left to show he had ever been there. He cupped her cheek, kissed her lightly, and headed for the door.

"You're going to leave!" she exclaimed, jumping to her feet. "Just like that?"

He glanced over his shoulder. "I thought you wanted me gone?"

"Well, yes, but…"

He lifted one brow. "But?"

"I…" Her gaze slid away from his.

Quinn smiled as he turned and closed the distance between them. "Are you saying you want to go with me?"

Still not meeting his gaze, she nodded. "Yes. But I wanted you to ask me."

"I don't have anything to offer you, Red. You know that, don't you?"

"I don't need anything."

"No?"

She looked up at him, her cheeks stained with embarrassment.

"You don't have to admit it," he said with a grin. "I like you, too. Any ideas about where we should go?"

Her brows drew together in a thoughtful frown. "Nardik has a place up in the Crystal Mountains on the far side of the Brynn Sea. We could stay there for awhile. I'm sure he wouldn't mind."

Quinn shook his head. "I don't think that's a good idea." The last thing he wanted was be indebted to the wizard.

"Have you got a better one?"

"Not really." It would be a great place to hide from the Enforcers, but they weren't the only threat they had to worry about. "What's to keep Serepta from following us there?"

"Nothing. She can follow us anywhere, which is why we need a real home. A place she can't enter without an invitation."

"I'm pretty sure Nardik wouldn't like the idea of me staying there."

"We'll worry about it when he finds out. Give me a minute to pack a few things. We should leave right away. Come along, Freyja."

* * *

Quinn had expected Seleena to use magic to transport them, but she had a different idea.

He followed her outside, waited while she locked the back door and warded the house with a protective spell.

"Now what?" he asked.

Smiling at him over her shoulder, she went to what Quinn had thought was a large storage shed. When she opened the door, he was surprised to see a new LandSkiff. Silver in color, it seemed to glow even in the shed's dim light.

Lifting Freyja into her arms, she asked, "Do you drive?"

"Since I was big enough to reach the controls." He opened the passenger door for her, then went around to the driver's side. The Skiff was loaded with every imaginable extra. The engine purred like one of Brynn Tor's white tigers.

"Where'd you get this?" he asked as he headed out of the village.

She shrugged. "It was a gift."

"From Nardik?"

"No. From a grateful father after I saved his daughter's life."

"Beats loaves of bread."

"Perhaps. But you can't eat the Skiff."

"Good point. But you could sell it for enough to buy more bread than you could eat in a lifetime."

Once clear of the village, he programmed the coordinates she gave him, then sat back, one hand resting lightly on the controls.

Seleena gazed out the window, absently stroking Freyja's head. The countryside passed by in a blur. What was it about men, she wondered, that they were constantly pushing the edge of the envelope?

She slid a covert glance in Quinn's direction. Was she making a mistake, running off with a man she hardly knew? It was one thing to be alone with him in her home in the village. She had friends there, neighbors who needed her help. Nardik's house was located high in the mountains, a solitary dwelling miles away from the nearest town. What would she do there, alone with Quinn?

Warmth curled through her belly as a host of ideas skittered across her mind.

Alone. With Quinn.

There were, she thought, worse fates.

* * *

Quinn smiled inwardly. He was keenly aware of Seleena's glances, of the sudden uptick in the beat of her heart, the flush in her cheeks. She wanted him. She might not be willing to say the words, she might not want to admit, even to herself, but all the signs were there. Thanks to his preternatural power, he could smell it on her. It spiked his own desire. And his hunger.

He squinted against the afternoon sun, which shone brightly through the Skiff's windshield. Though he could be awake during the day, the sun was not his friend.

He opened the throttle all the way. The sooner they reached Nardik's place, the better, he thought. Or was it?

The countryside changed dramatically as they left Seleena's village far behind.

Desert gave way to grassland and gently rolling hills. Luxurious homes located on large lots dotted the landscape. Three-story shopping centers sprang up here and there. They made a brief stop at one of them to eat a quick lunch and buy groceries.

Quinn loaded the boxes into the back of the Skiff and they were on their way again.

As the miles passed, houses grew scarce.

He caught a whiff of the Brynn Sea long before it was visible. And then they topped a rise and it was there, a splash of bright blue beyond an ocean of grass. And rising out of the Sea, the Crystal Mountains of Brynn Tor, the highest peak perpetually covered in snow.

Beside him, Seleena murmured, "I had forgotten how beautiful it is."

"Yeah. It's quite a sight."

"See that stand of timber, just there?" Seleena said, pointing. "A road runs alongside it. Follow it to the end. The Fortress is at the top."

"Gotcha."

The road, narrow and covered with dead leaves and pine cones, seemed to go on forever, gradually climbing higher and higher and higher, until the trail ended on a flat strip of land surrounded by ancient trees, most of them over a hundred feet high. A round house—four stories tall and painted a sparkling white trimmed in dark green—stood in the center of a verdant meadow. Sunlight glinted off dozens of stained glass windows.

Quinn whistled softly. "That's some place. Any particular reason why it's round?"

"It prevents outside magic from being effective on the inhabitants," Seleena said. "It's the reason many castles have round turrets and towers."

"I guess you do learn something new every day," he muttered as he pulled up in front of the house. Three stone steps led to a covered veranda that circled the main floor. The front door looked like solid oak strapped with iron. It had no visible latch.

"I forgot to mention that there's a cloaking spell at the foot of the mountain, although I'm not sure it's effective against uninvited vampires."

"I have my doubts that it would work against Serepta. She's tasted my blood. She branded me with this damn tattoo. I'm pretty sure she can track me anywhere, through just about anything."

Seleena nodded. "You might be right. But there's also a spell around the house that causes intruders and those intent on mischief to forget why they came."

"Mischief?" Quinn snorted. "She's got more than mischief on her mind."

"We should be safe enough. Even if none of Nardik's spells work, she's still a vampire. She can't enter the house without my invitation."

"Wouldn't Nardik have to invite her? For that matter, how did I get in without his invitation? It's his place, after all."

"Actually, I own half of it. He wanted it to be in my name, too, in case anything happened to him. Shall we?"

Quinn exited the Skiff, walked around the front to open Seleena's door, then moved to the back to unload the boxes of groceries.

Beckoning for him to follow her, she led the way to the front door.

"There's no latch. How do we get in?"

She smiled at him over her shoulder. "Leave that to me." Stepping forward, she placed her hand on the middle of the door and chanted softly.

Quinn heard the scrape of metal against metal as the interior locks disengaged. A moment later, the door swung open and Seleena crossed the threshold.

When he tried to follow, an invisible barrier kept him out. It was an odd sensation. Not painful. But not pleasant, either.

Seleena turned around when she realized he wasn't behind her. "Sorry. I forgot. Quinn, please come in. You are welcome in the Fortress until I decree otherwise."

"Thanks." He wasn't sure what he'd expected, but it was nothing like what he saw. The floor was black marble, the walls a blindingly bright white, until Seleena closed the door.

Quinn stared in disbelief as colorful images appeared on the walls—scenes of Brynn Tor's countryside at various times of the year - the mountains and trees covered in snow, the skies dark with clouds; hills and valleys verdant with new life - both plant and animal -in the spring; the leaves changing in a kaleidoscope of color in the fall. It was like an ever-changing movie.

"Amazing, is it not?" Seleena asked.

He nodded. A fireplace dominated one wall. Leather sofas and chairs - all well-worn and comfortable-looking, were grouped here and there. An arched doorway opened onto a spacious dining room. He assumed the closed door to the right led to a bathroom. A winding staircase with a wrought-iron banister led upward.

"The kitchen is downstairs," Seleena said. "The rooms on the second floor are bedrooms. The third floor rooms are empty. Nardik's private quarters are on the fourth floor."

"Why the empty third floor?"

"He wanted space between where he works his magic and the rest of the house."

"Did you live here with him?"

"Yes, for a time, while he was teaching me magic." She paused a moment, her expression pensive. "Serepta was conceived here."

More information than he needed - or wanted - to know, Quinn mused sourly. And then he frowned. "Was she born here, too?"

"Yes."

"Then why would she need in an invite?"

"Nardik revoked her invitation when she became a vampire, as did I. Come along, let's take those boxes down to the kitchen," she suggested. "I'd like a cup of tea."

The downward staircase opened onto a large room. Overhead lights came on automatically. The kitchen had all the usual equipment - sink, stove, refrigeration, a long, white, marble-topped counter, cupboards over and underneath.

Quinn unloaded the boxes and Seleena put the items away. When they were done, he sat at the table, content to watch her as she moved about, taking a kettle from one of the cupboards and a box of tea from another. She added a measure of tea to the kettle and filled the pot with water made hot by a word and a wave of her hand. While waiting for the tea to steep, she pulled a blue china cup and saucer from a shelf, then glanced at Quinn over her shoulder, a question in her eyes.

"You got any wine in this place?"

"Of course," she said, smiling as she opened another cupboard and retrieved a bottle. "Nothing but the best."

He stretched his legs out in front of him, admiring the beauty of her face and figure as she poured the wine in a crystal goblet. When the kettle whistled, she took it from the stove and poured herself a cup, then took the seat across from him.

He grinned inwardly, amused by the domestic scene and by her reluctance to meet his gaze. He figured she was probably reassessing the wisdom of the two of them staying in this big old house in the middle of nowhere. On the other hand, she was a powerful witch. Likely her magic was far more deadly than any power he could muster as a vampire.

But then, it wasn't his preternatural power she was afraid of. No, it was the growing sexual tension between them, a yearning that grew stronger with every passing day.

She looked up, a gasp escaping her lips when their gazes met.

And though he hadn't spoken the words aloud, they hung in the air between them.

It's gonna happen, Red. Sooner or later, it's gonna happen.

And this was just as good a place as any.

CHAPTER 13

Serepta woke with the setting of the sun. For a moment, she laid there, her senses reaching, probing the area surrounding her lair. But there was no one nearby. Rising, she left the cave and transported herself to her castle.

Her father's scent, along with her mother's and Quinn's, now days old, lingered in the air. Foolish of them, to think they would find her here, helplessly trapped in the dark sleep.

In her room, she cast off her gown and stepped into the shower. She smiled faintly as she wondered how Quinn was enjoying prison. But he wouldn't enjoy it long. She would go there tonight, drive a stake into his heart, and reclaim her magic. Without it, she felt as if she were missing a vital part of herself. The most important part. She hated being a vampire without it. True, she had a vampire's preternatural powers, but she detested having to drink nothing but blood, living only by night. She could still compel mortals to do her bidding, but it wasn't the same.

Stepping out of the shower, she changed into a pair of silky black pants and matching shirt, pulled on a pair of high-heeled black boots.

She grimaced as the hunger rose within her, undeniable, insatiable without her magic to control it.

Leaving the castle, she transported herself to Ironntown, where she fed on the first man she saw. She grinned inwardly. She could have made it pleasant for him, but why should she? It wasn't pleasant for her, feeding like some feral beast. And yet, the blood satisfied her hunger, while killing him satisfied another darker need.

She wiped her mouth with his shirttail, then tossed the body into a ravine. His death meant less nothing to her. She was a vampire, he was prey.

A thought took her to the Bosquetown prison. Outside the gate, she dissolved into mist, then floated over the wall, drifting above the heads of the guards who patrolled the perimeter. She entered through an open window and made her way down to the cells below.

She materialized in the shadows, then followed Quinn's scent to a cell near the end of the corridor, only to find it empty.

Fury rose within her, as hot as the lava that sometimes spewed from the volcano east of the snow-capped mountains of Brynn Tor.

Hands clenched at her sides, she took a deep, calming breath. He might not be here, but he couldn't hide from her forever.

Sensing a man coming up behind her, she spun around.

"Here, now!" the guard exclaimed. "How did you get in here?"

"Like this." Calling upon her preternatural power, she dissolved into mist.

"What the Hel!" Eyes wide with disbelief he stumbled backward.

Serepta quickly resumed her own form. Laughing softly, she trapped him in her embrace and buried her fangs in his throat. He was dead before he hit the ground. Wiping his blood from her lips, she strolled out of the prison.

Chapter 14

Seleena plumped her pillow, rolled onto her side, then onto her back, only to lie there, staring at the fresco on the ceiling.

She and Quinn had hardly exchanged a word since dinner but the tension between them had ratcheted up until she thought she might scream. Or go running into the night seeking relief. A foolish thought, when the only relief she was likely to find was in his arms.

What power did he hold over her, that she was so mesmerized by him? So eager to be in the embrace of a man she scarcely knew? A man who was not only a vampire, but one who had known her daughter intimately…But for that, she might have thrown herself into Quinn's arms earlier. Only it would have been like having three in a bed, she thought sourly. And no matter how much she wanted Quinn, Serepta would always be there between them, like a ghost.

Only she wasn't a ghost. She was alive again. Seeking vengeance.

Throwing the covers aside, she sat up. Pulled on her slippers and padded downstairs to the living room with Freyja at her heels.

As soon as she entered the room, a fire sprang to life in the hearth.

Startled, she took a step back. And bumped into Quinn.

"Easy," he murmured, his breath warm against her cheek. "I thought you might be cold."

"I'm quite capable of starting a fire on my own," she retorted.

He laughed softly. "You've certainly started one in me," he whispered, his voice husky.

His hands folded over her shoulders, slid up and down her arms. She shivered at the touch of his lips against her neck. "Quinn…"

"Shh. I'm not gonna hurt you."

"Aren't you?"

He nuzzled her neck again, reveling in its softness, in the warm rich scent of her desire.

Fighting to hold onto her self-control, Seleena stepped away from him.

Refusing to let her go, he captured her hand and led her to the sofa, drew her down beside him. "I'm not suggesting we go to bed together," he said, his hand lightly massaging her nape.

"No? What are you suggesting?" His hand was large and cool against her bare skin, soothing and arousing at the same time.

"I just want to hold you close, Red. I won't ask for more."

She looked up into his eyes - eyes she had once seen filled with pain and doubt were now filled with such longing it made her heart ache. His life had not been easy - growing up without a mother, raised by Jagg, enslaved by Serepta, turned into a vampire against his will. He could have let it embitter him, harden him, rob him of his humanity. Turn him into a true monster. And yet it hadn't. He had treated her with nothing but unfailing kindness and respect.

And, like it or not, she was falling in love with him.

* * *

Nardik gazed into his scrying bowl, his brow furrowing at what he saw. Seleena was at his retreat in the mountains of Brynn Tor and she wasn't alone. The vampire was with her.

It was wrong of him to spy on her. He knew it. He despised himself for it. But he did it, nonetheless. Did it in spite of the guilt that suffused him. He cared for Amerris. She was wise, beautiful, compassionate, loving. Everything a man could desire in a wife.

But she wasn't Seleena. Amerris stirred his affection. Seleena stirred his passion.

Amerris filled him with peace. Seleena filled him with excitement.

He was pledged to marry Amerris before the year was out, but it

85

was Seleena he yearned for. Was it merely because she had spurned him? The blow to his ego had been great. He had fathered her child, shared his magic with her, but it hadn't been enough to win her heart. There had been passion between them, but no love on her part. Perhaps if he had declared his feelings for her then, things would be different now. But he had thought there would be time enough for that. Compared to him, she had been young, with much to learn.

He stared into the bowl, eyes narrowing at what he saw: Seleena and Quinn, sitting side by side on the sofa, the vampire's arm around her, her head resting on his shoulder, as if they had known each other for years.

As if they were lovers…jealousy surged through him, swift and hot. *Were* they lovers?

He clenched his hands. No, she would never allow a vampire into her bed. He could live with the fact that she didn't want him. But for her to want another man, a man like Quinn…for a moment, the urge to destroy the vampire burned like bitter acid in his soul. It would be easy. So very easy.

He was on the verge of conjuring a spell of destruction when Amerris rapped softly on his chamber door.

"Nardik? Are you there?"

"A moment." He waved his hand over the bowl, obliterating the hateful images. Yet they remained seared into his mind.

Silently vowing to destroy the vampire if he violated Seleena, Nardik went to open the door for his betrothed.

CHAPTER 15

Freyja's rough tongue on Seleena's cheek woke her. It was a common occurrence. Lingering in bed, one hand scratching the cat's ears, she replayed the events of the night before—the sexual tension between herself and Quinn, the longing in his eyes when he kissed her, the yearning in his voice when he whispered he just wanted to hold her. He was lonely, she thought, and in that moment, she realized that she, too, was lonely, and had been for a long time, though she had never admitted it.

Where was he now? Was he sleeping in one of the other bedrooms? She was sorely tempted to slip out of her nightgown and into his bed.

As if reading her wayward thoughts, Freyja arched her back and hissed.

"Don't worry, I'm not going to do it. But, oh, Freyja, I want him so desperately!"

The cat stared at her through bright yellow eyes. Then, with an angry flick of her tail, she jumped off the mattress.

With a sigh, Seleena stepped into her slippers, pulled on her robe, and went downstairs to let the cat out.

* * *

A stirring in the air, the scent of sleep-warm skin, roused Quinn from the deep abyss that trapped him while he slept. While it was not as all-consuming as a vampire's normal daytime rest, it was not the kind of sleep mortals enjoyed. It was, he thought, like death. He didn't toss and turn. He didn't dream.

Without conscious thought, he rose and followed the sound of her footsteps down the winding stairway.

He paused on the last step, watching the gentle sway of her hips as she followed the cat to the front door. Her hair tumbled down her back in soft reddish-brown waves.

The cat meowed loudly when she lifted the latch, then bolted outside.

Seleena stood in the doorway, one hand braced on the jamb.

Quinn moved up behind her. A soft breeze carried the scent of grass and earth, of trees and flowers.

And vampire.

He cursed under his breath.

Hearing him, Seleena whirled around, her expression wary. "What's wrong?"

"Serepta. She's been here."

Seleena didn't ask how he knew. He watched her face pale as she pressed a hand to her heart. "I didn't think she would find us so soon."

"It's the blood bond between us. There's no way to break it." *Except death, his or hers.*

Freyja darted into the house as if she, too, had caught a whiff of something unpleasant.

Lips compressed, Seleena closed the door. As a precaution, she rescinded Serepta's invitation and re-established the wards. "Was she alone?" It was common knowledge that vampires sometimes mesmerized mortals to do their bidding because humans could cross thresholds warded against the undead.

"As near as I can tell."

"I hate this! No matter what she is, what she's become, she's my daughter and I love her!" Tears sparkled in her eyes. "I don't want to see her destroyed. I can't go through that again. And yet there doesn't seem to be any other alternative."

Filled with a sudden, unexpected compassion, Quinn gathered Seleena into his arms. With a sob, she pressed her face against his shoulder and wept.

Unable to think of anything he could say to comfort her, he stroked her back, brushed feather-light kisses to the top of her head. She felt so small in his embrace, fragile, and oh, so vulnerable.

She cried until she had no tears left. Stepping away, she pulled a lace-edged hanky from her robe's pocket and dried her eyes. "Crying never solved anything," she muttered irritably.

"True, but it usually makes you feel better."

"How would you know? I'll bet you've never shed a tear in your life."

"You think not?"

"Have you?"

"Well, only once," he admitted. "When my mother died." It was a day he would never forget. It had been raining. The roof of the squalid shack they lived in leaked like a sieve. He stood at his mother's bedside, clutching her hand as she writhed helplessly on the bed. Hour after hour, he stayed at her side, wiping the sweat from her brow, sometimes massaging her back, trying not to hear her screams as her body labored to expel the child. His hands had been swollen and sore by the time the infant slid into the world in a gush of blood and water. He washed the baby up as best he could, wrapped it in a towel that was none too clean, held it up so his mother could see it. She smiled faintly. Closed her eyes. And died. The infant—a girl— passed away an hour later. Surely a blessing, he thought later, when he was older.

Seleena laid a hand on his arm. "I'm so sorry for your loss."

"It was a long time ago."

She nodded. "I was on my way to make breakfast. Will you join me?"

"Sure."

He followed her downstairs to the kitchen, took a place at the table while she found a frying pan, pulled eggs and butter and milk from the refrigeration unit. He enjoyed watched her. She hummed softly as she worked.

"Would you like something to eat?" she asked.

"No, I think I'll go back to bed for a while. Wanna come with me?"

"Not this time." He was, she thought, the most exasperating man she had ever known.

With a woeful grin, he strolled out of the room. She had made it possible for him to be awake during the day, but it seemed he still preferred the night. Not that she could blame him. Spell or not, it wasn't normal for him to be awake when the sun was shining.

Seleena couldn't help admiring his backside as he walked away. He was the most remarkable looking man she had ever seen. Maybe she should have taken him up on his offer.

Humming softly, she bustled about the kitchen. She knew Quinn thought it odd that she didn't use her magic for simple day-to-day tasks, but she enjoyed cooking her meals and cleaning her house, pulling the weeds in the garden.

Breakfast was a simple affair - eggs and buttered toast washed down by a cup of hot chocolate. After tidying the kitchen, she climbed the stairs, planning her day as she went, though there was little to do other than shower and dress. Perhaps she would go through the grimoire again.

On her way to her room, she paused at Quinn's room door, sorely tempted to peek inside. To crawl into bed beside him. To run her fingertips over the hard expanse of his chest, his shoulders, his belly ridged with muscle. To cover his mouth with her own.

Annoyed with her wayward thoughts, she hurried into her own room and shut the door.

* * *

Quinn woke an hour before sunset. He knew immediately what time it was, that Seleena had just finished dinner, that Freyja was asleep in front of the fireplace.

Rising, he showered and combed his hair before making his way down to the kitchen. Seleena stood at the counter, wiping her hands on a towel.

She looked up, a smile curving her lips when she saw him. "Did you sleep well?"

He shrugged. "It's not really sleep."

Draping the towel over the back of a chair, she asked, "Are you hungry?"

His gaze settled on her throat, on the pulse beating there, slow and steady.

Seleena took a wary step backward. She really needed to quit asking him that question. "Stop looking at me like a hungry cat in front of a bowl of cream."

"Sorry," he said, stifling a grin. "Can I ask you something?"

"Of course."

"Promise you won't take it the wrong way, or get upset?"

She folded her arms over her chest. "I can't promise that until I hear the question."

He grunted softly. "Would your blood really make me sick?"

She hesitated for several moments, as if weighing her answer, then shrugged. "I honestly don't know. I was taught that witch blood made vampires violently ill. But I have no personal knowledge of such a thing. Better safe than sorry, though."

"I know a way to find out."

She knew what he meant. There was no mistaking the faint hint of red in his eyes. Hands clenched, she said, "I am *not* prey."

"I never said you were."

"But you want to feed on me!"

"No. No. I just want a taste. A sip, no more."

"Why? A sip will hardly satisfy your hunger."

"I'm not asking to make a meal of you. I just need a taste." He held up a hand when he saw the question in her eyes. "I don't know why. Sure, I'm a vampire. Drinking blood is what I do. But it's more than that."

"I don't understand."

"Me, either," he admitted with a rueful smile. "I just feel like tasting you is something I need to do.'

"It would create a bond between us, wouldn't it?" she asked. "The same kind that exists between you and Serepta."

"Yeah."

"Let me think about it for a little while. I want to search the grimoire some more."

"I don't know why. I think it's a lost cause."

"Maybe, but it will give me something to do." Something to take my mind off giving you a taste of my blood.

* * *

Quinn decided to tour the grounds while Seleena explored the pages of the old book. The house glowed in the moonlight like a jewel set against green velvet. Trees abounded, as did wildflowers and ferns. He felt the force of Nardik's spell as he strolled around the house.

Fortunately, it didn't have any effect on him.

Serepta had been here last night. A faint trace of her scent still lingered in the air. Whatever enchantment Nardik had conjured at the bottom of the hill hadn't kept her away. What about the other spell, Quinn wondered. The one that was supposed to make unwanted intruders forget why they came? Had that one worked?

Or would she be back again tonight?

On that unpleasant thought, he returned to the house.

CHAPTER 16

Seleena was still bent over the grimoire when Quinn returned to the house. He paused a moment to appreciate the way the light of the fire played over her face and hair, making her look almost otherworldly. And more desirable than ever. "Find anything useful?" he asked.

She didn't look up. "I'm not sure. I found something that's going to make you happy, but I'm not sure it will work because it's got nothing to do with tattoos."

"So, what is it about?"

"Vampires. Like I told you this morning, I was taught that vampires shunned witch blood because it made them violently ill." Leaning forward, she tapped her forefinger on a passage of text. "But it says here that the blood of an ancient witch will strengthen a vampire's power."

"Seems like vampires would know that," he remarked, sitting beside her on the sofa.

Seleena nodded. "Perhaps it was the witches themselves who spread the rumor about witch blood being poison. I mean, if vampires knew our blood would strengthen them...."

"They'd be hunting you for your blood."

"Exactly. But there's more, and this is the important part. It says here that the blood of an ancient witch can negate the forces of dark magic ."

"So, you're saying that your blood might counteract Serepta's magic?"

"Possibly."

Quinn's gaze moved to Seleena's throat. "You said the dragon holds some of your magic, as well as Nardik's."

"Yes."

"Wouldn't it neutralize that, as well?"

She considered that a moment, then said, "In all likelihood, I imagine it would."

"Is that a good thing?"

"I'm not sure, but I don't know of any way to separate my magic and Nardik's from hers."

"I don't suppose you found anything in there that tells how to make a vampire human again? Anything to indicate it's possible?"

"No." Rising, she closed the book. "I'm afraid not."

"Well, thanks for trying. Have you made a decision about what we talked about earlier?"

She shivered when his gaze met hers. "You mean letting you taste my blood?"

"Yeah."

"Will it hurt?"

"No."

"What if you can't stop?"

He jerked his chin at the silver dagger on the table beside the grimoire. "Just stick that in me."

Seleena stared at him in horror. "I couldn't!"

"It won't kill me, but it'll get my attention. Come on, Red, where's your spirit of adventure?"

She murmured a few words and the knife came to her hand.

"Damn, girl, that's a Hel of a trick."

"Just remember, there's more where that came from."

"I won't forget." Cupping her face in his hands, he kissed her lightly. "Relax, darlin'," he murmured.

Relax? How was she going to relax when he was looking at her like that, when his lips were moving over hers, when her whole body was inclining toward his. He kissed her again, her cheeks, her neck, until she forgot everything but the pleasure of being in his arms, the wonder of his kisses.

The prick of his fangs came as a surprise. As he had promised, it wasn't painful, just unexpected, and like nothing she had ever experienced before. It was surprisingly pleasant and over too soon.

She blinked up at him several times before asking, "Are you all right? How do you feel?'

"Never better."

She glanced at his shoulder. "What about the tattoo? Does it feel any different?"

With a shake of his head, Quinn peeled off his shirt. And frowned. The dragon appeared to be bigger, the scales blacker, brighter, than before. Looking up, he said, "That can't be good," as he met Seleena's gaze.

She bit down on her lower lip. Then, watching Quinn's face, she said, "Serepta."

He grimaced as the dragon bit him.

"It didn't help, did it?"

"Well, it's no worse than it was."

"Does it only bite you when someone mentions her name?"

"Yeah."

Seleena frowned. "I don't understand that. You would think the dragon would object when someone mentioned my name. Or Nardik's. Or even yours. But not hers. She's the one who cast the spell. It just doesn't make sense."

"Hel, none of this makes sense," Quinn muttered. Little had made sense since Seleena released him from that damn statue.

"I'm sorry."

"Hey, it's not your fault."

"She's my daughter. I can't help feeling a little bit responsible."

"Forget about it."

Seleena nodded. If only she could, she thought sadly. There was much in her past she wished to forget. Most of all, she wished she could forget that, willing or not, Quinn had once been her daughter's lover.

Chapter 17

Serepta stood at the foot of the Crystal Mountain, her brow furrowed in confusion as she gazed up at the Fortress. She remembered coming here, but she couldn't remember why. She shook her head, hoping to clear her thoughts, as she walked a few yards into the midnight-shadowed woods, felt the cobwebs clearing from her mind as she went. Pausing several yards away, she glanced over her shoulder, stared up at the house, now barely visible in the mist hovering over the top of the mountain.

Of course! Her mother and Quinn were lodging there. That was why she had come here. So, what was she doing, standing here in the woods?

Summoning her preternatural power, she willed herself to the top of the mountain, felt her mind grow cloudy as she walked slowly toward the massive structure.

She stopped abruptly. She might not be a witch any longer, but she recognized the shimmer of magic that hovered around the house. It was a spell, she thought irritably, most likely one of confusion or forgetfulness.

She cursed under her breath. If her parents hadn't deactivated her magic, she could have undone the spell with ease. As things stood, she was helpless to thwart it.

But that was about to change. Turning away from the Fortress, she hurried down the mountain. Her laughter filled the air as she transported herself to the nearest spaceport.

Inside, it was a simple matter to mesmerize a pilot to do her bidding.

A short time later, they were airborne, on their way to Caynn, a small planet not far from Brynn Tor. Caynn housed a secret coven of wizards known only to few witches who reveled in the Dark Arts. Why hadn't she thought of visiting them before?

After landing on a barren stretch of ground, Serepta ordered the pilot to wait for her return. A thought took her to a walled citadel located at the top of a barren rise.

Her parents might have won the last battle, Serepta mused as she vaulted over the high wall and rapped on the thick oak door. But they were about to lose the war.

She felt a shiver of anticipation as the door swung open, revealing a tall woman clad in a hooded brown robe.

She regarded Serepta through deep-set green eyes. "Who are you? How did you find this place?"

"I am Serepta, daughter of Nardik and Seleena."

The woman spoke a single word. It unleashed a surge of power that almost knocked Serepta off her feet. "Be gone. I detect no sentient magic within you."

"My father took it from me."

"Then be gone. You have no place here."

"Wait!" Serepta cried as the woman started to shut the door in her face. "I know there is someone here who can help me."

The woman shook her head. "No, you are mistaken."

Serepta pressed her hand against the door, preventing the woman from closing it. "I will not leave until I've seen him."

"Foolish child. Be gone, I say, before I turn you into a mouse and feed you to the cat."

Gathering her vampire strength, Serepta grabbed the woman's arm and flung her across the room. "I have power!" she shouted.

The woman never hit the wall. Lifting her hands above her head, she floated gently to the floor. "Vampire," she murmured, her voice tinged with surprise. "Tell me, were you witch and vampire at the same time?"

"What if I was?"

"I did not know such a thing was possible." Her expression of disdain changed to one of keen interest. "Come in."

Serepta felt an odd shimmer in the air as she crossed the threshold.

"I am Lanna. Follow me."

Serepta followed her down a long narrow corridor that opened onto a large square room furnished with several couches and low tables. An enormous fireplace took up most of one wall. Several ancient weapons and tools of torture adorned the other three walls. Most would consider them an odd choice for décor, she thought, but she found them vastly appealing.

"Wait here," Lanna said. "Sit, if you wish."

Serepta nodded. Her magic might be dormant, but the magical residue in the room was overpowering. With her nerves on edge, she paced the floor, pausing now and then to study the weapons, recognizing some of them as implements once used to torture men and women, and even children, suspected of witchcraft.

She turned at the sound of footsteps.

A man stood in the doorway. Small and slight, with a mane of snow-white hair, he wore a long black cloak, his hands tucked into the voluminous sleeves. Dark magic radiated from him, filling the whole room, making her feel small and helpless. And more afraid than she had ever been.

He floated toward her, his feet not touching the floor.

It took all her courage not to flee his presence.

"I am Wyrick." His voice echoed like thunder, unexpected from such a diminutive figure. "Who are you?"

"I am…" She swallowed hard. "Serepta."

"Illegitimate daughter of Nardik and Seleena."

"Y…yes."

"And a vampire."

Serepta nodded.

He looked at her for stretched seconds that seemed like an eternity before asking, "What do you want of me?"

She took a deep breath. "I want you to restore my magic."

"To what end?"

"I want to avenge myself on those who have wronged me!"

"Your parents?"

"Yes!"

"And what will you give me in return?"

"Anything."

He placed his right hand over her womb, then shook his head. "Barren."

Serepta stared at him in shock. He wanted a child? "There must be something else I can offer," she cried, her voice thick with desperation.

"Bring me a woman of child-bearing age. She must be young, untouched, of pleasant demeanor, and lovely of face and form."

"And you will restore my magic?"

"Yes."

He waved his hand, murmured a quick incantation, and Serepta found herself outside the walls of the citadel.

Serepta stood there a moment, weak with relief because vampires were unable to conceive. She would rather remain without her magic than share her bed with that frightening little man.

With a shake of her head, she returned to the Airship. So, Wyrick wanted a woman, she mused as she settled back in her seat. Someone to give him a child.

She smiled as the pilot took off.

She had the perfect woman in mind.

CHAPTER 18

Seleena rose to her feet. Arching her back, she stretched her arms overhead. She had spent the last two days searching the grimoire for answers, but she was rapidly losing hope. There were spells to neutralize real dragons, but no information on dragon tattoos other than what they had already learned. She found spells to repel vampires, spells to weaken their power, but nothing to cure a human of being undead.

Nardik had sent word that he was continuing his search for Serepta, but to no avail. If she still resided in her castle, she was well hidden.

Quinn had grown increasingly restless. He hunted more frequently, a fact which bothered Seleena greatly. The tension between them was palpable. She knew he was avoiding her and it broke her heart. She wanted him desperately and yet she was reluctant to give herself to him, not only because he had been her daughter's lover, but because she was afraid of how bereft she would feel if he decided to leave. Love was a powerful force, strong enough to topple kingdoms and change the course of history.

And then there was the dragon tattoo. It troubled her deeply. Sometimes she thought of it as a living entity - one that was just biding its time, waiting to strike.

Sometimes, to her complete and utter shame, she almost wished Serepta was really dead and buried.

She thrust the horrible thought from her mind. No mother worthy of the name would ever think such a despicable thing.

Sighing, she went to the window and drew back the curtains. Where was Quinn?

She hadn't seen him since last night and this night was nearly gone. Had he left for good?

Tears stung her eyes. Surely he wouldn't leave without a word? Then again, what reason had she given him to stay?

Sinking down on the floor, she murmured, "Oh, Freyja, what am I going to do without him?"

Meowing softly, Freyja rubbed her head against Seleena's cheek.

And that was how Quinn found them when he materialized in the room.

"Here, now," he said, hunkering down beside Seleena, "what's wrong?"

She sniffed back her tears, her heart giving a little leap of joy at the sound of his voice. "Nothing."

"Nothing?" He lifted one brow. "Really? Nothing's making you cry?"

She shook her head. "I'm fine. Just…just…"

He trailed his fingertips down her cheek, pushed a lock of hair behind her ear. "Did you really think I'd leave you without saying goodbye?"

She looked up at him, eyes wide. "How…how did you know…?"

"Apparently tasting your blood allows me to read your thoughts."

"What?" She sprang to her feet, hands fisted on her hips. "Don't you think you should have told me that?"

"Hey, I didn't know."

"I don't believe you!"

Quinn frowned up at her. Now that he thought about it, it seemed he could always read her mind, or at least grasp an inkling of what she was thinking, feeling.

Rising, he reached for her, but she backed away, her expression furious.

Shoving his hands in his pants' pockets, he said, "Tell me what you want, Red. Do you want me to stay? If not, just say the word."

"Of course I want you to stay!" she snapped.

"Then what are you so mad about?"

She looked at him as if he was some kind of idiot. "Because you were gone and I didn't know where you were, or if you were coming back, and…"

This time, when he reached for her, she went into his arms. "I'm sorry." He brushed a kiss across her cheek. "I won't do it again."

Nodding, she sniffed back the last of her tears. "Where were you?"

"I went to Serepta's castle. I thought maybe I could find her lair. I searched every inch of that damn place. I have to agree with Nardik. If Serepta's holed up in there, she's sure as Hel well-hidden." Grimacing, he said, "Damn, he's here."

"Nardik?"

Quinn nodded as the door flew open and the wizard strode into the house.

Taking a deep breath, Seleena smoothed a hand over her hair. "Nardik, what brings you here so late?" she asked, then bit down on her lower lip. He had every right to be here at any time of the day or night. It was, after all, his house.

"Annis has been kidnapped."

"Kidnapped!" Seleena exclaimed. "Who would do such a thing?"

"Who, indeed?" he muttered.

"Serepta?"

He nodded.

"But why? And how?"

"A man attired in the garb of the Queen's guard arrived at the convent last night with a letter from Gryff saying that Marri is desperately ill and desired to see her sister before it was too late. Naturally, the Reverend Mother agreed that Annis should go home."

"How did you find out?"

"In the morning, one of the young nuns found the guard's body lying outside the walls, drained of blood. She sent word to the castle. There is no doubt that the guard was killed by Serepta."

"But why would she take Annis?"

Nardik shook his head. "Marri is beside herself. Every knight in her service is scouring the countryside searching for the girl."

"Have you tried locating her?"

"Of course."

Seleena sank down on the sofa. If Nardik couldn't locate the girl, there were three possibilities. Annis was dead. She was hidden behind a powerful ward of some kind. Or she was no longer on Brynn Tor. "So, what do we do now?"

"We wait," Nardik said. "This must have something to do with regaining her magic, although I fail to see how kidnapping Annis could help to accomplish that. If I hear anything, I will let you know."

Seleena walked him to the door and bid him goodnight.

Returning to the living room, she curled up in a corner of the couch. Meowing softly, Freyja jumped onto her lap. For a moment, Seleena stared into the hearth, one hand absently stroking the cat's head as she tried to make sense of the kidnapping.

"Worrying won't help," Quinn remarked, taking a seat at the other end of the sofa.

"I know, but Annis is so young, so innocent. She knows nothing of the world. She must be terrified."

"Yeah."

Seleena regarded him a moment. "You said the dragon bites you when you mention Serepta's name."

"Yeah, it happened just now."

"Is it an actual bite?"

"What do you mean?"

"Does it draw blood?"

"I don't know. I've never paid any attention. Why?"

"Take off your shirt."

"What are you getting at?"

"I'm not sure," Seleena said. "Maybe nothing."

Quinn tossed his shirt on the side table. "Now what?"

"Serepta."

The dragon lashed its tail, then bit into the muscle on Quinn's arm. Several drops of blood oozed from the tiny wound. The dragon lapped them up.

Seleena nodded, as if she had known such a thing would happen. "Because of its black color, I was sure it was a fire dragon. But it's not. It's a blood dragon, even though they're usually red."

Quinn glanced at the tattoo. "So?"

"I think Serep….I think she conjured the wrong dragon."

"What do you mean?"

"Fire dragons are fiercely loyal to their masters and will only do their bidding. No matter how you tried, no matter if you were the most powerful wizard in the land, a fire dragon would never obey your wishes."

"So?"

"A blood dragon will only serve the first person - man or woman - whose blood it consumes."

"So even if she kills me, she won't be able to reclaim her magic."

"Exactly."

"How could she make such a mistake?"

"The spells are quite similar, almost word for word. If she mispronounced a word, or said it in the wrong order while conjuring a fire dragon, the result would be a blood dragon."

Quinn ran his fingertips over the ridges along the dragon's back. A low rumble, reminiscent of Freyja's purr, issued from its throat. "That's not going to help me if I'm dead."

Seleena sighed. "It doesn't help us now, either. And it doesn't explain why she took the girl."

Quinn dragged a hand over his jaw, his brow furrowed. "I hate to say it, but maybe she's discovered another way to get her magic back."

CHAPTER 19

Annis paced the tiny, windowless cell that imprisoned her. It held no furniture, only a quilt that had seen better days. She had no idea where she was or how she had come to be there. The last thing she remembered was walking out of the cloister with one of Marri's guards. She had no memory of what had happened between then and now.

There was no light in the dungeon. No way to determine whether it was day or night. No way to know how long she had been there. She fought down the panic trying to engulf her. She told herself there was no need to worry. When she didn't show up at the castle, her mother would send Nardik to look for her. She would pay whatever ransom was being asked. Perhaps the wizard was on his way, even now.

What if he didn't come? What if there was no ransom demand? What if some twisted creature had kidnapped her with some other motive in mind?

Fighting tears, she wrapped her arms around her middle and sank down on the quilt. "Nardik, please find me. Please. I'm so afraid."

"No one will find you."

Annis' head jerked up, her gaze searching the gloom. "Who's

there?" She squinted against the light that suddenly appeared in the cell.

A woman clad in black, her face as pale as death, stood in front of the cell door.

Annis took a step back. "Who…who are you? Why have you brought me here?"

"I am Serepta. Perhaps you've heard of me."

"Serepta." Annis murmured the word with the same sort of horror people used when they spoke of the plague.

The woman's laughter filled the air. "So, you *have* heard of me."

Annis stared at her as if seeing a ghost. And perhaps she was. Marri had told her that the witch was dead, killed by Gryff's hand.

Serepta laughed again though there was no humor in it. "Told you I was dead, did they?"

Annis nodded. How was it possible for the witch to know what she was thinking?

Serepta shrugged. "I can read your thoughts child, because I drank your blood."

Eyes wide with horror, Annis lifted a trembling hand to her neck. "Is that why you brought me here? To…to feed on me?"

"No." The witch licked her lips. "It was just a nice bonus." Unlocking the cell with a flourish, she grabbed Annis by the arm and dragged her into the corridor. "Come along," she said. "We're going to take a little trip."

Before Annis could protest or even ask where they were going, they were there. Serepta hustled her into an Airship and pushed her into a seat.

The pilot shut the doors, ran his hands over the controls, and, in moments, they were airborne.

Annis stared out the window. "Where are we going?"

"To see a dark wizard about getting my magic back."

* * *

If Lanna was pleased or surprised to find Serepta and a young girl standing outside the coven's door, it didn't show on her face. With a beckoning hand, she invited them into the house.

"Wyrick is expecting you," she said. "Wait here."

Wide-eyed, Annis stared at her surroundings, her legs so weak with fear, she was afraid they would collapse beneath her at any moment. She knew little of magical power, but it was here, in this room, weighing her down like an invisible hand.

There was a whoosh in the air and a man appeared before them. He was shorter than she, with long, snow-white hair and penetrating dark eyes. Power radiated from him, stronger than that which already filled the room.

When he moved toward her, his feet didn't touch the floor. He stopped directly in front of her. Annis flinched when he placed his hand over her womb.

"A virgin," he murmured. "Pure and perfect. And lovely."

"We have a deal then?" Serepta asked.

"Done and done." Taking Serepta by the hand, he led her a few steps away. And with each step, his form grew taller, wider, until he towered over her. As he grew larger, so did his power. He drew Serepta into his arms and his cloak wrapped around her, like the wings of a giant black bat. When he spoke, his voice rumbled like thunder, though Annis didn't understand the words.

Power swirled through the room like a whirlwind, growing even stronger, heavier.

Fearing certain destruction, Annis fell to the floor, her eyes tightly closed, her arms over her head.

Time lost all meaning. Gradually, the power drained away, and with it, the sense of impending doom. When she risked opening her eyes, the wizard was again a small, seemingly harmless old man. But Serepta…Annis blinked up at her. She looked the same and yet…her eyes blazed with new life. The vampire pallor had left her skin, her hair appeared thicker, more lustrous.

Serepta smiled at the wizard. "I wish you many strong sons."

The wizard inclined his head. "I wish you the fulfillment of all your dreams. And should you ever wish to join us, we would welcome you into our coven."

"My thanks, Lord Wyrick. But first I have several scores to settle." A wave of her hand, and she was gone.

Annis shrank back when the wizard reached for her. Voice trembling, she asked, "What do you want with me?"

"A child," he said. "Come along. Your rooms await."

* * *

A child. The thought made her shudder. She had never been intimate with a man. Never even been kissed. Occasionally, her wayward thoughts had led her to wonder what it would be like to be with a man. Of course, she had pictured him man as tall and blonde, with beautiful blue eyes and a kind smile. Someone who would love her. Someone who would patiently teach her the ways of love. Instead, she would be forced to surrender her virtue to an old man who scared her half to death.

A child. The wizard's words continued to play and replay in her mind as he led her down a long, winding corridor and into a suite of rooms fit for Marri herself. The walls were a pale blue. A carpet of a slightly darker shade covered the floor. A matching spread covered the bed. Lights set in the ceiling filled the room with a warm, golden glow. A small fire crackled in a white stone fireplace.

"I think you will be comfortable here." He gestured at a wardrobe. "You will find clothing in there. Your bath is through that door. If you need anything, you have but to ask."

"I need to go home."

He smiled sympathetically. "I am afraid my need for a child outweighs your need for home." Bowing in her direction, he left the room. The door closed with a quiet click.

She waited a moment, then went to try the handle. She wasn't surprised to find it locked.

Curious, she opened the wardrobe doors. Inside, she found a dozen gowns in a variety of colors, as well as shoes, boots, undergarments, hats and gloves. All in her size. She shook her head. How was that even possible when he had only just met her?

Turning, she surveyed the room again. If she had to be a prisoner, she thought, she couldn't have asked for a nicer jail. But this place would never be home. She would never see Marri or Nardik again. Never again know the peace and serenity of the convent.

Her life, as she had known, had been ripped away. And nothing would ever be the same again.

With a sob, she sank down on the floor and wept.

CHAPTER 20

Serepta stood in the center of the Black Castle's great room, her arms uplifted, her laughter filling the air as she magically rearranged the furniture and repainted the walls. Copying a bit of Wyrick's home decor, she had gathered several of her old instruments of torture and hung them over the fireplace.

She had her magic back! And it was stronger and more potent than ever. Her dungeon was filled with handsome young men, all eager to do her bidding. All very tasty. She had never felt better, been stronger, or more certain of victory. She had warded the castle and the grounds against intruders, cast a spell over it that prevented the use of magic by other witches within its walls.

Soon, all those who had thwarted her would pay the price for their treachery - her mother, her father. Quinn.

Ah, Quinn. He would be the first to die. As strong as she was, it wouldn't hurt to have the dragon's power at her beck and call when she confronted her parents.

But there was no hurry. Lowering her arms, she regarded her handiwork. Everything looked fresh and new again. As it should be. Because she felt new again. Reborn.

Leaving the castle, she went into the garden to bask in the sun's light. How she had missed it! The grounds seemed barren without the statues, she mused. But that was easily remedied. But, again, all in good time.

Reclining on one of the benches, she turned her thoughts to her parents. Wouldn't they be surprised when they saw her again, stronger and more powerful than ever before.

She hoped they were enjoying what little time they had left.

CHAPTER 21

Annis scrambled to her feet, her heart pounding with trepidation, when the bedroom door opened. Would this be the night the wizard forced himself upon her?

She froze, more frightened that she had ever been in her life, as a man appeared in the doorway. She had expected Wyrick. She had seen no one else in the three days she had been here. But this man…She blinked up at him. He was tall and blonde and, except for the fact that his eyes were dark brown instead of blue, he could have been the man of her dreams.

He smiled when he saw her - a warm friendly smile that made his eyes twinkle. "Annis?"

"Y…yes."

"I am Rajj."

She nodded, uncertain of what her response should be.

He closed the door behind him and moved toward her, forcing her to look up to see his face.

"I see Wyrick has not told you about me. I should have guessed as much." He laughed softly. "My father told me of you, but his words did not do you justice. You are quite lovely." He cocked his head to the side. "Do you know why you are here?"

"Yes," she said, blushing. "To give the wizard a child."

Rajj threw back his head and laughed.

"I see nothing humorous in this situation," she snapped, her fear momentarily swallowed up in her anger.

"You are not here for Wyrick," Rajj said, still chuckling. "You are here for me."

Annis stared at him. "For...*you?*"

"My father told me if I did not find a suitable woman by summer's end, he would find one for me. And here you are. I hope you are not too disappointed." He circled her, like a hungry tiger studying its prey. And then he frowned. "You have no magic."

She shook her head. Maybe he wanted a witch for a wife. Maybe he would let her go home. But his next words dashed her hopes.

"It matters not. My magic will pass to our child. The maids will be here soon to help you prepare."

"Prepare? Prepare for what?"

"For our mating. Tonight."

"Tonight?" The word emerged from her throat as little more than a high-pitched squeak.

Nodding, he drew her into his arms. "I will be gentle, sweet Annis," he promised.

"But...can't we wait a few days? To...to get acquainted?"

He smiled indulgently, like a parent humoring a child. "You will know everything you need to know about me when the night is over."

And with those parting words, he kissed the top of her head and left her standing there, not knowing whether to be terrified or relieved.

A trio of women descended on her a short time after Rajj's departure. One prepared a fragrant bath. One stripped her of her clothing. The third removed the sheets from the bed.

The one who had prepared her bath scrubbed her thoroughly from head to foot.

The second woman laid out a long, white gown that sparkled like diamonds in the candlelight.

The third remade the bed with black silk sheets, then pulled a small crystal bottle from the bag she had brought with her.

Annis stared at the bottle, fearful of what it might hold.

The first woman helped her out of the tub, wrapped her in a

warm, fluffy towel, dried her hair, then brushed it until it shone like liquid gold.

The second woman slipped the gown over her head.

The third applied a bit of makeup, then sprayed her with sweet-smelling perfume.

Then, as one, they bowed and left the room.

Standing in front of the mirror, Annis studied her reflection. She had never thought of herself as pretty, but the woman gazing back at her was lovely. Her blond hair seemed to shimmer in the light, her eyes looked larger, darker, her lips were glossy and pale pink. And the gown…it clung to her like a second skin. Not quite transparent, it outlined every curve. What would Marri think if she could see her now? What would Reverend Mother think? No need to worry, she thought bleakly. She would never see her sister or the cloister at Aisly again.

She felt the sting of tears at her eyes, quickly brushed them away when Rajj stepped into the room.

He paused, his gaze moving over as if he were examining a piece of merchandise he was thinking of buying. And then he smiled. "Annis. You are truly beautiful."

"Am I?"

"The most beautiful woman I have ever seen."

She basked in the admiration she read in his eyes, felt her heart skip a beat when he took her in his arms.

His fingertips caressed her cheek, threaded through her hair. "Do not be afraid."

She could fight him, she thought. But he was bigger, stronger. And he had magic. There was no way to win. And yet, how could she simply surrender her virtue to a stranger?

"Annis. You have nothing to fear from me."

His voice sank into her very being and when she looked into his eyes, she knew he would never hurt her.

"I don't know what to do," she murmured. And then frowned when he blushed.

His amused laughter poured over her like summer sunshine as he hugged her close. "Neither do I, my lovely lady. We will learn together."

CHAPTER 22

Serepta lapped up the last of her victim's blood, then cast the dry husk aside. In the beginning, when she had first been turned, she had preferred blood to mortal food, but no more. She wasn't sure what had caused the change, nor did she care. Still, unpleasant as it was, there was no denying the occasional need for blood if she wanted to survive.

But now it was time to destroy Quinn and reclaim the fire dragon's power. How best to accomplish it? She could send him a message, asking him to meet her, but she doubted he would oblige, and if he did, she was certain he wouldn't come alone. She didn't want her parents to show up, not yet, not until she had decided how best to avenge herself on them. No, she wanted Quinn alone, bound and helpless. She wanted to hurt him, humiliate him, before she destroyed him.

She paced the great hall, considering and rejecting a dozen ideas.

And then she smiled, wondering why she hadn't thought of it sooner.

CHAPTER 23

With a sigh, Seleena rested her head on Quinn's shoulder. "I heard from Nardik while you were out. He says there's still no sign of Serepta or Annis. I don't know what else we can do." She paused. "Do you think she killed Annis?"

Quinn rubbed his shoulder where the dragon had just bitten him. Maybe they needed to find a code name for Serepta. "I wouldn't put it past her. But I think she's toying with us. Just biding her time, hoping we'll relax our guard."

"I just wish it was over. It's been three days. Amerris must be worried out of her mind. Marri, too."

"Yeah." But he was more worried about Seleena. She was in danger as long as Serepta lived. And even though he would willingly sacrifice his own life to save hers, he wasn't sure he was strong enough to defeat Serepta. And that bothered him more than he wanted to admit.

With a wave of her hand, Seleena lit a fire in the hearth. "I made a cake today. Would you like a slice?"

He brushed a kiss across the side of her neck. "I'm not really hungry for cake."

"No?"

He shook his head. "What do you taste like, I wonder?"

"I'm sure you can guess."

"Is that a no?"

She smiled up at him. "How could I refuse?"

"You've refused me plenty of times," he muttered.

"Quinn…"

"Hey, it's okay. I understand."

"Do you?"

"Not really. I want you. I know you want me." He shook his head. "Are you holding out for marriage?"

"Are you proposing?" She placed her fingertips over his mouth before he could reply. "Forget I said that."

"It's gonna happen, Red. I knew it the first time I saw you. I wish you'd tell me why you're so reluctant."

"You really don't know?"

He started to say no and then, in a flash of inspiration, he knew. He leaned back a little so he could better see her face. "It's Serepta, isn't it?"

She nodded. "I can't forget that you slept with my daughter."

"Believe me, it wasn't my idea."

"It doesn't matter. It happened and I can't forget it."

Just one more reason to kill the witch, he thought.

Seleena chafed at the tense silence that fell between them. Maybe she shouldn't have said anything. She worried her lower lip between her teeth, then stood abruptly. "I'm going outside for a bit."

"Is that a good idea?"

"I just need some air."

And some time away from me, Quinn thought. He sat back, his gaze on the wall of moving pictures across from him, though not really seeing the ever-changing images of land and sea and sky. All this time he had assumed she was reluctant to share his bed because he was a vampire. Apparently, he couldn't have been more wrong. Was it jealousy that made her hesitate? Perhaps some moral objection? Or both? And what was he going to do about it? Hel, what could he do? He couldn't undo the past.

She had been outside about twenty minutes when he started to worry. Serepta had made her way up the mountain once before. Maybe she had again.

He hurried outside, breathed a sigh of relief when he saw Seleena standing a short distance away, gazing at the twin moons. Moving up behind her, he slid his arms around her waist. He had expected a little resistance; instead, she turned in his arms, clasped her hand behind his neck, and kissed him.

As soon as her mouth covered his, he knew it wasn't Seleena. It was the last thing he remembered before darkness swallowed him whole.

* * *

He woke to find himself nearly naked in a room that was all too familiar. His arms were stretched over his head, his wrists manacled to an iron bar suspended from the ceiling, his ankles secured to bolts in the floor. The shackles, made of silver, burned his flesh and weakened his preternatural powers. The only furniture was a single chair. There were no windows. There was a grate directly beneath him surrounded by ugly, brown stains.

How long had he been here? The ache in his arms told him it had been more than minutes. Hours, perhaps. He called on his preternatural powers. Though weak, he sensed no one else within the castle walls.

Where was Seleena?

How had Serepta managed to bypass both of Nardik's spells?

Where was Serepta?

How had she managed to overpower him so completely, so quickly?

Questions for which he had no answers.

Chin resting on his chest, he closed his eyes and shifted from one foot to the other. Minutes stretched into hours as time marched on, intensifying the ache in his arms and back and shoulders. He wondered how long it would take before the silver burned all the way through his flesh.

Quinn's head jerked up at the scent of blood. Someone screamed, the sound filled with such torment it made his stomach clench. The blood scent grew stronger. His fangs extended as his hunger sprang to life. His hands fisted around the iron bar as another scream punctuated the silence, followed by the pungent scent of death.

His senses reached out, searching, but in spite of the cries and the overpowering smell of blood, he detected no one inside the castle. How was that possible?

He tensed as the door swung slowly open. Serepta stood in the doorway, as beautiful as he remembered, her hair falling in red waves over her shoulders. A long black gown outlined the curves he remembered so well.

She held a glass of dark-red liquid in her hand.

"Where's Seleena?"

She smiled faintly. "Worried about my dear mother, are you? I've seen the way you look at her. The way she looks at you."

"Where is she? If you've hurt her…"

"You'll do what?"

"Rip your black heart out of your chest."

She laughed softly as she closed the distance between them. "That hardly seems likely now, does it?"

He tensed when she walked behind him, flinched when she dragged her nails down his back. Blood trickled down his spine.

Quinn tracked her footsteps as she moved to stand in front of him again. He licked his lips when she lifted the glass and took a drink.

"Thirsty, are you?" she asked with a knowing grin.

He shook his head, a bald-faced lie. "Whose blood is that?"

She looked at the glass, then shrugged. "I didn't ask his name."

"What do you want?" It was a foolish question.

"I wanted you to love me," she said, "but we can't always have what we want, can we? Then, again, maybe we can."

Eyes narrowing, he focused his senses on her, felt the shock of raw power that slammed into him. "Your magic!" he exclaimed. "How did you—?"

"You noticed!" She smiled, as if he had just paid her an unexpected compliment. "How I missed it. And now it's stronger than ever." She glanced at the dragon tattoo. "And when you're dead, I will be the most powerful witch in all of Brynn Tor and beyond."

"Beyond?"

She laughed again. "Nardik was so certain he was the most powerful wizard in the universe. But he was wrong." She drained the glass in her hand and flung it against the wall, where it burst into a thousand shards of crystal. Humming softly, she ran her fingers over his belly, hissed when he flinched at her touch. "Worried I'll make you a statue again?" .

"No," he retorted. "I'm worried I'll have to sleep with you again."

"Before I'm done with you, you will beg to come to my bed!"

"No way, witch. You might as well kill me now, because it will never happen."

Face contorted with rage, she slapped him, hard, twice, and then vanished from his sight.

Quinn sagged against the chains that bound him, the pain in his body forgotten. Damn the witch! If she had Seleena imprisoned somewhere within the castle, he would do whatever Serepta asked of him. He would make love to her night and day, crawl on his belly like a snake, humiliate himself in any way she saw fit, because his life meant nothing to him if he couldn't share it with the woman he loved.

CHAPTER 24

Seleena hesitated a moment before opening her front door. She had told Quinn she just needed some air, which had been partly true. But mainly, she had wanted to go home and make sure everything was all right in the village. It had been foolish, perhaps, to go alone, but she needed some space. Time to think. It was all out in the open now - her real reason for refusing to let him make love to her. When she said it out loud, it seemed inadequate, and yet she couldn't seem to get past it. Sometimes, she dreamed of the two of them - Quinn rising over Serepta, his body sheened with sweat, his hands and lips caressing her daughter, their arms and legs tangled in silken sheets... Dreams, she thought. More like nightmares!

She wandered through her house. All was as she had left it. She stood in the doorway of Quinn's room, wondering how long he would stay with her, now that he knew her innermost feelings. Her heart sank at the thought of a future without him. Until he came into her life, she hadn't realized how empty her days were. How lonely she had been. How much she would miss him when he was gone.

Earlier, she had checked her mailbox, but there were no letters. No messages from any of the villagers asking for her help.

She took a last look around, fortified the wards on the house and all points of entry, then murmured the incantation that would take her back to Nardik's.

Back to Quinn.

* * *

Seleena knew Quinn was gone the moment she stepped inside the Fortress. Even worse, she could have sworn she detected Serepta's presence. But that should have been impossible. Nardik's wards were still in place. Still strong. How had Serepta breeched them? It should have been impossible. Unless…

Returning to the yard, she murmured an incantation that allowed her to see the image of anyone who had recently been there. A gasp rose in her throat when she saw her own image standing beside Quinn. Another incantation showed the real people behind the images. Quinn remained the same, but the other image morphed into that of her daughter. How had Serepta regained her magic? And where was Quinn? She bit down on her lower lip, trying not to panic. She took several deep breaths, forcing herself to think, to concentrate. He could read her thoughts.

Was he able to read hers? Quinn? Quinn, can you hear me?

Red? He had never heard anything more beautiful than the sound of her voice. For the first time, he was truly glad to be a vampire.

"Where are you?"

It doesn't matter. There's nothing you can do. Stay inside the Fortress and be safe.

I know you're hurting.

I'll be all right.

Maybe I can help with the pain. He heard her chanting softly, caught the faint scent of a candle, of rosemary and sage and rue. Was it his imagination or could he almost feel her hands on his skin? Imagination or not, the pain lessened, became bearable. Disappeared.

Did it work? she asked anxiously.

Yes. Bless you, woman. You're amazing.

Tell me where you are.

Not a chance. I don't know how it happened, but she's got her magic back, and it's stronger than ever.

The dragon, Quinn. You have to wake the dragon. It's the only way you can hope to defeat her.

Just wish I knew how.

Trust your instincts.

Yeah...I've got to go. She's coming.

Serepta had changed out of the black dress she had been wearing and into a long white gown trimmed in white fur. Nearly transparent, it hinted boldly at the lush figure beneath. And tempted him not at all.

"White?" he drawled with all the disdain he could muster. "Really?"

She snarled at him and then, with a wave of her hand, opened a long, shallow gash the length of his left arm.

His blood dripped to the floor. A new stain, he thought, wondering how many others were his from times past.

She glared at him, her anger a palpable presence in the room. "I am going to kill you an inch at a time," she promised, biting off each word. "And I am going to make my mother watch."

Knowing she was trying to goad him, he said nothing.

She raked her nails down his cheek, then slammed out of the room, leaving the threat hanging in the air.

Quinn blew out a sigh of relief. When he had first met Serepta, she had ever been in control of her emotions. Even when furious, she had projected an outward calm. But she had no such control now. Perhaps he could turn her lack of restraint to his advantage.

And perhaps not.

* * *

Seleena's heart went cold. Serepta had Quinn. Hadn't she known, all along, that it would happen sooner or later? That no matter what they did, Serepta would somehow prevail. Brow furrowed, she doused the candle, then climbed the stairs to the fourth floor. Nardik's presence was stronger here than anywhere else in the house.

Seleena made her way along the corridor to the room where he practiced his magic, with Freyja at her heels. Memories assaulted Seleena as she stood in the doorway. The room looked exactly as she remembered - large and square, the walls a pristine white, the floor made of gold-veined black marble. A narrow shaft of moonlight shone through the room's small, round window. A long, oak table held an assortment of magical implements. It had been here that

Nardik had shared his knowledge and his magic with her, here that he had seduced her. Here that Serepta had been conceived.

Shaking off thoughts of the past, she found a scrying bowl and filled it with water. It had been Nardik who taught her the ancient art. Egyptian magicians had used ink or blood or other dark liquids. Others used water. Many witches insisted on scrying within a magic circle to prevent outside influences. But that wouldn't be necessary here.

She gazed into the bowl, her whole being focused on locating Quinn. For a moment, the water remained clear; then, gradually, it darkened and his image appeared. He was in a room, his arms stretched over his head, his wrists shackled to an iron bar. There was dried blood on his back, his cheek, and along his left arm.

Her tears dripped into the cauldron when she saw the burned flesh of his wrists and ankles. It was at that moment, seeing the results of Serepta's cruelty, that her love for her daughter shriveled and died.

She brushed her tears away, her anger rising with her determination to free the man she loved, for love him she did. She smiled at Freyja, who sat patiently at her feet. "Best get used to him," she said. "Because when I get him back, I'm never letting him out of my sight again."

And she would get him back. She knew where he was. She had seen that room before, when they searched the Black Castle. "I'm coming, Quinn," she murmured as she descended the stairs to the first floor. "Hold on."

Anxious as she was to rescue Quinn, she wasn't foolish enough to go alone.

Moving to the desk in the corner of the main room, she found a sheet of paper and an enchanted pen, scribbled a note to Nardik, dropped it into a bowl and set it on fire. A plume of thick yellow smoke rose from the bowl and wafted out the nearest window.

All she had to do now was wait.

CHAPTER 25

Annis lay curled in Rajj's arms, happier than she had ever been in her life. She had never imagined that making love could be so pleasurable, so wonderful. So exciting. How was it possible to have fallen in love with him so quickly? Was it love? Or had he cast a spell on her? How was she to know? Whatever it was, she never wanted to leave him…

She sat abruptly as the afterglow of his lovemaking melted in the face of reality. "Nardik will come for me."

"Is that your father?" Rajj asked, apparently unconcerned.

"No, but he's engaged to my mother. My sister is Marri, Queen of Brynn Tor."

He chuckled softly. "I've fallen in love with a princess!"

"You love me?"

"How can I help it?"

"This could start a war! I have to go home."

"Nonsense." His fingers stroked her cheek. "No one will ever find you here."

"You don't understand. Nardik is a powerful wizard."

"Not as powerful as my father."

"If you truly love me, you'll let me go home, at least long enough to let my mother and sister know I'm well."

His hand skimmed her breast, her thigh. "Perhaps I'll suggest it to my father in a day or two. But first we must wed so that you will truly be mine. With our marriage consummated, no one can take you from me."

She blinked at him. "Married? You and me?"

"Of course. Had you not pleased me, had we not bonded together so well…" He shook his head. "Never mind."

"What would have happened to me?"

"You would have been given to another. But do not worry, my lovely one. That will never happen now. You are mine, always and forever. No one will ever harm you or take you from me. No one."

CHAPTER 26

Nardik stood on the wall of Brynn Castle, gazing into the distance. Notice of Annis' disappearance had been sent to every city and village in Brynn Tor. Many of the guards sent to find her had returned. None bearing good news. There had been no demand for ransom. Amerris had taken to her bed. Marri hoped for the best even as she prepared herself to accept the worst.

As worried as he was for Annis, his major concern was for Seleena's safety. There was no telling what evil Serepta had in mind. Unbidden, came the memory of his daughter as a little girl, taking her first step, saying her first word, conjuring her first spell. How had his lovely, innocent, child turned into such a depraved creature? Would she have turned out differently if he had been the one to raise her? He thrust that thought aside. Seleena had been a devoted mother.

It pleased him that Seleena was staying at the Fortress. Was she remembering their time together? The nights they had surrendered to the passion that had smoldered between them? He should never have let her go. Too late, he had realized that what he had assumed was only a passing fancy for a beautiful woman had been stronger, deeper. But she had left him, and his foolish masculine pride had kept him from going after her.

He frowned as a wisp of yellow smoke drifted into view. He held out his hand and it settled in his palm, the smoke inscribing letters on his hand. *Nardik, I need you.*

Hurrying to his room, he penned a short note for Amerris. After donning his cloak, he spoke the words that would carry him to the Fortress.

* * *

Seleena opened the door before he knocked. "Thank you for coming."

"What is wrong?" He followed her into the living room, removed his cloak, and tossed it on the back of a sofa. "How can I help?"

"Serepta has Quinn."

"I see. You are certain of this?"

"Of course!"

"What do you want of me?"

"What do you think?" She fisted her hands on her hips. "I know you don't like him, but that doesn't matter. We can't leave him there." She swallowed the growing lump in her throat. "If you won't help me, I'll go alone."

"No, you will not."

"She's torturing him. We have to go, now, before it's too late. Before she grows weary of her sport. Before she kills him and unleashes the dragon's power. I'm afraid there will be no stopping her then."

"There can be no hesitation on our part this time," he said. "No mercy. I will take her heart and her head and burn what is left. If you cannot condone her destruction, then you should stay here."

"I am going with you." Not long ago, she would have been horrified to even contemplate such a thing. But Serepta was their daughter. They had brought her into the world. And although they weren't responsible for her devotion to the dark arts, it was up to them to put an end to her reign of terror before Serepta took any more innocent lives.

Before she caused Quinn any more pain.

* * *

He writhed on the floor of his cell in a pool of his own blood, the silver that bound him rendering him helpless to resist as Serepta dragged a razor-sharp blade over his flesh. Had he not been shackled, the cuts, though painful, would have healed instantly. But they did not heal quickly now. The loss of blood weakened him still further.

Worse than the pain was the way she gloated as she tormented him, describing in vivid detail how she planned to kill him, promising it would be more excruciating than anything he could imagine. Promising that her mother would be there to watch every glorious moment.

He prayed fervently that Seleena would stay locked in the Fortress, that Nardik could keep her safe. That, hopefully, between the two of them, they could put an end to Serepta's evil.

Quinn remained as stoic as he could, refusing to grovel, biting back the desire to give voice to the agony she inflicted.

Relief washed through him when, with a grimace of displeasure, she left the dungeon in a cloud of black smoke.

Curled in on himself, he closed his eyes, seeing respite in sleep. But sleep wouldn't come.

It took him a moment to realize it wasn't the pain keeping him awake, but the restless dragon on his shoulder.

* * *

Standing in front of Serepta's castle, Seleena fought a growing sense of despair as another of Nardik's spells failed. She gasped when he breathed out an oath. Swearing was something he rarely did and only served to emphasize his anger and frustration. Separately and together, they had tried to breach the wards around Serepta's castle, but to no avail.

"There has to be a way!" Seleena cried.

"Her magic is stronger than it ever was," he replied, his brow furrowed. "I do not understand how that is possible."

"Me, either. If only we knew who restored it."

He nodded. "I can think of no wizard or witch on Brynn Tor who possesses greater magic than we do. Even with the addition of her vampire powers, we should be able to break any spell she can conjure."

"Perhaps she didn't get help from anyone on Brynn Tor."

Nardik grunted thoughtfully. "Centuries ago, there was a coven of dark witches on Caynn."

"Where are they now?"

"Still there, perhaps, though no one has heard anything about them in decades."

"They might be our only hope. Do you know any of them?"

"No."

"What are we waiting for? We should go there now! There's no time to waste."

"It could be dangerous."

"I don't care. I'm going, with or without you."

* * *

With Nardik's magic, it took only moments to arrive at the nearest spaceport. He found a pilot who was willing to transport them to Caynn, for the right price. Again using his magic, the required number of credits appeared in the pilot's account. Half an hour later, the Airship was fired up and ready to go.

Seleena sat rigid in her seat. She had never traveled through outer space before and vowed there and then she would never do so again. She didn't like not being in control.

She glanced out the window. The photos she had seen of Caynn depicted mountains and valleys and vast swaths of green. But the landscape below looked bleak and inhospitable.

The Airship landed smoothly on a barren stretch of ground beneath a dull gray sky. Seleena disembarked gratefully, relieved that the trip had been remarkably, blessedly, short.

She glanced around as Nardik stepped out behind her. She was about to ask him how they would find the coven when she sensed it - the unmistakable signature of black magic. She turned toward the east, where it was strongest.

"You sense it, too?" Nardik asked, moving up beside her.

Seleena nodded. "Let's go."

"Wait." Nardik drew his wand from inside his cloak, waved it once, then murmured an incantation. "She is here."

"What you talking about? Who's here?"

"Annis." He smiled grimly. "Perhaps we can solve two problems with one visit."

* * *

Serepta's scent preceded her into the dungeon. But it was another scent that brought Quinn to his feet. He swayed unsteadily, the scent of fresh blood - human blood - stirring a hunger already roaring out of control due to the blood he had lost and the pain thrumming through him.

"I brought your dinner," Serepta said as she unlocked the door and thrust a young girl inside. She was no more than fifteen or sixteen, with stringy blonde hair. Blood leaked from a long gash in her left arm. "Enjoy."

Quinn backed away as far as the chain would allow. "Get her out of here!"

"Not your type?" Serepta asked.

"Get her out of here!" He clenched his hands. He had never known a hunger like this. He had to resist the urge to kill her. She was young, innocent, her eyes wide with terror. The pounding of her heart called to him. Fresh blood. An end to the pain ripping through him. "No!" He had promised Seleena he wouldn't take a human life.

"I'll just leave you to it," Serepta said. "Think of it as your last meal."

Her laughter trailed behind her as she left the dungeon.

Tears welled in the girl's eyes. "Please, don't."

"Put something over that cut." He ground the words through clenched teeth.

She stared at him then removed her torn shirt and wrapped it around her arm.

It didn't help.

Quinn cursed under his breath as blood quickly soaked the cloth. The smell was just as strong. Just as tempting. With a low groan, he turned his back on her and dropped to his knees. He hadn't uttered a prayer since the night his mother died. But he prayed now, desperately pleading for the strength to resist the siren call of the girl's blood.

Chapter 27

Seleena stared at the walled citadel that crouched like a lion on the flat rise before them. This close, the signature of Black Magic was overpowering. It crawled over her skin, made her insides clench with revulsion.

"Do you want to wait out here?" Nardik asked, sensing her reluctance to enter.

"No."

With a nod, he started up the hill.

Seleena followed him. It would have taken little effort to transport themselves to the top of the rise, but it was never wise to use one's magic in another's territory. A narrow path led from the top of the rise to the wall, which rose one hundred feet into the air.

There was no visible entrance.

"What do we do now?" she asked.

"The wall is to keep invaders and non-magical folk out," Nardik said.

Seleena frowned. "So, we need to go over it. But you said we shouldn't use magic."

"In this instance, they will be expecting it. Together," he said, reaching for her hand. A murmured incantation carried them over the wall into a barren courtyard. A large gray stone dwelling stood at its center.

A thick oak door swung open at their approach. A man clad in a long, black robe stood in the doorway. Slight of stature, he had regular features, devil-dark eyes, and hair as white as the snow atop the mountains of Brynn Tor. Power radiated from him.

With a slight now, Nardik introduced himself, then inclined his head in her direction. "And this is Seleena."

"What brings you here, uninvited?"

Though he was small of stature, the wizard's voice rang like thunder in Seleena's ears.

"I am Serepta's father. And this is her mother."

Face void of any emotion, Wyrick said, "I have been expecting you."

"Indeed?"

The wizard nodded. "I am Wyrick. Please, come inside."

Seleena followed Nardik and the other wizard down a long narrow corridor and into a large, square room furnished with a number of couches and tables. A large stone fireplace took up one wall. Ancient weapons and instruments of torture rested on shelves and adorned the walls.

"Please, sit," the wizard invited. A wave of his hand, and a tray holding three crystal goblets and a decanter appeared on a table. He filled the three glasses, offered one to Nardik and Seleena. Keeping the third for himself, he sat on the sofa opposite theirs. "How may I help you?"

"Our daughter was here," Nardik said.

Seleena wondered if the wizard would deny it, though it would be foolish to do so. The signature of her magic lingered in the room.

"Yes," Wyrick said. "She asked that I restore the magic you took from her."

"She is stronger now than before."

"Of course. That is why she came to me. You think to destroy her, do you not?"

"It must be done, though we take no pleasure in it. Is there a way to weaken her powers?"

Wyrick shrugged. "Perhaps."

"Will you tell me how it can be done?"

"No."

"What did she give you in return?"

"That is for me to know."

"It was a young woman, was it not?" Nardik asked. "A young woman by name of Annis. Sister to the queen of Brynn Tor."

The wizard said nothing.

"Serepta kidnapped Annis from the cloister where she had taken her vows."

Surprise flashed in the wizard's eyes.

"She is here," Nardik said.

Wyrick sipped from his glass, then put it aside. "Yes. No harm has come to her. She is to wed my son."

"What?" Seleena leaned forward. "She is already married to the church."

"That is unfortunate," Wyrick replied. "The date of the marriage has been set."

"You cannot force her to marry against her will!" Seleena exclaimed.

"She willingly accepted my son's proposal. Their union has been consummated."

Seleena stared at Wyrick.

"I wish to speak with her," Nardik said. "I wish to hear from her own lips that she comes to this union of her own free will."

"As you wish. Follow me."

Wyrick led them through a warren of corridors and up a flight of stone stairs. He paused before the only chamber on the floor and knocked once.

Several moments passed before the door opened. A tall, handsome man stood on at threshold. He smiled at Wyrick, then frowned when he saw Nardik and Seleena. "Father?"

"These two wish to speak with Annis."

"To what end?"

"They have come to assure themselves that she is not being forced into this marriage."

The man glanced over his shoulder. "Annis, we have guests."

Smiling, she came to his side, her eyes growing wide when she saw their visitors.

"Nardik! What are you doing here?"

"I have come to take you home."

Annis looked at Rajj. "You're sending me away?"

"Only if you wish to go."

"But I don't!" She looked at Nardik, her eyes wide. "I want to stay here, with Rajj."

Nardik's gaze searched hers. He detected no hint of witchcraft compelling her to lie, no sense that she spoke anything but the truth. No mistaking the fact that she was truly happy.

"I was afraid at first," she said, taking Rajj's hand in hers, "but I'm not any more. I know it sounds unbelievable, but I know we were meant to be together."

"Is there anything you need?" Seleena asked. "Any message for your family?"

"Yes. Please tell Marri and my mother I'm well and happy and that I send them my love." She smiled at Rajj. "And that we hope to visit them soon."

* * *

Seleena was pensive as she and Nardik left the citadel. "Did you believe her?"

"Yes. She was not compelled in any way."

To her surprise, an opening appeared in the wall when they approached. Nardik hesitated a moment, then passed through. Seleena stared after him. Her body tingled with foreign magic as she followed him. The opening closed silently behind her.

"We're no better off now than we were before," she remarked as they made their way down the hill toward the Airship. "We still don't know how to defeat Serepta or how to breach the wards she's set round her lair."

"At least we know Annis is well," Nardik said matter-of-factly. "No doubt our daughter will be displeased to learn that, quite inadvertently, she has made someone happy."

"I'm not worried about her," Seleena said, settling herself inside the craft. "Right now, I can't think of anyone but Quinn." Leaning forward in her seat, she spoke to the pilot. "Please, hurry!"

Sitting back, she closed her eyes. Going to see Wyrick had been a waste of precious time. Time they didn't have to waste.

"When we get back to Brynn Tor, I want you to go to the Fortress and wait for me," Nardik said.

"No! I'm going after Quinn."

"You cannot go alone. I need to let Amerris and Marri know that Annis is safe."

Seleena stared at him. "Surely Quinn's life is more important that allaying their fears!"

"Do not argue with me. We have not been able to breach her wards. You will accomplish nothing by going there now. Sooner or later, she will come to us."

Seleena nodded.

"I will return as soon as possible. Consult the grimoire. Perhaps you will find an answer there."

She nodded again, hands clenched at her sides. Nardik could do whatever he wished.

She was going after Quinn.

CHAPTER 28

Quinn huddled in the corner of his cell , eyes tightly shut. Even though he couldn't see the girl, he heard every ragged breath she took, the slow, steady beating of her heart, the enticing scent of her fear. Like a wild animal smelling its prey, it only increased his desire to bury his fangs in her throat and ease the incessant hunger burning through every fiber of his being.

"Girl."

"Wh…what?"

"Tell me your name."

"Why?"

"Tell me, dammit!"

"Larrah."

He repeated it, hoping it would help him to think of her, not as prey, but as a human being, a young woman who needed his protection. "I need you to trust me."

She said nothing, but her skepticism was palpable.

Quinn opened his eyes and took a deep calming breath. "I want you to come here and sit beside me."

She scrambled into the far corner, legs drawn up to her chest, hands protecting her throat.

"Come here."

She crawled toward him, her whole body trembling, her eyes wide with terror.

"Listen to me," he said. "I'm going to drink from you. You must not fight me. I want you to sit very still and say nothing. Do nothing." If she allowed him to drink from her, perhaps he could take only a little. If she fought him, he knew he would kill her. "Larrah, do you understand?" If his powers weren't so weak, he could have mesmerized her, but he lacked the strength to do so.

She nodded once, then closed her eyes. Her lips moved. He watched her a moment and realized she was praying.

Thinking, *Heaven help us both*, he grasped the girl's shoulders and lowered his head to her slender white throat.

* * *

Serepta cursed at the sight that met her eyes when she materialized outside Quinn's cell. She had expected to see the girl dead, drained of blood, her prisoner filled with self-loathing. Instead, the little whore was asleep, her head resting on Quinn's lap.

He looked up, an impudent grin playing over his lips. "Thanks," he drawled, stroking the girl's pale cheek. "I needed that."

Serepta glared at him. Then, overcome with rage, she materialized inside the cage and broke the girl's neck.

Strengthened by the girl's blood, Quinn sprang to his feet. "Damn you, Serepta! That was uncalled for!"

At the mention of the witch's name, the dragon stirred to life, its teeth sinking into Quinn's shoulder. Overcome with anger, he hardly noticed it.

But Serepta did. She smiled triumphantly. It was what she had been waiting for.

Now, she thought, her hand reaching for the dagger hidden in the folds of her cloak. Now was the time to destroy Quinn and unleash the dragon's power.

She lunged toward him, smiling triumphantly.

Quinn stumbled backward and darted to the left. The blade, meant to pierce his heart, sliced into his shoulder instead, opening a shallow gash across the dragon's tail.

The dragon let out a roar that shook the walls. Its tongue, long and black and forked, lashed out amid a white hot flame, searing Serepta's arm from wrist to elbow and setting her cloak on fire.

With a shriek, she dropped the dagger and vanished from the cell.

Dropping to his knees, Quinn tore a strip from the hem of the girl's skirt, intending to use it to staunch the blood flowing from his shoulder. But there was no need. Like a kitten with a bowl of cream, the dragon lapped it up, and as he did so, strength flowed into Quinn. The wound healed without a trace. The dragon snorted a puff of gray smoke and resumed its normal position on Quinn's shoulder.

Quinn stared at the tattoo. Why had it defended him against Serepta? Wasn't she supposed to be its master? She had created it, after all.

With a shake of his head, he closed Larrah's eyes, removed her shirt, and covered her face and neck with it. "I'm sorry," he murmured. "So damn sorry."

Picking up Serepta's dagger, he turned it in his hands. He spent the next several minutes trying to pry open the lock of the shackles on his wrists, but to no avail.

And then he looked at the tattoo on his shoulder. "Dragon?"

Nothing happened.

Using his fingers, he stroked the creature's back. "Dragon, awake!"

The tattoo rippled. He flinched when the dragon's claws raked his skin, but it didn't draw blood. And then it raised its head and stared at him through dark, fathomless eyes.

"Well, shit," Quinn muttered. "Listen, dragon, I need you to melt these shackles. Can you do that?"

With a shake of its head, the dragon unleashed a narrow flame of white hot fire. It burned through the silver link between the chains and the silver cuffs at his wrists, freeing his hands. Surprisingly, the flame didn't burn the skin beneath.

Stroking the dragon's neck, Quinn summoned its power and his own, felt it flow through every nerve and cell of his body. "All right, buddy, let's get the hell out of here."

* * *

Serepta kicked her ruined gown aside, then stared at the blackened skin of her rm. Not only did it burn like the fires of Hel, but it wasn't healing. She summoned the woman who served as her maid, sank her fangs into her neck, and drained her dry. And still the burn did not heal.

The dragon had attacked her. Why? She had conjured it. It carried her magic. Why had it turned on her? And why wasn't the burn healing?

* * *

Quinn was feeling pretty good by the time he returned to the Fortress. He called Seleena's name as he stepped inside, realizing as he did so that she wasn't there. Damn and blast, where could she be?

Seleena? Can you hear me?

Quinn? Oh, Quinn, just sit tight. I'm on my way.

On your way where?

To Serepta's.

Forget that. I'm at the Fortress.

How did you get away?

The dragon, Red. He got me out of there. Hurry home and I'll tell you all about it.

She walked in the door on the last word and flew into his arms, her hands moving over his back, his shoulders, his face.

"You're all right?" she asked, her gaze searching his.

"Never better, now that you're here."

"I was so afraid!"

"Yeah, me, too. Afraid I'd never see you again."

Taking him by the hand, she led him to the sofa and pulled him down beside her. "Tell me everything." She noticed the dried blood for the first time. "Are you sure you're all right?"

He nodded. "She cut me up a little, that's all."

"That's all?"

"That's not the worst of it." He paused, thinking of the dead girl. "Are you sure you want to hear this?"

"Tell me everything."

"Serepta brought me a young girl to feed on. Her name was Larrah. I fed on her, but I didn't kill her. It made Serepta angry and she broke the kid's neck."

Seleena's face paled at his words. Taking a deep breath, she blew it out in a long, slow sigh. "I've resigned myself to the fact that my daughter is beyond redemption. The dragon, Quinn, tell me about the dragon."

"Serepta pulled a dagger, intending to kill me, I guess. When I dodged out of the way, the blade cut the dragon's tail. I guess he didn't like it. He struck before she got a second chance. It burned her hand and her arm. She let out a shriek, dropped the dagger, and vanished. The dragon melted the shackles that held me and we came here." He held up his hands. "Think you could magic these cuffs off me?"

"Of course." She murmured a few words and the restraints fell away.

He kicked them aside, then rubbed his wrists. "Where's Nardik?"

"We went to Caynn in search of the wizard who restored Serepta's magic, hoping he could tell us how to thwart her. He refused to help, but we learned that Serepta had given him Annis in exchange for the return of her magic. Nardik hoped to bring Annis home, but it seems she's quite happy there. She's going to marry the wizard's son."

"No shit? Wasn't she a nun or something?"

"Yes. Nardik's gone to tell Amerris and Marri that she's all right." Seleena cupped his face in her hands and kissed him lightly. "I missed you."

"No more than I missed you." He glanced at his blood-stained arm. "I need a shower."

"Would you like me to wash your back?"

Quinn stared at her, wondering if he was reading more into her offer than she meant. "And my front, if you've a mind to." He had expected her to blush and stammer. Instead, she took his hand and led him into the bathroom.

Once there, she turned on the shower, adjusted the temperature, pulled several towels from the shelf.

Quinn reached for his belt, paused when she didn't leave the room. He tossed it aside, unfastened his trousers, let them rest on his hips. And still she didn't take her leave.

Keeping his gaze on her face, her cheeks now very pink, he shucked his pants and briefs and stepped under the spray, felt his mouth go dry when, several moments later, the door opened and she moved in behind him.

Quinn sucked in a breath when she took the soap from his hand

and began to run it up and down his spine. "Red…do you know what you're doing?"

"Washing your back. Isn't that what you wanted?"

He groaned softly. "Damn, woman, I'm not made of stone any more, you know."

She laughed softly, her soapy hands moving tantalizing over his shoulders and back, sliding lower, lower.

"You'd better stop now, Red," he growled, "or you're going to wind up flat on your back in about ten seconds."

"Isn't that what you've been wanting all this time?"

"Yeah, but you'd better be sure it's what *you* want, 'cause once we get started, there'll be no going back."

He tensed as she dropped the soap, then leaned into him, her bare breasts pressed against his back as she scattered butterfly kisses across his shoulders.

Muttering, "Time's up," he turned off the water, swept her into his arms and carried her swiftly into her room. "Last chance," he warned as he lowered her onto the mattress.

Pulling him down on top of her, she whispered, "Stop talking," and covered his mouth with hers.

It had been years since she had shared a bed with a man. She had been certain that there could be no better lover than Nardik, which just proved how wrong you could be, she thought, as Quinn kissed and caressed her. She had shared passion with Nardik, but never love. Never given him her heart. It made all the difference. Why had she waited so long for this? Her fears had been groundless.

She reveled in his caresses, in the slick feel of his damp skin against her own, the touch of his hands in her hair, on her skin, the husky sound of his voice as he whispered that he loved her, needed her, wanted her more than life itself.

Time lost all meaning as they came together, hearts and souls blending, melding, until, with one final thrust, he made her his. Pleasure exploded deep within her. His body shuddered a moment later and then, spent and sated, they fell asleep in each other's arms.

* * *

Quinn woke abruptly, aware of movement in the house. He tensed a moment, then relaxed when he realized it was Nardik. And tensed again when he heard the wizard's footsteps in the hallway. Grabbing the blanket from the foot of the bed, he drew it over Seleena, covering her from head to heel.

He was sitting up, his back against the headboard, the blanket draped over his hips, when Nardik opened the door.

A look of utter hatred twisted the wizard's features when he saw Quinn.

The dragon on Quinn's shoulder moved, undoubtedly stirred to life by the tension between the two men.

Quinn met the wizard's gaze. It was all he could do not to laugh in the other man's face.

With a hiss, Nardik closed the door.

Quinn smiled. Score for one me, he thought.

Seleena stirred beside him.

Sliding under the covers, he said, "Hey, sleepy head. We've got company."

Her eyes widened. "Nardik!"

"Yeah. He doesn't look too happy."

"He knows? About us?"

"You could say that. He poked his head in here a minute ago."

She groaned softly, obviously uncomfortable at having her former lover and her current lover under the same roof.

"It's not a secret you could keep from him," Quinn remarked.

"I know, but…"

"You're not having regrets, are you?"

She considered it a moment. She had expected to feel guilty or uncomfortable knowing Quinn had made love to her daughter first, but the thought hadn't even crossed her mind. And it didn't bother her now.

"Red?"

"No, of course not. It was wonderful." She smiled up at him. "You said it was bound to happen sooner or later. I just wish it had been sooner."

"Not my fault it took so long," he said, kissing the tip of her nose. "I was ready the day we met." He brushed a lock of hair behind her ear, thinking how beautiful she looked with her hair sleep-tousled, her lips swollen from his kisses, and how lucky he was to have found her. He muttered a mild oath when he heard Nardik in the kitchen, slamming cupboard doors. "We might as well get up and face the music," he said, tossing the covers aside. "He's not leaving until we do. But first, how about another shower?"

* * *

Seleena took several deep breaths. She could hear Nardik pacing the floor in the living room. She didn't have to see his face to know he was angry. And jealous. Though he had no reason for his jealousy, she thought, since he was engaged to be married to Amerris as soon as her mourning period was over.

"Hey, there's nothing for you to be afraid of." With a wink and a smile, Quinn slipped his arm around her waist. "I'm here."

Warmth flooded her whole being, and with it a strong sense that, whatever else the future held, deciding to be with Quinn was the wisest decision she had ever made.

They found Nardik pacing the living room floor, his robes swishing around his ankles, his face a cold mask of barely-controlled rage.

At the wizard's request, Quinn told him all that had happened while he had been Serepta's prisoner. "She's vulnerable," he said when he'd finished. "The dragon burned her and the wound isn't healing." He glanced at Seleena. "You were right. She conjured the wrong dragon. He's mine now and she's afraid of it."

"How do you know her wound isn't healing?" Nardik asked.

"I'm not sure, but I think it has to do with the dragon. Even though she conjured the wrong one, it still possesses some of her magic. I can sense her pain and her confusion. The dragon's burn isn't healing. Instead, it's spreading." Quinn paused. "She's drained a half-dozen people but it's not helping."

Seleena looked at Nardik, her brow furrowed. "Is there anything that will heal the wound?"

"Nothing that I know of. Nor would I offer it to her if I had the remedy."

Seleena bit down on her lower lip. She thought her love for Serepta had died. Yet, even knowing their daughter was evil and that there was no hope of turning her away from the dark path she had chosen to follow, it grieved her to know her child was hurting.

Perhaps dying. In spite of the pain Serepta had caused, the lives she had taken, she was still her daughter. Her only daughter. Perhaps the only child she would ever have. She turned away, not wanting Nardik or Quinn to see her tears.

"If she shows up, let me know," Nardik said, his voice icy cold. "I'll be at Brynn Castle." Then, sending Seleena a look of disappointment - or was it disgust? - he stormed out of the Fortress.

CHAPTER 29

"Well, that was fun," Seleena muttered later, when her tears had dried, along with her last hope of saving her daughter.

"He was bound to find out about us sooner or later. I'm pretty sure it didn't come as a surprise."

"No, I suppose not."

Quinn folded her into his arms, his chin resting lightly on the top of her head. Her hair smelled of honey and almonds. She fit in his embrace as if she had been made only for him.

"I wish it was over, once and for all," she said quietly. "Is it awful of me to feel that way? It hurts to know I can't help her. That no one can help her."

"I know these last months have been difficult for you. I don't guess mothers ever stop loving their children."

"I thought I had. When I saw her torturing you, causing you such pain and enjoying it with such obvious delight, I was sure I hated her. But all I feel now is pity. And sorrow for what might have been."

Quinn stroked her hair, wishing he could find a way to ease the pain in her heart, knowing it would only get worse once Serepta had been destroyed. And if he was the one to do it, what then?

It was something he didn't want to think about.

* * *

Serepta raced through the dungeon in a killing spree. In a matter of minutes, she had drained every prisoner dry, and still the ugly black burn on her arm didn't heal, or stop spreading. It was up to her shoulder now, inching its way down over her breast.

Hurrying upstairs, she gathered her athame and her cauldron, lit a fat, black candle, then lifted her arms overhead and invoked a new spell of self-healing.

Throwing her gown aside, she stood in front of the mirror and stared at her reflection. At first, nothing happened, and then, to her immense relief, the blackened skin on her shoulder and the curve of her breast faded to gray and disappeared. It took longer for the burn on her arm to heal.

Feeling suddenly weak in the knees, she sank down to the floor, her head cradled in her hands. Her magic was still strong. Next time they came for her, she would know what to expect and she would be ready.

Rising, she dressed quickly and headed for Bosquetown. She needed an army and that lawless city was the best place to assemble one.

And then she needed bait for the trap.

* * *

Seleena sat on the sofa beside Quinn, her legs curled beneath her, her head resting on his shoulder. At her insistence, they had returned to her home in the village. There was no point in trying to hide from Serepta any longer, and Seleena wasn't comfortable making love to Quinn in the house she had once shared with Nardik.

Quinn hadn't argued when she suggested leaving the Fortress, making her think he felt the same.

It was, she thought now, good to be home. A fire crackled in the hearth, soft music filled the room. Earlier, they had made love in front of the fire. Now, feeling cherished and content, she gazed into the flames, utterly at peace. For these few hours, she refused to worry about the future.

She was on the brink of sleep when there was a frantic knock at the door.

"It's Kerry Frazzier," Quinn said, sitting up. "I hope she doesn't need help with another pregnant cow."

"She just has the one." Seleena made a face at him as she went to answer the door.

Kerry Frazzier stood there, her eyes red-rimmed from weeping, her hands clasped tightly together. "What is it?" Seleena asked, suddenly certain she didn't want to hear the answer.

"Lonn's gone."

"Gone? You mean he ran away?"

Sniffling, Kerry shook her head. "Your daughter…she took him."

Seleena grabbed the edge of the door as the strength drained out of her legs.

"She said….she said she would carve my boy up and send him back to me a piece at a time unless you and Mr. Quinn went after him. She…she wouldn't…wouldn't do that, would she?" Kerry grasped Seleena hands in hers. "Tell me!" she screamed. "Tell me she would never do such a terrible thing!"

Quinn moved up beside Seleena and slipped his arm around her waist. "Of course she wouldn't," he said, his voice calm, soothing, as he captured the other woman's gaze with his. "I want you to forget you saw Serepta. Forget what she said."

"Forget," Mrs. Frazzier repeated. She shook her head. "How can I?"

"You will," he said, exerting his power over her mind. "Now. You're going to go home and take a nap."

"Yes, a nap."

"You will sleep until Lonn returns or until I release you. Do you understand?"

"Yes, understand." Expression blank, Kerry Frazzier turned and walked away.

Seleena took a deep breath. Straightened her spine. "We have to go," she said, her voice rock steady. "Now."

"I'm ready when you are."

It took them a minute to decide which mode of transportation to use - his or hers. Quinn decided his was quicker. Wrapping his arm around her shoulders, he willed the two of them to the outskirts of the Black Castle.

He knew immediately that Serepta was expecting them. The wards around the castle were down. The doors stood ajar. No lights were visible within.

Quinn opened his preternatural senses. There were a number of people inside. The boy was there, too, his heartbeat different from that of the adults. He was alone in the dungeon.

Serepta was in there somewhere, lurking in the darkness. And so were a dozen others…Quinn frowned. There was something odd about them. They were human, but not.

Beside him, Seleena chanted softly, her eyes closed, her hands raised, palms facing outward.

"Are you getting anything?" he asked.

"She has created a small army of zombies," Seleena said.

"Zombies," Quinn muttered. "How the hell do you kill a zombie?"

"I'd rather not find out."

"I don't see as how we have any choice. I'm pretty sure they aren't there to make us feel welcome."

"No. But they're connected to Serepta. There's a slim chance we can spare their lives if we…if she…"

"Go on. What happens if she's out of the picture?"

"The spell will…will die with her."

"And the zombies?"

"It depends on the kind of spell she cast. Either it will release them, or they will cease to exist when she does."

"Good to know. Can you make yourself invisible? And if you do, will she be able to detect you?"

"Yes, I can, and no, she won't know I'm there."

Quinn nodded. "Okay. Here's the plan. You go to the dungeon and grab the boy and get the hell out of here. I'll take care of the rest. You ready?"

"Ready." The voice should have been low and sweet; instead, it was a deep growl.

Glancing over his shoulder, Quinn saw Nardik standing a few feet behind him. As usual, the wizard was clad all in black.

"What the hell are you doing here?" Quinn asked. "Are you stalking us?"

Nardik glared at him. "I've naturally been keeping myself informed of your plans."

"Naturally," Quinn muttered dryly.

"I came to back you up, for Seleena's sake. I don't want her to get hurt."

"That makes two of us." Drawing Seleena into his embrace, Quinn hugged her close. "Be careful, Red."

"You, too."

"No worries," he said. "Just get in, grab the boy and get out the hell."

Seleena murmured an incantation that shrouded her with a cloak of invisibility. When she was out of sight, Quinn and Nardik approached the castle doors. As one, they paused briefly before crossing the threshold.

The great hall was dark and quiet. Quinn detected the slow, steady sound of beating hearts all around him. There was no trace of Serepta, but she was there. The scent of dark magic hung heavy and unmistakable in the air.

Nardik murmured an incantation that lit the end of his wand.

In the faint glow, Quinn saw a dozen men - all young and strong, all in their prime. They lined the walls of the room, eyes blank, faces slack. They were all equipped with the latest firearms.

"Can you work some kind of spell to counteract whatever Serepta's got planned?"

Quinn asked.

"I can try." Chanting softly, Nardik turned in a slow circle, pointing his wand at each man in turn..

He had gone about half-way around when a burst of laughter rang off the walls.

It sent a chill down Quinn's spine. There was nothing human in the sound, no hint of amusement, only a wild, maniacal cackle filled with hatred.

It roused the zombies. Lifting their weapons, they began to fire.

Nardik vanished.

Quinn did likewise. He had expected the zombies to slaughter each other, but the witch had apparently erected some kind of protective shield around each one of them. The bullets never touched them.

Quinn left the great hall. Materializing on the second floor, he made his way from room to room, but the rooms were cold and empty.

* * *

Seleena found Lonn in the last cell at the far end of the dungeon. He was hunkered down in a corner, arms wrapped tightly around his middle, his cheeks wet with tears, his eyes wide and afraid.

Murmuring his name, she materialized outside the cell. A word unlocked the door. When she held out her arms, he ran to her, sobbing incoherently.

"Hush, now, it's all right," she said, patting his back. "I'm taking you home."

"You're not taking him anywhere."

Seleena froze at the sound of Serepta's voice. Putting Lonn behind her, she turned slowly to face her daughter.

"How nice of you to drop by," Serepta said, her eyes filled with madness.

"I'm here now. Let the boy go."

"I'm afraid not. Young blood is so very tasty."

"I will not let you hurt him."

Serepta snorted. "As if you could stop me."

"Maybe she can't, but I can."

Relief swept through Seleena as Quinn materialized out of the darkness.

Serepta whirled around. She shouted an incantation and as she did so, she grew taller, larger, until she towered over Quinn, her head mere inches from the high stone ceiling.

A wave of her hand sent him to his knees but Quinn held his ground, all his anger and energy focused on calling forth the dragon. It stirred beneath his shirt, its claws raking his shoulder. Quinn felt a wave of heat and then his shirt disintegrated. He glanced at the dragon, hissed a curse as it stretched and grew. And grew larger still, until it leaped from his arm and took shape.

Still on his knees, Quinn could only stare at the creature. It was an amazing and beautiful thing to see, its tail whipping back and forth. Sleek and black and powerful, its scales iridescent even in the darkness.

Serepta let out a shriek as it lumbered toward her, wings folded tightly against its body, eyes blazing. She backed away, but she had nowhere to go. She raised her hand again, perhaps to incant a spell, but she was too slow. With a mighty roar, white-hot flames poured from the dragon's mouth.

They enveloped the witch from head to heel. She screamed once, a horrible, agonized cry that Quinn knew he would carry to his grave, and then she was gone.

A sob was torn from Seleena's throat. Turning away, she wrapped her arms around Lonn, whispered a few words, and vanished from the dungeon.

Quinn rose slowly to his feet, his gaze fixed on the dragon. It wasn't overly large as dragons went. Perhaps nine feet tall.

The beast swung its head around, black eyes meeting Quinn's.

Quinn swallowed hard, wondering if he was next.

Slowly, the dragon moved toward him, until it stood within arm's reach. And then it lowered its head.

Lifting a tentative hand, Quinn patted the dragon's neck.

Several moments passed and then the dragon grew smaller. When it was the size of a large rat, it scurried up Quinn's arm and melted into his skin.

Loosing a sigh, Quinn made his way up the stairs to the great hall.

Nardik stood in the center of the room, surrounded by a dozen dead men. Quinn grunted softly. Knowing Serepta, he had been pretty sure that whether she lived or died, the men wouldn't survive. Even as he watched, their bodies disintegrated, until there was nothing left but dust. And then that, too, disappeared.

"Seleena has gone home," Nardik said.

Quinn nodded.

"You are in love with her."

"Yes."

"And she loves you," the wizard said, resignation thick in his voice.

Quinn nodded again. "I'm going to marry her, if she'll have me."

"If you hurt her in any way...."

"Yeah, I know. You'll turn me into a newt."

A faint smiled quirked the corner of the wizard's mouth and then he vanished in a puff of smoke.

Quinn glanced around the room. The air was still, the castle quiet. There was no lingering trace of evil or dark magic, no indication that men had died here, or that a black witch had ever walked its hallways.

It was over. Closing his eyes, he willed himself to Seleena's house.

He paused outside the blue door. Ordinarily, he would have just walked in, but at the moment, he wasn't sure of his welcome. Would she be glad to see him, or would the dragon on his shoulder forever be a reminder of her daughter's fiery death?

CHAPTER 30

Seleena took Lonn home. Kerry Frazzier woke from the spell she was under at the sound of her son's voice calling her name. As if nothing untoward had happened, Kerry rose from the couch and gave him an affectionate hug, then offered Seleena a cup of tea, which she declined.

Seleena managed to hold back her tears until she was in her own house, and then she took refuge in her bed. Freyja curled up at her side, purring softly in an effort to comfort her mistress.

Seleena's tears came then, so many she thought they might never stop. Not that she cared. Her daughter was truly dead this time. No magic in the world, black or white, would ever bring Serepta back.

She wept bitterly, blaming herself, blaming Nardik, blaming Quinn, even though she knew, deep in her heart, that it was Serepta herself who was responsible for the dark, twisting path she had followed, the terrible decisions she had made. So much blood spilled at her hands. So many needless deaths.

Seleena was almost asleep when she sensed someone at her front door and knew it was Quinn.

Freyja let out a hiss of displeasure as Seleena threw back the covers and hurried to let him in.

Choking back a sob, she wrapped her arms around him as a fresh wave of tears poured down her cheeks.

There was no need for words as he carried her into her room, laid her gently on the bed, then cradled her in his embrace.

He held her close, lightly stroking her back, her hair, whispering meaningless words until she fell asleep.

All under the watchful yellow eyes of the cat.

* * *

Quinn didn't sleep that night. He spent the long dark hours watching Seleena sleep, soothing her nightmares, listening to the soft, even sound of her breathing, the slow, steady beat of her heart. Except for his mother, he had never loved anyone, never really cared for anyone. He couldn't imagine the pain of losing a child, even one like Serepta.

He had been a little surprised at Seleena's reaction when she saw him. He hadn't expected her to fall into his arms. But the more he thought about it, the more natural it seemed. Except for the cat, she had no one else to comfort her.

He was in love with her, he admitted, heart and soul. She was like a miracle, one he had never thought to find. Certainly one he didn't deserve. He wanted to marry her, spend the rest of his life with her, if she would have him.

Quinn glanced at the dragon, sleeping peacefully on his shoulder. He had never expected the thing to come to life the way it had. He couldn't help wondering, if they had been in a building with a higher ceiling, if it would have grown even larger. Maybe one day he would find out.

His eyes grew heavy as the sun climbed over the horizon. Murmuring, "I love you, Red," he fell into the waiting darkness.

* * *

Seleena woke slowly, gradually becoming aware that Quinn was lying beside her, his arm around her shoulders, her head resting on his bare chest.

The dragon stared at her.

Seleena stared back, images of her daughter flashing through her mind - Serepta taking her first step, saying her first word. Serepta blossoming into a lovely young woman. Serepta, writhing in the heat of the dragon's flames.

She started to get up but something in the dragon's eyes - pity, compassion - held her immobile. The dragon extended one wing and images danced across it - images of the future if Serepta had won the battle. One scene of carnage after another, each worse than the last, until Seleena felt as if she were drowning in a sea of blood. A single tear shone in the dragon's eye and then the images were gone.

Seleena wiped the tears from her own eyes. There had been no joy in the scenes she had witnessed, no future happiness, no love. Just misery and death. Had Serepta foreseen such a future for herself? Had her subconscious purposefully conjured the wrong dragon?

Murmuring, "I hope she's found peace at last," Seleena stroked the dragon's head. Then, pressing closer to Quinn, she closed her eyes, content to lie in his arms until he woke.

* * *

Quinn came awake instantly, all his senses alert. His inner clock told him it was mid-afternoon. He was surprised, but pleased, to find that Seleena was still in bed beside him. Glancing to the side, he met the warmth of her gaze. No words were necessary.

She melted into his embrace with a sigh, her eyelids fluttering down as he kissed her lightly and then again, longer, deeper. Their clothes disappeared with a wave of her hand. There was nothing like it, she thought, the touch of skin against skin, when it belonged to the one you loved. And she loved Quinn. She wasn't sure how or when it had happened, knew only that she could no longer imagine her life without him.

Their lovemaking was slow and leisurely, as if they had all the time in the world. And maybe they did, Quinn thought. He was virtually immortal, and some witches lived hundreds of years.

Cupping her face in his hands, he whispered, "I've never loved anyone before, Red. Maybe I'm not very good at it. But I know that I need you. Will you marry me?"

She smiled up at him, her gray eyes filled with love and happiness. "I thought you would never ask."

"I'll understand if you want to wait awhile."

"I don't think that's a good idea," she said, a mysterious grin playing over her lips.

"Why is that? Not that I'm complaining. I'm willing to tie the knot tonight."

She laughed softly. "I'm glad to hear you say that, because in about nine months you're going to be a father."

"What?" Quinn bolted upright. "Are you saying you're pregnant?" He frowned as his gaze moved over her. "How?"

"In the usual way, I would imagine."

He shook his head. "Vampires can't reproduce. And even if it was remotely possible, which it isn't, how could you know so quickly?" Hell, they had only made love a couple of times, and then only in the last few days.

"I *am* a witch, remember?"

He fell back on the bed. A baby.

"I thought you would be happy. I am."

"Happy?" He rose up on one elbow, his other hand resting lightly on her belly as his gaze caressed her face. "I'm beyond happy, Red. I never thought…never expected." He cocked his head to the side, a grin twitching his lips. "So, is it a boy or a girl?"

"You'll just have to wait and see."

"Don't you know?"

"I'm not sure I want to. Do you?"

"Hell, yeah."

Seleena closed her eyes a moment, then smiled. "It's a boy."

Quinn hugged her close. A son, he thought exultantly. And then he frowned. He didn't know a thing about being a father. Vampires weren't supposed to be able to reproduce. What if the baby was born dead? Deformed?

Seleena cupped his face in her palms and kissed him lightly. "Stop worrying. He will be perfectly healthy and whole. Did you mean it when you said you would marry me tonight?"

He nuzzled her neck. "The sooner the better."

* * *

It was near dark when Quinn left the house. Seleena had suggested he go for a walk while she made arrangements for the wedding and he hadn't argued. He needed to feed, and truth be told, he needed a little time alone to come to terms with being a father.

He had never known the man who sired him. Had never had a fatherly influence in his life. Jagg hardly qualified.

A baby. What if Seleena was wrong and everything wasn't all right. What if the kid was part vampire? He muttered an oath as he imagined a baby who slept all day and drank fresh blood instead of mother's milk.

He thrust the nightmare images aside. Seleena had assured him the child would be all right. Determined to hold tight to that thought until it proved false, he willed himself to the nearest town.

He had just honed in on possible prey when Nardik fell into step beside him.

Quinn clenched his hands at his sides. There could only be one reason for the wizard to be there. "I don't suppose you've come to offer your congratulations."

"Hardly."

"So, why the hell are you here?"

"I want you to leave this place and never come back."

Quinn shook his head. "That's not going to happen. And what the hell do you care? Aren't you engaged to another woman?"

"I never stopped loving Seleena," Nardik said. "She means more to me than she could ever mean to you. We had a child together. No matter what happened since then, there's a bond between parents that cannot be broken."

Quinn blew out a sigh. "I'm glad to hear that."

Nardik frowned. "What do you mean?"

"She's pregnant. With my son."

Nardik came to an abrupt halt, his eyes blazing with disbelief which quickly turned to jealousy and then rage. Sparks erupted from the tip of his staff.

Shit! Quinn gathered his power, felt the dragon stir beneath his jacket.

The air between vampire and wizard pulsed with supernatural energy.

"You really want to do this?" Quinn glanced around. They were in a residential area. Several nearby houses had lights in the windows. He could hear conversation, the sound of laughter. "Here and now? Even if you destroy me - and I'm not sure you can - she'll never be yours."

The wizard glared at him; then, as the truth of Quinn's words apparently hit home, the tension between the two of them dissolved.

Eyes narrowed, Nardik said, "If you hurt her…"

"You know I'd never do that."

All the tension drained out of Nardik. "You are right. I do know. Just as I know that if you walked out of her life, she would never love me the way she loves you."

Something that might have been a grin flashed behind the wizard's eyes. "But be warned, there are worse things that being turned into a newt."

Quinn snorted. "Yeah? What could possibly be worse?"

"A eunuch!" Laughter rumbled deep in Nardik's throat as, with a wave of his hand, he vanished in a puff of black smoke.

CHAPTER 31

Quinn paused outside when he returned to Seleena's house. It looked the same, and yet different. There was a glow about it that hadn't been there before. The flowers in the yard were larger, brighter. A wreath of sage, apple, orange blossoms and lavender hung on the door.

Another surprise awaited him inside. Tiny white lights floated near the ceiling. A dozen white candles were scattered around the room, their flickering light casting shadows on the walls. An arch adorned with white roses stood in front of the hearth. Lonn and Kerry Frazzier stood on one side, a priest on the other.

The priest stepped forward, his hand outstretched. "Quinn?"

"Yes."

"I am Father Dixxon. Seleena asked that we start the ceremony as soon as you arrived."

Quinn nodded. "Pleased to make your acquaintance, Father."

Kerry Frazzier smiled at Quinn then began singing in a language he didn't understand, her voice pure and clear.

At the soft sound of Seleena's footsteps in the hallway, he turned.

His bride stood in the doorway. She wore a long, blue gown and a matching veil. Her hair fell in soft waves over her shoulders.

Quinn's breath caught in his throat as her gaze met his. She looked like an angel, he thought. And she was his.

As the last notes of the song faded away, Seleena walked toward him, her dove-gray eyes alight with love.

Stepping forward, he took her hand in his and gave it a squeeze and then they turned to face the priest.

"We are gathered here this evening to join Seleena and Quinn together. They have pledged their love one to another, and it is that love, stronger than mere words, that will bind them together from this night forward. Seleena, will you have this man as your husband?"

"Yes, I will."

"Quinn, will you have this woman as your wife?"

"Yes, I will."

"Then I hereby proclaim that you are now husband and wife, legally and lawfully wedded, forever and always." He smiled at Quinn. "You may kiss your bride."

Quinn's gaze moved over her face, as if to memorize how she looked at the very moment she became his. Taking her in his arms, he whispered, "I will love you as long as I live," and then he kissed her, ever so gently.

He surrendered her momentarily so that Mrs. Frazzier and her son could offer their congratulations while he shook hands with the priest, who wished them a long and happy life.

Kerry Frazzier had baked a cake for the occasion. She served it, first to Seleena and Quinn, then to Father Dixxon priest and her son.

Shortly thereafter, amid more hugs and good wishes, their guests took their leave.

Murmuring, "Alone at last," Quinn drew Seleena into his arms once again and claimed her lips with his. And then, frowning, he drew back. "Is it okay for us to make love, now that you're pregnant?"

"Of course, silly. I'm not made of glass."

Sweeping her into his arms, he carried her swiftly to their room. Twinkling fairy lights bathed them in a warm golden glow as they crossed the threshold. Music played in the background, soft and oddly erotic. The faint scent of musk teased his nostrils.

"You're beautiful, Red," he murmured as he set her on her feet. "The most beautiful woman I've ever seen."

She smiled with pleasure as she went up on her tiptoes and kissed him. And then, taking a step back, she began to undress him. The dragon on his shoulder stirred at her touch, a soft purr issuing from its throat.

"I think he likes you," Quinn said, his voice husky with desire. "I know I do."

She tossed his clothing aside, then ran her fingertips across his chest. "You're beautiful, too."

"Uh-huh. My turn." He undressed her slowly, his gaze moving over every inch as it was revealed. She blushed from head to heel in a way he found most endearing. And arousing. Whispering her name, he lifted her into his arms.

She wrapped her legs around his waist as he carried her to bed, where he made slow, sweet love to her.

Later, holding her close, he thought of his past, of how, not so long ago, his only thought had been to avenge himself on Serepta. The dragon had accomplished that, but it hadn't given Quinn the satisfaction or peace of mind he had expected. It was Seleena who had brought him joy and a sense of inner tranquility. Seleena who had taught him what it meant to love someone with his whole heart and soul. She had given him a reason to view the future with hope. And soon, she would give him a child. He secretly hoped for a son.

Quinn gasped with pleasure as she began to caress him, her hands working a familiar magic, her lips like velvet against his skin as she aroused him again.

If his luck held, he thought, perhaps, in a year or two, she would give him a daughter.

Epilogue

Moved beyond words, Quinn held his newborn son in his arms. He had never believed in miracles, until he met Seleena, and now he couldn't help wondering what he had ever done to be so richly blessed. He had been gifted with a child, healthy and whole. He had a wonderful wife who loved him unconditionally in spite of his faults and his past. He could ask for nothing more.

As Seleena had only moments before, Quinn counted each tiny finger and toe before pressing a kiss to his son's cheek. It was downy soft, as was his thick black hair.

Quinn looked at his woman, now sleeping peacefully. She had never looked more beautiful, and he had never loved her more.

After dropping a soft kiss on her brow, he tiptoed out of their bedroom. In the living room, he lowered himself into the rocking chair, his gaze lingering on the face of his son.

With a low purr, Freyja curled up at Quinn's feet, all her former animosity apparently forgotten.

Quinn closed his eyes, content to rock the baby as his thoughts wandered over the changes the last few months had wrought.

Seleena had enlarged her bedroom - now their room - and redecorated it in shades of pale blue and dark green.

With the aid of her magic, she had added a nursery to their home, then furnished it with every possible thing a new baby might need.

Nardik had wed Amerris as soon as her mourning period was over. When Quinn had last seen the wizard, he seemed content.

Annis appeared to be blissfully happy. She and Rajj were expecting a baby in a few months. Wyrick proclaimed it would be a girl.

Marri and Gryff were expecting their second child.

Brynn Tor was at peace under Marri's reign.

And life was good.

Quinn's Revenge

PROLOGUE

Annis paced the floor of the windowless room. Five steps from one end to the other. Back and forth. Back and forth. She had no idea where she was or how long Rajj intended to keep her there. All she remembered was falling into a dark abyss after the baby was born and waking up in this small, windowless chamber that was not a cell with iron bars, but was definitely a prison.

Thus far, she has been well taken care of. The room, painted a pale green, was furnished with a comfortable bed, a small wooden table, and a rocking chair. A thick sage-green carpet covered the floor. She had books to read and movies to watch. But, save for the witch known as Lanna who brought in meals three times a day, Annis never saw another soul.

She had begged Lanna to tell her why she was being kept in this place, but to no avail. Gradually, Annis came to believe that Rajj had bespelled her into loving him, that he had never cared for her at all, that their marriage had been nothing but a sham. All he had ever wanted from her was a child.

In the beginning, she refused to believe that everything that had happened since she met Rajj had been a lie.

He had told her it didn't matter that she had no magic.

A lie.

He had assured her that he had never been with another woman, that they would learn the intimacies between a husband and wife together.

Another lie.

He had vowed that he loved her.

And that had been the biggest lie of all.

How could she have been so blind to the evil that resided within? So gullible to his promises and lies?

She sank down on the bed, her arms aching to hold her daughter. Annis knew Corrie was nearby. Lanna brought her in every few hours so Annis could nurse her, but the witch refused to leave the baby any longer than necessary. Daily, Annis pleaded with Lanna to let her care for Corrie. Babies needed a mother's love and attention, but the witch only shook her head.

Annis' heart skipped a beat when she heard the rasp of the key turning in the lock. A moment later, she held Corrie in her arms. She rocked gently as the baby nursed, her eyes drinking in the sight of her daughter, her fingers lightly stroking the fine gold of Corrie's hair, her downy cheeks.

She lived for these few precious moments, knowing, deep in her heart, that when the child was weaned, Rajj and the coven would have no further need for her.

CHAPTER 1

It happened so gradually that, by the time Quinn became aware of it, months had passed and then one morning, as the twin suns rose in the sky, he realized he was no longer subject to the Dark Sleep of his kind. The hunger for blood remained, but the Dark Sleep no longer had any power over him.

At first, he suspected Seleena had conjured a new spell to allow him to spend more time with their son, a charm similar to the one that allowed him to eat mortal food, but when questioned, she had assured him she had nothing to do with it, leaving him to believe it had to be the black dragon tattoo's doing.

Standing in front of the large, oval mirror in the bedroom, Quinn studied the tattoo on his left shoulder. It had grown larger in the last few months. Once the dragon's body had covered only the top of his shoulder, with the forked tail twining around his bicep. Now, the body covered not only his shoulder, but his upper arm and a portion of his back, as well. The tail trailed past his elbow all the way down to his wrist.

He turned away from the mirror when Seleena stepped into the room. "Is something wrong?" she asked. "Breakfast has been ready for twenty minutes."

He ran his fingertips back and forth over the dragon's head, heard the creature's faint growl of pleasure. "It's getting bigger. What do you think it means?"

Her gaze moved to the tattoo, a constant reminder of a past she would rather forget, but was now a part of the man she loved more than life itself. "I have no idea."

He heard the note of worry in her voice. The tattoo had been conjured by Seleena's daughter, who had been a powerful witch in her own right. Serepta had infused the tattoo with a part of her dark magic, intending to use it to increase her magical powers. Instead, it had been her undoing. Neither Quinn nor Seleena had spoken of Serepta since the dragon incinerated her, but he knew Seleena wondered, as did he, if all of Serepta's dark magic had died with her.

"It seems odd that she would saddle me with the thing and then encase me in stone, don't you think?"

Seleena nodded. "I never thought about it, but now that you mention it, it does seem peculiar. But then, she often made rash decisions without thinking them through. And I'm sure..." She took a deep breath. "I'm sure she expected to be able to retrieve the dragon's power at some time in the future."

A future her daughter had never had. Guilt knifed through Quinn. The dragon had incinerated Serepta, but Quinn felt responsible, since the dragon had acted to save his life.

Seleena moved into Quinn's embrace, her hands locking behind his neck. Rising on her tiptoes, she kissed him. "Worrying doesn't help. Neither does dredging up the past."

His arm tightened around her waist. Although they had been together over a year, he still couldn't believe she was his. Or that the child born of their love slept in the next room. Now three months old, Steffon appeared to be a normal, happy baby and yet Quinn couldn't help wondering if some hint of darkness lurked in his son, born of the mating of a witch—even a white witch—and a vampire. He had voiced his concern when Seleena first told him she was pregnant. She had assured him that their son would be healthy and normal and yet, in spite of her repeated assurances, doubts lingered in the back of his mind.

Stepping back, Seleena tugged on his hand. "Come on. Your breakfast is cold."

He let her lead him into the kitchen, sat at the table while she reheated their meal.

With Serepta's death, their life had settled into a comfortable routine. Seleena continued to use her magic to help the villagers - healing their sick, blessing their cattle and crops, listening to their problems. She was a remarkable woman, beautiful, patient, kind, always busy with their son, eager to be of help to others, whether they were Queen or peasant.

Quinn knew he should have been content, but the truth was, except for the hours he spent with his son, he had little to occupy his time. Though he hated to admit it, he was rapidly growing bored with life in the village. He needed to be busy. Needed to feel he was contributing to the household. A man needed a job, a sense of purpose. Sadly, he had little qualifications for employment. There wasn't much call for assassins in their small village and that was the only thing he was good at. Occasionally, he went deer hunting, but with only himself and Seleena to feed, a haunch of venison lasted a good long time.

"You look troubled," Seleena remarked. "Is it the tattoo?"

"Yes. And no."

She put breakfast on the table, then slid into the chair across from his. "What does that mean?"

His gaze met hers. "The truth?"

"Of course."

"I'm feeling restless. There's nothing for me to do here, you know? Don't get me wrong. I love being with you and Steffon. But I need a job. Something to keep me busy."

Seleena nodded. Hadn't she secretly feared this very thing might happen? Her village was small, with little excitement. The men raised crops and cattle, the women sold produce in the marketplace. Unlike the big cities of Fenton, Bosquetown and Tarnn, life here was quiet and uneventful.

Keeping her voice steady, she said, "I've known for some time that you're not happy here."

"I'm not unhappy." Reaching across the table, he took her hand in his and kissed her palm. "Don't think that, Red. Don't ever think that."

Worry shadowed her eyes. "Do you want to leave?"

"Only if you go with me."

Her relief was a palpable thing. "Where would we go?"

"I don't know. I haven't really given it any thought." He leaned back in his chair, arms crossed. "You wouldn't be happy anywhere else, would you?" How could he even think of asking her to leave? She was a part of this place, as much at home here as the trees and the grass.

"I've lived here a long time. My neighbors accept me. Most other towns don't trust witches, or want them around. And big cities…" She shook her head. "I'm not comfortable there."

"I don't reckon vampires are welcome anywhere." He snorted softly. "We make a hell of a pair, don't we?"

"This is my home," she said quietly. "I won't keep you here if you want to go."

Pushing away from the table, Quinn pulled her into his arms. "Unless you send me away, I'm not going anywhere," he said, his voice a growl.

And then he kissed her, long and slow and deep. She melted against him, her flowery scent familiar and enticing, her breasts warm against his bare chest. She looked up at him, her dove-gray eyes shining with love and desire.

Murmuring her name, he swept her into his arms and carried her swiftly to bed.

At a word from Seleena's lips, their clothing fell away. Her gaze moved over him, filled with longing and admiration as her hands slid across his chest and down his arms, reveling in the strength she felt there. Her fingers delved into the thick dark hair at his nape, then skated down his back, her nails lightly raking his skin. He groaned softly as she writhed beneath him, hips lifting to receive him.

Their coming together was as explosive as the colliding of two stars - full of sparks and fury.

Quinn whispered her name as she shuddered beneath him, then let out a sigh of deep contentment. She was the best part of him, the other half of his soul. The anchor that kept him grounded, kept his infernal hunger at bay.

If he died of boredom in this little backwater town without a name, so be it.

But he was never leaving her side.

CHAPTER 2

Seleena frowned as she read Gryff's letter a second time.

Seleena ~

Marri has not yet recovered from the birth of our second child and knows nothing of what I am about to tell you. Last month, Amerris went to Caynn to visit Annis and the baby. When she arrived, she was told that her daughter and granddaughter were 'unavailable' at that time. When Amerris said she would wait, she was told, in no uncertain terms, that she was not welcome to do so.

A week later, she sent a letter to Annis. It was returned, unopened. The next day, she returned to Caynn and a detail of the Queen's Guard to find the citadel apparently abandoned. On her return to the castle, Nardik invoked a spell to locate Annis, but to no avail.

With Marri in ill-health and our newborn fighting for her life, I cannot leave Brynn Castle. Which brings me to the reason for this letter. I'm hoping that Quinn will accompany Nardik to Caynn to find out what's going on.

She blew out a sigh of resignation. If Gryff required their help, then, for the sake of their friendship, they must give it to him.

Life had just settled into a quiet routine, she thought, and now trouble again loomed on the horizon, demanding their attention.

Feeling a twinge of guilt at entertaining such an uncharitable thought, she quickly shook it away. She had much to be thankful for. Her son slept peacefully in the nursery. She was married to a wonderful man who loved her. She was respected by her neighbors.

She looked up from her chair when Quinn entered the room, her heart lifting at the mere sight of him.

He jerked his chin at the letter in her hand. "Bad news?"

"I'm afraid so." Offering him the letter, she said, "It's from Gryff. Annis and her daughter seem to have gone missing."

Quinn read the note quickly, then folded it in half and dropped it on the side table. Sitting on the sofa, he stretched his legs out in front of him. "What do you think happened to her?"

"I have no idea, but it seems very suspicious to me. I suspected there was something not quite right when Annis fell in love so quickly, but Nardik told me that when he visited her before the wedding, he didn't detect any hint of coercion, or any kind of enchantment that would have compelled her to fall in love with Rajj."

Quinn nodded. Nardik was Queen Marri's chief advisor. He was rumored to be the most powerful wizard on Brynn Tor, but that didn't mean he was infallible. "Maybe he was mistaken. Or maybe the witches of Caynn are more powerful than he is."

"I suppose it *is* possible," she said, though she looked doubtful.

"Have you tried to locate Annis?"

"Yes, while you were out." Seleena shook her head. "But if Nardik couldn't find her…" Her voice trailed off. "Are you going to go with him?"

"Not if you don't want me to. But what's the point, if the place has been abandoned?"

"Wyrick could easily have tricked Amerris into thinking that the place was deserted. She has no magic to detect any kind of magic."

Quinn considered that for a moment. "Will you be all right while I'm gone?"

Amusement twinkled in her eyes. "Of course."

Quinn grunted softly. Sometimes he forgot she was a powerful witch in her own right.

"So? Are you going?"

"I reckon so." He wasn't looking forward to spending time with Nardik. Seleena and the wizard had a long history together. Years ago, they had been lovers. Serepta had been the result. They had loved the child, worried when she turned toward dark magic, shared their grief when she had to be destroyed. Though Nardik had wed Amerris, Quinn knew the wizard still harbored tender feelings for Seleena.

"I'll send word to Nardik and let him know you'll go with him and that you'll be ready tomorrow," she said. "You will be careful, won't you?"

Tugging her out of her chair and into his arms, he asked. "What do you think?"

"I think I'll worry the whole time you're gone."

"I don't know why." He pushed a lock of hair behind her ear. "You have the ability to know what I'm doing every minute I'm away."

She nodded. Quinn had tasted her blood. It had formed an unbreakable link between them, which allowed them to communicate mentally over long distances. If she wanted to know where or how he was, all she had to do was open that link. Or use her own magic.

At the sound of their son's cry, she kissed Quinn's cheek then hurried into the nursery. "Here, now, my sweet baby boy," she crooned, lifting Steffon into her arms. "There's no need to fret."

She hugged him close as she carried him into the living room. Taking a seat in her favorite rocker, she felt a wave of love sweep over her as he nuzzled her breast. Was there anything stronger or more enduring than the love of a mother for her child? The pain of losing Serepta was a constant ache in her heart, a soul-deep sorrow that could never be healed or forgotten.

She rocked gently as the baby nursed, her gaze drinking in the sight of him. He looked so like his father. The same dark brown hair and tawny skin. His eyes were dark blue, like Quinn's, and she knew somehow that they would not change color as Steffon grew older, as a baby's eyes often did.

His eyes. When he looked up at her, as he was now, she sometimes felt as if he was reading her mind, probing the innermost feelings of her heart. But, of course, that was impossible.

She glanced up at Quinn and smiled. Not so long ago, her life had been empty, but now her arms and her heart were overflowing with love.

* * *

In answer to Seleena's letter, Nardik arrived at their door the following day just after sunset. The wizard was tall and thin but solidly built. Long gray hair framed a narrow face with flat cheeks, an aquiline nose, and eyes the color of honey. Quinn had rarely seen the man smile, never heard him laugh. In spite of the color of the man's hair, it was difficult to judge his age.

Jealousy tightened Quinn's gut when the wizard took Seleena's hands in his, then bent to kiss her cheek.

Nardik held her hands longer than was necessary before turning his attention to Quinn. "Amerris extends her gratitude," he said. "Gryff, too, sends his appreciation for your willingness to help."

Resisting the urge to slug the wizard, Quinn nodded.

Seleena laid her hand on Quinn's shoulder. "Be careful. Both of you."

"Don't worry about us." Knowing it would irritate the wizard, Quinn drew Seleena into his arms and kissed her soundly. "I love you, Red."

"I love you, too."

Nardik cleared his throat impatiently. "Shall we go?"

Quinn grabbed his jacket, kissed Seleena one more time, and followed the wizard out the door. The sky was overcast, the east wind blustery. "So, where is this place?"

"It is on a neighboring planet. We will need an Airship to take us there. It is only a short hop. I have a pilot waiting nearby."

* * *

The pilot, Dixx, turned out to be a big bear of a man, with a shock of unruly red hair and a full beard. He shook Quinn's hand when Nardik introduced them, waved his two passengers aboard before settling into the cockpit.

The trip to Caynn passed uneventfully. Nardik didn't seem inclined to talk and that suited Quinn just fine. There was little love lost between them, and no good memories.

The pilot put the ship down on a stretch of barren ground, nodded his understanding when Nardik instructed him to wait for their return.

Quinn looked around, wondering if the whole planet was as barren as this stretch of ground. At first glance, there was no sign of life, human or otherwise. No trees, no plants or flowers. Nothing but white sand as far as the eye could see until, lifting his gaze, he glimpsed a walled citadel at the top of a distant rise.

Nardik struck out at a swift pace.

After a moment, Quinn fell in behind him, content to follow, though curious as to why they were walking when they could so easily transport themselves to the citadel. The wizard had been here before. He hadn't. Maybe the wizard knew something he didn't. Quickening his pace, he caught up with his companion.

"Do you sense that?" Nardik asked as they drew nearer the foot of the mount.

Quinn nodded. "Magic. Dark magic." He had been on the receiving end of it more times than he cared to admit. It wasn't a sensation he was likely to forget. "I thought the place was supposed to be abandoned."

"A powerful coven lives behind those walls. Their leader, Wyrick, is the most powerful witch I have ever met. He would have had little trouble convincing Amerris and the Queen's guard that no one was home."

"You think this guy, Wyrick, is behind Annis' disappearance?"

"I am almost certain of it."

"Seleena said the girl was happy with her new husband. Why would they get rid of her?"

"I do not know that she is dead."

"You don't know if she's alive, either. When was the last time anyone heard from her?"

"Shortly after the birth of her child six months ago."

"No word since then?"

"None."

Quinn jerked his chin toward the rise. "That's a hell of a climb."

The wizard nodded. "True, but it is often dangerous to use one's magic in another witch's territory."

"What about vampire magic?"

"I do not recommend it."

Quinn followed Nardik up a narrow, winding trail to the top of the hill. A stone wall, at least a hundred feet high, surrounded the stronghold. This close, only the turrets were visible above the enclosure. There was no sign of an entrance.

"What now?" Quinn asked, glancing around.

"We go over the wall."

"Won't we need magic for that?"

"At this point, it is expected."

"How did Amerris get in the first time?"

"She sent Annis a letter, advising of her impending visit. Wyrick met Amerris outside the wall and turned her away."

"How did they get through the wall the second time?"

"She mentioned an opening."

"I don't see one now."

"We don't need one. Ready?"

Using magic, both preternatural and magical, Quinn and the wizard cleared the wall and landed on the other side.

The courtyard was as barren as everything else Quinn had seen. A large gray building, reminiscent of a fort with turrets at all four corners, stood in the center of the yard.

A thick oak door was set between a pair of tall, leaded windows. Nardik lifted his hand, but before he could knock, the door swung open on silent hinges.

A man clad in a flowing, black robe stared out at them, his dark eyes narrowed with obvious displeasure. "Nardik." His voice was deep and strong, a surprise coming from a man of such small stature.

"Wyrick."

"Why have you come?"

"Amerris, mother of the Queen of Brynn Tor, is worried by the lack of response to her last letter to her daughter. I have come to ascertain Annis' good health."

"Alas, it grieves me to inform you that Annis passed away shortly after her mother's visit."

No sign of emotion or doubt crossed Nardik's features. "Why did you not inform Amerris of her daughter's death when she visited the second time?"

"I have no knowledge of a second visit. Please accept our condolences."

"I would like to take the body home to be buried with her family."

"I am afraid that is not possible. It is our custom to burn our dead."

"Then I must insist on seeing the child so that I might assure the Queen's mother that her granddaughter is alive and well."

"I am afraid that, too, is impossible at this time. My son is naturally heartbroken at the loss of his wife. Rajj has taken his daughter and gone into seclusion. Perhaps, when he has recovered from his loss, he will consider taking the child to Brynn Tor for a visit."

Quinn shifted from one foot to the other. He didn't know what Nardik was thinking, but there wasn't a doubt in his mind that every word Wyrick had spoken thus far was a bald-faced lie.

For stretched seconds, Nardik and Wyrick stared at each other, unblinking. Power thrummed in the air, raising the hairs along Quinn's arms, arousing his instinct for self-preservation. The dragon stirred restlessly beneath his shirt.

Quinn tensed as Wyrick's sharp gaze shifted from Nardik to himself.

"Another vampire," Wyrick remarked. "They seem plentiful on your planet."

"You got a problem with that?" Quinn asked, holding the man's gaze.

"You have no inherent magic," Wyrick said, frowning, "and yet…" Closing his eyes, he went suddenly still.

Quinn tensed, the hair on the back of his neck standing at attention as Wyrick's magic moved over him. It took every ounce of willpower he possessed not to flinch.

Lifting his head, Wyrick breathed in Quinn's scent. "Serepta!"

Quinn flinched when the dragon bit him, something it did whenever it heard the witch's name.

Wyrick's eyes snapped open, wide with shock. "You carry her magic. How is that possible when she is dead?"

Quinn started to ask how Wyrick knew of her death, then realized it was a foolish question. The wizard had obviously been keeping track of Nardik's daughter. What he didn't know was why.

A glance at Nardik showed he was wondering the same thing.

Wyrick gestured at Quinn's left shoulder. "This may seem an odd request, but would you humor me by removing your shirt?"

Quinn hesitated a moment, wondering at the wisdom of exposing the dragon, and then shrugged. "Not at all."

As Quinn slipped his shirt off, Wyrick leaned forward, a look of anticipation on his face.

Quinn glanced at his shoulder. There was nothing there. Why had the dragon disappeared, he wondered as he shrugged back into his shirt. And was it gone for good?

Wyrick's expression was one of curiosity and confusion as he tucked his hands into the sleeves of his robe. He studied Quinn for a long moment, and then he smiled. "Vampire, and yet you have a child," he remarked. "Unusual. Most unusual. The mysteries of magic never fail to amaze me. If there is nothing else," he said briskly, "I will bid you good evening."

With a curt nod, Nardik backed away from the threshold, his hooded gaze remaining on the door until he heard the click of a lock.

Quinn huffed a sigh of relief when Wyrick was out of sight. It had been disturbing, standing in the presence of two powerful wizards. Though there had been no outward sign, the two had been probing each other's magic, silently pushing against each other, testing which was the more dominant.

Moving several paces away from the entrance, Quinn lifted his shirt away from his shoulder, pleased to see the dragon had returned. He grinned when the beast winked one ebony eye at him.

A faint murmur of astonishment rose in Nardik's throat.

"Why do you suppose it disappeared?"

"Besides being powerful, your dragon is quite intelligent," the wizard replied.

"It is never wise to reveal one's secrets to your enemy, something the beast seemed to realize. Had you refused Wyrick's request, he would have been suspicious. He might have insisted, which could have provoked the dragon. No telling what the consequences might have been if that happened."

Quinn considered Nardik's words a moment, and though he didn't say so, he would have put his money on the dragon in any confrontation with Wyrick or anybody else.

Heedless of his own admonition about using magic in another witch's territory, Nardik bespelled them back to the Airship. As soon as they were onboard, the pilot lifted off.

"Looks like this trip was a waste of time," Quinn remarked irritably.

"I think not. Annis may well be alive." Nardik leaned back in his seat. "No scent of death lingers in the air. If she did indeed, pass away, it was not inside the citadel. If she is still alive, she is behind a powerful veil. Either that, or they have imprisoned her elsewhere. The child, too, perhaps."

Quinn settled into the seat beside the wizard as the ship leveled off. "Why bother to marry the girl if they intended to kill her all along?"

"For the child, obviously."

"That doesn't make sense. Why would they need Annis for that? Wouldn't any woman in the citadel have served the purpose?"

"It is a small coven. I sensed only six men—all of whom are well past their prime—and a handful of women. None of the females are of child-bearing age. They need fresh blood. They have Annis' daughter. As she matures, she will inherit her father's magic." Nardik fixed his gaze on Quinn. "I would not be surprised if they intend to acquire a boy, as well."

Quinn sucked in a deep breath, fear knotting in his gut. Wyrick knew he had a child. No doubt he also knew it was a boy. Only one parent needed to possess magic to pass it on. Wyrick already had a girl. "You don't think…?"

The wizard nodded. "I would keep a close eye on Seleena and your son. Wyrick is clearly driven to repopulate his coven. There is nothing he will not do to achieve his goal."

CHAPTER 3

Seleena was waiting at the front door for Quinn when he returned home. "Any news of Annis?" she asked anxiously.

Quinn shook his head. "According to Nardik, there's no way to prove if she's alive or dead. And no way to ascertain if she was inside the citadel. He said if she's dead, she didn't die there. When he asked about the baby, Wyrick said Rajj had taken his daughter and gone into seclusion. How's Steffon?"

"Sleeping. I've hardly let him out of my sight since you left."

"Why? Have you sensed something?"

"No, but..." Seleena shrugged as she moved to the sofa and pulled Quinn down beside her. "Marri and Amerris must be worried sick. Does Nardik have any idea about what we should do next?"

"If he does, he didn't share it with me. All he seemed to know for sure was that the marriage was a ploy, and that Annis was nothing more than a means to an end."

Seleena considered his words for several minutes and then frowned. "So, all they wanted was a baby?"

"Seems that way. According to Nardik, all the men in the coven are past their prime and all the women are past child-bearing age."

"They need fresh blood," Seleena murmured.

"Yeah, that's what Nardik said."

"Their coven must be dying out."

Quinn nodded, thinking about what Nardik had said, wondering how long it would take Seleena to put two and two together and realize Wyrick would also need a male child and that Steffon was the right age. Wondering if he should tell her. It would only make her worry, and yet, she needed to know. If something happened and she found out he had kept this from her…it didn't bear thinking about.

Rising, he said, "I need to see my boy."

Tiny and perfect in every way, Steffon lay on his back in his crib, eyes closed, arms flung out to the side, tiny hands fisted. Quinn felt a familiar catch in his heart as he drew a blanket over his son. Even now, months later, he found it hard to believe he had fathered a child, or that he could love something so small so much.

He glanced over his shoulder as Seleena came up behind him.

"He's beautiful, isn't he?" she remarked, slipping her arms around his waist.

"Like his mother."

"Like his father."

Quinn snorted. Then took a deep breath. "Wyrick knows we have a son," he said, picking his words carefully. "Nardik warned me to be careful."

Eyes widening with alarm, she asked, "How could he know?" and then shook her head. "How could he not? He seems to know everything."

"That's not all. He knows I carry Serepta's magic." He muttered an oath as the dragon bit him.

"Again, hardly surprising that he would recognize it, since he restored it to her." She released a long, troubled sigh. "Steffon's in danger, isn't he?"

Quinn gathered her close, his hand stroking up and down her back. "Remember what you told me. Worrying doesn't help."

A very unladylike sound escaped her throat. "Not worry? When the most powerful wizard I've ever met is looking for a male child born of a witch? Right."

"Maybe we should leave here for a while," Quinn suggested. "Go back to the Fortress."

"Do you really think we'd be any safer there than we are here?"

He frowned. "Have you got a better idea? If you do, I'm listening."

"We'll think of something."

CHAPTER 4

Amerris wept bitter tears after hearing Nardik's report of his journey to Caynn.

"Do you believe Wyrick?" she asked between sobs. "Do you think Annis is dead?"

"I do not know. I sensed no hint of recent death within the citadel, nor any trace of Annis or her child. All I know is that, if she is truly dead, she did not die there."

Amerris wiped her eyes on a white lace handkerchief. His words brought little comfort. Even if Annis was yet alive, how would they ever find her if even Nardik's powerful magic had failed?

"Should I call off the search?" he asked.

"No! Send out fresh troops. I cannot stop looking until I know there's no hope of finding her."

"We should advise Marri," Nardik said.

Amerris nodded. "Yes, of course. She needs to know, though it will break her heart."

* * *

Amerris smiled faintly as she stepped into Marri's bed chamber.

Marri was in bed, propped up by several pillows as she nursed her infant. Amerris felt a surge of relief at seeing the color in her daughter's cheeks. For weeks, everyone in the household had feared for her health. This birth had not been as easy as the first. Marri had labored a day and a night to bring the child into the world. There had been complications, a great loss of blood. But she seemed well on the road to recovery now, as did the baby.

Amerris pulled the covers up over the baby's feet. Leslee was finally gaining weight. She had her father's dark hair. It was too early to tell what color her eyes would be, but Amerris hoped they would be the same blue-green as Marri's.

Amerris pulled a chair up beside the bed, her smile fading as she considered how best to deliver her bad news. Perhaps she should have let Gryff do it. She worried her lower lip a moment, then said, "I'm afraid I have some rather troubling news."

"Can't Gryff take care of it?"

"It isn't something to be taken care of," Amerris said, choosing her words carefully. "Nardik went to Caynn to visit Annis."

"Is she well? I can't wait to see her again. How's the baby?"

Striving for calm, Amerris took a deep breath. "Wyrick said Annis passed away shortly after the birth of her daughter."

Marri stared at her mother, eyes wide with disbelief. "How can that be? The letter before last said she and the babe were in good health. She was planning to come here for a visit." She bit down on her lower lip. "What if it's true? It would explain why there was no answer to my last letter. But surely Rajj would have let us know, invited us to the funeral. Did Nardik…did he see her grave? How's the baby?"

"It seems Rajj has taken his daughter and gone into seclusion. As for the grave…it seems it's their custom to burn their dead and scatter the ashes."

"No!" The people of Brynn Tor considered such a thing to be an abomination.

Seeing the color drain from Marri's cheeks, Amerris said, "There may yet be hope."

"How can there be?"

"Nardik thinks Annis may yet be alive."

"What makes him think that?"

"He detected no scent of death inside the citadel. He believes they could be keeping her elsewhere, or hidden behind a powerful veil."

"One so powerful even Nardik can't detect it?" Marri blinked back her tears, then shook her head. She would not give up hope. Annis was alive. She had to believe that. Surely she would know if her little sister was dead. "I want you to tell Nardik and Gryff to do whatever it takes to find her!"

Amerris smiled, pleased to see the color return to her daughter's cheeks, the spark of fire in her eyes. "We are all everything we can to find Annie."

Marri nodded as she patted her daughter's back. "I know you are," she said quietly.

"I've ordered your personal guards to keep a close watch on your private quarters, especially the nursery."

"Why? Do you think we're in danger here?"

"It's just a precaution. Nardik said Wyrick is looking for children with magic, and even though I'm not sure shape-shifting is considered magic, I thought it wise to double the guard."

"Where's my son?" she asked anxiously. "Where's Rory?"

"I looked in on him before I came to see you." The boy, almost two, was the very image of his father. "Don't worry, he's in his room with his nurse."

Marri nodded, some of the tension easing out of her shoulders. Surely even Wyrick wouldn't attempt to storm the castle and kidnap the future king of Brynn Tor. She reached for her mother's hand. "You've done everything I would do."

"Try not to worry. Gryff and Nardik are meeting now, trying to decide what to do next." Amerris gave her daughter's hand a reassuring squeeze. "Get some rest now, daughter. I'll look in on you again in a little while."

Nodding, Marri held her baby closer as she whispered a fervent prayer for the safety of her sister and her niece.

* * *

Gryff stepped into the bedroom, quietly closing the door behind him. He tiptoed toward their bed; then, seeing that Marri's eyes were closed, he started to turn away, only to pause when she whispered his name.

Sitting on the edge of the mattress, he took her hand in his. "I thought you were asleep." She looked tired, he thought, her beautiful blue-green eyes shadowed with anxiety and stress.

"I was waiting for you."

He pushed a lock of hair behind her ear. This birth had been hard on her. In spite of her assurances that she would soon be as good as new, he had decided there would be no more children. He couldn't risk losing her, not now, not after everything they had been through together.

"What did you and Nardik decide?" she asked.

"We're still discussing our options. But don't worry, we won't rest until we bring Annis home or find out the truth of what's happened. In the meantime, our most trusted guards are patrolling the grounds inside and outside the walls. And Nardik has warded the whole place against intruders."

Marri nodded, but she still looked worried.

"If it will make you feel better, I'll keep watch, too."

She smiled at him. Her husband was more than just a handsome man. He was also a shape-shifter. She had seen him morph into some amazing creatures.

"I don't think we need to worry," he said. "According to Nardik, Wyrick wants children with magic. I don't think shape-shifting qualifies, since it's something you're born with. And until our kids reach puberty, there's no way of knowing if either one of them inherited the ability."

Marri squeezed his hand. She knew he was trying to calm her fears and she loved him the more for it. "What about Corrie? We need to find her."

Gryff blew out a sigh. "Rajj is her father. He has every right to keep her with him."

"I don't care about his rights! If they've killed my sister, they aren't fit to raise her child!"

Leaning forward, Gryff brushed a lock of hair from her brow. "All right. I'll tell Nardik. You rest now."

Nodding, Marri closed her eyes. She was tired. But she wasn't going to rest until she learned the truth about her sister. And Wyrick had been destroyed.

CHAPTER 5

Quinn slipped his arm around Seleena's shoulders and drew her closer. Dinner was over, the dishes were done. The baby was asleep for the night. Two crystal goblets and a bottle of fine wine waited on the side table.

Purring softly, Freyja settled herself on the rug in front of the hearth, yellow eyes staring at the flames.

It had been a long day. Seleena had spent the morning and most of the afternoon assisting one of the village women in the birth of her first child. It had been a difficult delivery, the fate of both mother and child still uncertain. Without Seleena's healing powers, he knew both would have surely died.

"I'm glad everything turned out all right," he remarked. There had been times, though thankfully few, when even her magic wasn't enough. Times when Death would not be stayed.

"I was worried the baby wouldn't survive. It's always so sad, when a new life ends before it's even begun."

He sifted his fingers through the silky fall of her hair. Married a year and he knew so little about her. "Tell me about your parents. Are they both witches?"

"Yes. My father is incredibly powerful, much like Nardik. My mother practices Earth Magic."

"Where are they now?"

"They went to live on Gaxton Four several years ago. My father runs a school for young warlocks there." At his questioning look, she said, "It's a small planet on the far side of the galaxy."

"And your mother?"

"She grows things," Seleena said, smiling. "Beautiful things. Amazing things."

"Do you have brothers and sisters?"

"No. There's just me." She locked her fingers with his, her expression thoughtful. "I haven't seen them in years."

"Have you told your folks about Steffon?"

"There's no way to contact them, except by going there. My father erected a barrier around the planet to protect the young warlocks. Nothing from outside worlds are permitted inside."

"So, you can't write or call him?"

"Yes, but only when Gaxton Four and Brynn Tor are in alignment."

Quinn dragged a hand over his jaw. He had never heard of the planet. Or of a barrier that would repel all outside contact. Leaning forward, he opened the wine, filled their glasses, and handed one to Seleena. "To good parents," he said, lifting his glass and touching it to hers.

It was an odd toast, coming from him, she thought. Quinn's mother had died when he was very young. He had never known his father. The man who raised him had been the worst cutthroat and slave trader in Bosquetown, a city known far and wide as the armpit of Brynn Tor. Jagg had raised Quinn to be an assassin. Thankfully, in spite of Jagg and the evil that surrounded him, Quinn remained a decent man.

Seleena sipped her wine; then, putting her glass aside, she stood and took Quinn's hand in hers, a come-hither look shining in her eyes.

Smiling, he set his glass on the table and followed her into their bedroom. In the time he had known her, they had made love often, yet the passion between them had not cooled. It flamed to life when he took her in his arms, his hands skimming up and down her back as he rained kisses on her cheeks, the tip of her nose, before capturing her lips with his.

She moaned softly as they fell back on the bed, arms and legs entwined, everything else forgotten as they gave themselves over to the desire that sparked between them.

* * *

Careful not to jostle Seleena, Quinn slid out of bed and pulled on his shirt and pants. Though he could be awake during the day, the night often called to him, whispering secrets, promising delights mortals never knew.

Leaving the house, he stood in the moonlight, felt the darkness settle around him like the welcome touch of an old friend. The east wind caressed his face, carrying with it the scent of earth and foliage. Hands shoved in his pockets, he strolled toward the village square. He heard the faint sounds of beating hearts, soft snores, the whimper of a hungry infant, a child's frightened cry.

But it was the siren call of warm, fresh blood that drew him toward a narrow dirt path lined with trees that led to a solitary house. It was a place he had visited once before, shortly after meeting Seleena. As he had the first time, he knocked on the woman's door, mesmerized her with a glance, and compelled her to invite him inside.

Crossing the threshold, he felt a whisper of power that, without her invitation, would have prevented him from entering her home.

After closing the door behind him, he placed his hands on the woman's shoulders, his voice low and compelling as he assured her that he meant her no harm. Her blood was satisfying, though not as sweet as Seleena's. He took only a little, just enough to satisfy the need that was ever there, just under the surface. Sometimes he felt like he was cheating on Seleena when he drank from another woman, but it couldn't be helped. He was what he was.

Before leaving the house, he ran his tongue over the twin puncture wounds in her neck, then spoke to her mind, telling her she would remember nothing of what had happened. And then he vanished from her sight.

He made his way back to the village square, the woman's blood singing in his veins.

At home again, he went into the nursery to look in on Steffon. The boy slept on his back, one arm flung out to the side, his thumb in his mouth.

His son remained a miracle in his eyes, a gift he surely didn't deserve after the life he had led when he lived with Jagg. It had been the slave trader who sold him into slavery to the black witch Serepta. At the time, Quinn had considered it the low point in his life. Oddly enough, it had turned out to be a blessing in disguise. Had he not been Serepta's slave, he never would have met Seleena. Never have known love. Never known what it was to be a father.

Brushing a lock of hair from his son's brow, he returned to his bed.

And the warmth of his woman's arms.

CHAPTER 6

"You went out late last night."

Quinn looked at Seleena across the breakfast table. She always knew when he left the house. Was it because of the blood bond they shared? Or her own magical powers? Not that it mattered. There was no hiding his midnight exploits from the woman he loved.

A smiled teased the corners of her lips. "I smelled her scent on you when I woke up this morning. You drank from her once before, didn't you?"

He nodded, since there was no point in denying it. "Does it bother you?"

"No, but only because I know you didn't hurt her. And because she means nothing more than nourishment. But you could have come to me."

"I know." He tasted her from time to time, for the sheer pleasure of it, but he had never taken enough to ease his hunger. Nor would he.

Setting her tea cup aside, she leaned toward him, one brow raised. "But?"

"You're my woman," he said, slowly. "My wife. You're not prey."

She frowned at him and then, as her eyes lit up with understanding, she reached across the table and squeezed his hand. "So when you drink from me, it's not to satisfy your thirst?"

"Right. It's…" He shrugged. "It's kind of like she's meat and potatoes and you're a cherry tart."

"I love you."

"Good to know, Red, because I love you, too. Shouldn't Steffon be awake by now?"

"I fed him earlier this morning and he dozed off, so I put him back to bed." But there were none of the funny little noises his son made in his sleep. A hint of unease slid through Quinn's mind as, brow furrowed, he opened his preternatural senses. With an oath on his lips, he raced down the hallway to the nursery. Swore again with the realization that the crib was empty. His son was gone.

How was it possible? Using his own preternatural powers, he had warded the house and Steffon's room. Seleena, too, had erected magical barriers against intruders. Yet someone had breached all their wards and done it with such stealth and skill, neither of them had noticed.

It could only have been Wyrick.

Seleena ran into the room, a wordless cry of denial erupting from her lips when she saw the empty bed. "No!" She screamed the word as she sank down to her knees, arms wrapped around her waist as she rocked back and forth.. "No. No. No!" With tears cascading like rain down her cheeks, she looked up at Quinn.

Dropping down beside her, he drew Seleena into his arms. "I'll find him," he vowed. "And when I do, I'll kill Wyrick with my bare hands."

Seleena dashed the tears from her eyes. Took a long, shuddering breath. "Let's go."

"That's my girl." Rising, he drew her to her feet and into his arms. "Just wish I knew where to start."

"Caynn." A wave of her hand transformed her nightgown, robe, and slippers into a pair of black leather pants, a black silk shirt, and boots. "I'm ready."

Nodding, he took her hand and transported the two of them to the same space port he and Nardik had used. He found the pilot, Dixx, sitting alone at the bar, drink in hand.

"I didn't expect to see you again," Dixx remarked, glancing over his shoulder. "Is the wizard with you?"

"Not this time."

The pilot tossed back the last of his drink, then shrugged into his leather flight jacket. "Ready when you are."

* * *

The citadel was exactly as Quinn remembered it—a large gray dwelling at the top of a desolate rise. He followed Seleena over the wall, then cautiously led the way to the entrance.

The place looked deserted, he thought, but then, it probably always looked that way. He opened his preternatural senses. And frowned. On his last visit, the weight of dark magic had been oppressive. He had no such feeling this time. No sense of any wards protecting the citadel or preventing them from entering. No sense of any living creature, human or otherwise.

And no sense of his son's presence.

"Steffon's not here." His bond to his son was stronger than that of just father to child. His blood ran in Steffon's veins. If the boy had been there, he would have known. He had been tempted once to taste his son's blood, but at the time, it had seemed horribly wrong to drink from an infant. Had he done so, he would now be able to follow that blood link to Steffon's whereabouts. Then again, perhaps Wyrick might have been able to prevent that, too. The wizard's power seemed limitless. "Where do you suppose they would have taken him?"

Seleena shook her head, the pain in her heart growing with every passing moment.

"We might as well go…" Quinn's voice trailed off as he detected a faint heartbeat. "Wait! There's someone's in there."

Hope filled Seleena's eyes. "Steffon?"

"No. It's a woman."

"Could it be Annis?"

"I don't know. I never met her, but whoever's in there is unconscious and barely breathing. Can you magic that door open, if necessary? If not, I can probably break it down."

"It might not be locked."

Moving forward, Quinn placed the flat of his hand on the door and gave it a push.

It opened on silent hinges.

Seleena stepped inside. A wave of her hand lit two of the candles on the mantel. She glanced over her shoulder. "Can you come in?"

Quinn shrugged. "Only one way to find out." He hesitated a moment, then took a step forward. He felt a faint whisper of power slide over his skin as he crossed the threshold.

"I didn't think you'd be able to pass."

"They've abandoned the place. The threshold no longer has any power to repel intruders." Lifting his head, he took a deep breath. "This way." He glanced into the rooms that lined the corridor as they passed by. All were empty.

The woman's scent led them down a spiral staircase to a small open area with a tile floor. A single door opened into a large square room. A young woman clad in a dark blue robe lay sprawled face-down on the floor. Her long blonde hair was tangled, her feet bare

Seleena let out a horrified gasp as she hurried to the girl's side and turned her over. "It's Annis."

"Are you sure?" Her face was deathly pale, her heartbeat thready.

"Yes." Seleena knelt beside the girl. "She looks very much like Marri."

"Can you do anything for her?"

"I'm afraid she's too far gone." Seleena looked up at him. "Can you...?"

"Would she want that?"

"I don't know."

Quinn knelt beside Seleena. "It's a hell of a decision to make for someone else, Red. Believe me, I know."

She looked up at him, her eyes filled with compassion. "We can't just let her die."

Muttering, "Maybe we don't need to do anything so drastic," Quinn propped Annis up, her back against his chest. After forcing her mouth open, he bit into his wrist, then dribbled a few drops of his blood onto the girl's tongue.

Seleena clasped her hands in her lap, her lips moving in silent prayer.

At first, there was no change. Quinn dribbled more of his blood into Annis' mouth. Seconds melted into minutes. And then Annis swallowed. Licked her blood-stained lips. And swallowed again. Gradually, the color returned to her cheeks. Her breathing grew regular.

Her eyelids fluttered open as Quinn lowered her to the floor. She blinked at him, her expression turning to one of terror.

"Annis, it's all right," Seleena said quickly, taking the girl's hand in hers. "Marri sent us."

Annis stared at Seleena. "Where's my baby?" she wailed. "Where Corrie?"

Seleena glanced helplessly at Quinn.

"They took her, didn't they?" Tears trickled down Annis' cheeks. "They took my baby girl."

Rising, Quinn heaved a sigh. "This isn't getting us anywhere. Come on," he said, lifting Annis into his arms, "let's take her to Brynn Castle and let Marri and her mother look after her."

Her eyes empty of hope, Seleena gained her feet. "How will we ever find Steffon now?"

"Beats the hell out of me," Quinn said, his voice raw as he started up the stairs. "But I swear I'll find our boy if it's the last thing I do in this life."

* * *

Quinn came to an abrupt halt when he stepped out of the citadel and found Nardik standing in the courtyard. "What the hell are you doing here?"

The wizard raised one brow. "The same thing you are, I imagine," he replied, his voice dust-dry. He glanced from Quinn to the woman bundled in his arms and back again. "The child?"

Quinn shook his head. "No sign of her."

Nardik turned in a slow circle. "They have wiped away every trace of their presence," he said with some surprise. "Wyrick is even more powerful than I imagined."

Voice tinged with bitterness, Seleena said, "More powerful than *any* of us imagined."

"They've taken Steffon, too," Quinn said in answer to the wizard's inquiring look.

"I am sorry," Nardik said.

"Any idea where the coven would go?" Quinn asked.

Nardik shook his head, his brow furrowed in thought. "I am aware of only one other outpost inhabited by dark witches."

Seleena tugged on the sleeve of Nardik's robe. "Where is this place?"

"Callidori. I know nothing of it other than it is located on the other side of the galaxy."

"I've never heard of it," Quinn said.

"Few have."

"How do we get there?" Seleena asked.

"I do not know. It does not appear on any known map, and is said to be shielded by a powerful veil. To my knowledge, only one witch has gone there and returned to tell the tale."

"Then how do we find the place?" Quinn asked.

"Isn't it obvious?" Seleena asked. "We need to find that witch. But first we need to get Annis home."

* * *

Seleena begrudged every minute it took them to return to the Airship, impatiently tapped her foot until they landed back on Brynn Tor.

Nardik's magic carried the four of them to Brynn Castle.

There was a flurry of excitement when they entered the Great Hall. Amerris jumped out of her chair and ran across the room, crying and laughing at the same time as she was reunited with her youngest daughter.

She quickly instructed servants to draw a bath for Annis, to warm her bed, to prepare her favorite foods.

Once Annis was settled in her room, Amerris returned to the Great Hall to express her gratitude to Quinn and Seleena. "You found no sign of Corrie?"

Quinn shook his head. "I'm sorry."

"And no sign of your son?"

"No."

Amerris took Nardik's hand. "Is there anything we can do?"

"Not at this time," Quinn said. "If you'll excuse us..."

"I will join you in a few minutes," Nardik said. "Wait for me outside."

"Do we really need him?" Quinn asked as they left the Hall.

"I think so," Seleena said. At any other time, she might have found his jealousy amusing, but not now. They needed all the help they could get. "Unless you know how to find the witch."

Quinn scowled at her. Like it or not, she was right.

"Sorry I took so long," Nardik said, joining them. "Are we ready?"

"The dark witch you mentioned," Seleena said. "How do we find him?"

"Her," Nardik said. "The witch we seek is female."

* * *

It was all Quinn could do to keep a lid on his temper as they left Brynn Castle. It galled him that, once again, they needed Nardik's assistance. He knew he was being foolish, childish, to resent the man's presence when he should he grateful for all the help they could get. Instead of feeling resentful, he should be thanking his lucky stars for the wizard's willingness to help.

After Nardik said his farewells to Amerris and the Queen, the three of them had returned to Seleena's house where they gathered in the living room.

Now, Nardik sat hunched over the coffee table, making a list of witches he knew who might have information regarding the whereabouts of the dark witch they sought.

Seleena had settled in her rocking chair, her eyes filled with worry and doubt. Freyja lay curled on her lap, purring softly. Earlier, with Freyja's help, she had tried to locate Annis. The cat had often assisted her in the use of her magic before, but even with the aid of her familiar, Seleena had found nothing. Wyrick was a powerful wizard, indeed.

Quinn stood near the fireplace, a glass of wine in his hand. He didn't miss Nardik's furtive glances in Seleena's direction, knew that it was more than concern the wizard felt for his former lover.

Dropping his pen on the table, Nardik sat back. "To the best of my recollection, there are nine witches who might know Alexxa's current location. Of course, I do not know if any of them will share that information."

"So, how do we contact them?" Quinn asked. Knowing they needed Nardik's help, he tamped down his dislike of the wizard, but it galled him to have to depend on another man for anything. Especially this man.

Nardik shrugged. "The usual way."

"He's going to send a message on the wind," Seleena explained. "It's sort of like witch air mail."

"I am going to spend the night at the Fortress," Nardik said. "If I hear anything, I will let you know." A wave of his hand, and he was gone.

"I guess all we can do now is wait," Seleena remarked glumly.

Filled with frustration, Quinn ran his fingers over the dragon tattoo. He hated waiting. He wanted to be out there, doing something—anything but sitting here, feeling helpless.

The dragon stirred at his touch, as if it was as ready for action as he was.

With the dragon's movement, Quinn received the strong impression that, one day soon, he would have need of the dragon's power again.

Chapter 7

Annis stood at the window of her chamber, her arms aching for the weight of her child, her heart empty of hope. She had been kidnapped from the convent where she intended to spend her life. Bespelled into loving a man who had no true affection for her. Lost her sweet baby girl.

Opening the window, she stared down at the empty courtyard below. The wind stirred her hair as she leaned out just a little farther. What would it feel like, falling, falling, her body striking the paving stones, bones shattering? Would she die instantly?

"Annis! What are you doing?" Darting into the room, Amerris grabbed her daughter's arm and pulled her away from the window.

Annis blinked at her mother, then dissolved into tears.

"Hush, now," Amerris crooned, leading the girl back to her bed.

Annis burrowed into her mother's arms, sobbing uncontrollably. "I'll…I'll never…see…her…again."

"Of course you will." Amerris stroked her daughter's hair, her own heart aching with loss. "Nardik will find her. Have you ever known him to fail at anything? It might take him a little while, but I know he'll find Corrie. And Seleena's little boy, as well. Cook baked your favorite chocolate tarts this morning. Why don't we get some and go sit with Marri for a little while? I know she would love to see you."

"No!" Annis shook her head vigorously. "I don't want to see her or…or her baby!"

"Perhaps you'd like to go riding? It's a lovely day. We could take a turn along the river."

The river. She could ride to the old bridge…

Annis nodded slowly. "I'd like that. But I'd rather go alone, if you don't mind."

Amerris regarded her daughter for several moments, then nodded. "Of course. But don't go too far."

"I won't."

* * *

Clad in pants, boots, and a short-sleeved shirt, and mounted on a gentle bay mare, Annis rode along the river's edge. The water was shallow here, near the keep, gradually growing deeper as it meandered toward the ancient wooden bridge half a league away.

In spite of her mother's words, she had no hope that Nardik would find Corrie. She had lived with Wyrick and Rajj long enough to know that their dark magic was far more powerful—and frightening—than any spell or charm her step-father could conjure. She had seen things she wasn't supposed to see—curses and enchantments that had given her nightmares—until she could no longer turn a blind eye to the truth.

Convinced that she was in danger, she had made a desperate attempt to escape from the citadel. And it had cost her everything.

At the bridge, she dismounted, then looped the reins over the pommel.

Leaving the horse behind, she walked to the middle of the rickety wooden structure to stare down into the swirling, dark water. Perhaps, if she hadn't tried to run away, Rajj would not have turned against her. Yet, even as the thought crossed her mind, she knew it wasn't true. He had never loved her. And the love she had thought she felt for him had not been real, but induced by magic.

Tears blurred her eyes as she peeled off her boots, then climbed over the railing. Praying that it would be painless and quickly over, she plunged head first into the roiling water.

* * *

Gasping for air, lungs on fire, she fought the arms that pulled her out of the water.

"Easy now, Princess," coaxed a deep, male voice. "Just relax and take slow, deep breaths. You'll be all right."

Opening her eyes, Annis found herself lying on the grass beside the river, staring up at one of the Queen's guards. Beating against his chest with her fists, she cried, "Let me go. Let me go!"

A smile crooked his lips. "I think you'll be fine now."

"I am *not* fine. And I'll thank you to go away this instant and mind your own business!"

"Ay, Princess, that's what I'm doing. Your mother put me in charge of your safety."

Annis glared at him. She didn't recall seeing him before. Surely she would not have forgotten that face, those eyes.

Rising, he offered her his hand.

She hesitated several moments before reaching for it.

He pulled her gently to her feet, his gaze sweeping over her. "Can I trust you not to dive back in?" he asked.

Cold and wet from head to heel, she glowered at him.

Keeping one eye on her, he went to his horse and removed the blanket lashed behind his saddle. Shaking it out, he wrapped it around her shoulders.

Annis huddled into it, grateful for its warmth. Looking beyond her rescuer, she saw her mare grazing in a patch of sunlight.

"Let me know when you're ready to return to the keep."

"What if I don't want to go back?" she asked, wringing the water from her hair.

He shook his head. "I'm afraid you have no other choice."

"Why did my mother send you after me?"

"She feared you might do exactly what you tried back there," he replied candidly. "Is life in the castle so dreadful that you wish to end it?"

He didn't know about Corrie or the hell she had endured in the citadel, she thought, relieved. And she wasn't about to tell him.

"Since you seem reluctant to return home, why don't you sit down and rest while I build a fire?" he suggested. "I've some meat and cheese and a bottle of wine in my saddlebags."

"Do you always leave the castle with provisions?" Sinking down on the grass, she watched him gather sticks and pine cones. Moments later, he had a cheery blaze going. She held her hands toward it, basking in the heat.

"It often pays to be prepared," he said, smiling.

She couldn't help noticing that it was a very appealing smile. As were his dark brown eyes. And the dimple in his chin.

He fetched the food and drink, then sat across from her. They made a fine pair, she thought, both dripping wet, though he wasn't shivering.

To her surprise, Annis found her appetite had returned. In addition to meat and cheese, he had half a loaf of bread. She watched him prepare two sandwiches. It was the first time a man had ever served her and she discovered she rather liked it.

He had only one cup, and though it was unheard of for royalty to share with a servant, she nevertheless insisted they do so. It gave her an odd jolt of pleasure, watching him drink from it after she did.

"Have you a name?" she asked.

"Doesn't everyone? Even my horse has a name."

She made a face at him.

He laughed, a deep, rich sound that made her insides curl. "I'm Killian. And you are the Princess Annis, sister to Marri, the Queen."

They ate in silence for several minutes. It was peaceful here, Annis thought, with only the crackle of the flames, the gurgle of the river, and the stamp of a horse's hoof to mar the stillness. Overhead, a bird chirped.

"Would you care to talk about what troubles you?" Killian asked after a while. "I'm told I'm a very good listener."

It was tempting, she thought, so tempting. She had told no one, not even her mother, of the horrors she had seen inflicted on others. She had always been treated well, especially once Rajj learned of her pregnancy. After all, she had been carrying Wyrick's grandchild. But after she tried to run away, they had locked her up. She had spent day and night confined in her chambers until Corrie was born, and then she had been taken to another room, seeing no one save for the witch who brought her meals each day. All anyone at Brynn Castle knew was that she had been found, alone and near death, in the bowels of the citadel, and that Corrie had been taken from her.

She gazed into Killian's eyes. Dare she trust him? Dare she trust her feelings? She had put her faith in Rajj and he had betrayed her in the worst way possible. Was she making the same mistake again?

"Whatever you tell me will stay with me," Killian said. "I vow it on my honor as a knight and as your loyal servant."

Haltingly at first, she told him of how the dark witch, Serepta, had taken her to Caynn. How Serepta had traded her to Wyrick with the promise that he would restore the witch's magic. How Rajj had bespelled her into believing she loved him and that he loved her. Words tumbled from her lips as she told Killian of the men, women, and children who had been sacrificed to strengthen Wyrick's dark magic. How she had feared for her own life once Corrie had been born.

She broke down then, hot tears cascading down her cheeks as she described being imprisoned in her chambers, of the long hours of childbirth, of having Corrie taken from her arms just hours after the birth.

Lost in the past, blinded by her tears, she hardly noticed when Killian took her in his arms. His voice was low, soothing, as he whispered words of hope and comfort, vowing that he would do whatever he could to help find her daughter.

Annis knew she shouldn't let him hold her so closely, but for the first time since being rescued from the citadel, she felt safe. Protected. As if nothing could ever hurt her again as long as he was near.

Looking up, she met Killian's gaze and knew, deep in her soul, that she could trust him with her life.

* * *

Annis found herself stealing looks at Killian time and again as they rode back to the castle. He was incredibly handsome, with his thick brown hair and deep brown eyes. She knew a moment of regret when they arrived. Although her hair and clothing had dried, she was certain that, with her muddy clothes and scraggly hair, she looked like a drowned rat. Luckily, there was no one in the stable yard to see her when they arrived.

She placed her hands on his shoulders as he lifted her from the back of her horse. He held her several seconds longer than necessary. She should have berated him for his impudence, but how could she, when she wished he had held her even longer?

"Be well, Princess," he said, giving her shoulder a squeeze.

"Thank you for today." She watched him lead their horses toward the stable, the warmth of his touch, the caring in his voice, etched deep in her memory.

Hurrying into the keep, she dashed into Marri's chambers.

Marri looked up, startled, as the door burst open and Annis rushed inside. "Is something wrong?" she asked, then frowned at her sister's appearance. "Merciful heavens, what happened to you?"

"What? Oh. I...I went riding by the river and I...I slipped on a rock and fell in."

"You're lucky you didn't get hurt."

Annis nodded. "I...um, have a request."

"Of course, what is it?"

"I should like to have Killian posted as my personal bodyguard."

Marri lifted one brow. She had assumed the flush in her sister's cheeks came from the exertion of running up the stairs—until she remembered how handsome Killian was. "I'm sure that can be arranged."

"Thank you." Annis' excitement faded when she saw the baby cradled at Marri's breast. Tears stung her eyes as she wondered if she would ever hold her own sweet little girl again.

"They'll find her," Marri said quietly. "I know they will."

Nodding, Annis returned to her own chambers, the brief happiness she had known with Killian swept away by the pain of not knowing where Corrie was, or if she would ever see her daughter again.

Chapter 8

Marri regarded Killian, who knelt before her in the Throne Room, his head bowed. He had been in service at the castle for the past five years and though she had only seen him from a distance, his good looks were often the subject of conversation between all the single women in the keep, and some of the married ones, as well. He was even more handsome than she had supposed. "Please, rise."

He stood in one lithe movement, a tall man, broad through the shoulders. He had a reputation as a skilled hunter and swordsman. "How may I be of service, your majesty?"

"My sister asked that you be her personal bodyguard."

Killian's surprise was evident in his expression.

"What happened between the two of you today?"

"Your mother requested that I follow Princess Annis when she left the keep."

"Do you know why?"

He cleared his throat as he shifted from one foot to the other "I think she feared your sister might attempt to take her own life."

Marri leaned forward, hands gripping the arms of her chair. "And did she?"

Killian hesitated, then nodded. "She jumped off the bridge near the crossroads."

Stunned, Marri stared at Killian. She knew Annis was horribly distressed at the loss of her daughter, but to try to take her own life! Had she truly abandoned all hope? Was that why Annis had asked that Killian be her bodyguard? Because she was afraid she might attempt to take her own life again? Or was it merely that she was young and heart-broken and Killian was a much-needed distraction?

"Majesty?"

"I had no idea Annis was so distraught. Under the circumstances, I think it wise that you take on the duties as her bodyguard. You will accompany her whenever she leaves the keep. You will stand watch outside her door. And you will let me know immediately of any suspicious behavior."

"Yes, your majesty."

Marri sat back, hands folded in her lap. "Do you have feelings for my sister?"

Killian's eyes widened in shock. "I...I..." He paused as he searched for the right thing to say.

"Please, speak your mind."

"We've only just met, your majesty, and not under the best of circumstances. She is a lovely young woman, and I..." He shrugged. "I would be lying if I said I was not attracted to her."

Marri nodded. "I expect you to protect her from anyone who seeks to do her harm. Anyone, including yourself. Do you understand?"

"Yes, Majesty. Completely."

"Very well. You may go."

* * *

Killian breathed a sigh of relief as he left the Throne Room. Though he willingly served the Queen, he had never been in her presence before. When he had received her summons, he could think of no reason for it. Though Marri and her consort, Gryff, ruled with justice and fairness, he had always found it wise to be cautious in the presence of royalty.

He smiled faintly as he considered his new post. Bodyguard to the Princess Annis. Even though she was far above him in station, he could think of no better way to spend his days than in her company. In spite of all she had been through, there was an innocence about her, a sweetness, that he found appealing. In a world of greed, treachery, and intrigue, she was like a child, still innocent in many ways in spite of the horrors she had seen.

He hand changed his clothes before his meeting with the Queen. Now, he straightened his uniform jacket and ran a hand through his hair as he made his way up the spiral staircase to his charge's chamber door.

* * *

Sitting in an overstuffed chair in front of the hearth, Annis stared into the fire. But it wasn't the flames she saw, but the face of her husband as he wrested their newborn daughter from her arms. She had looked at Rajj and seen the face of a cruel stranger. Gone was the façade of love and concern he had worn during her pregnancy. For the first time, she had seen the man behind the mask and wondered how she had ever thought he loved her. Or that she loved him. That had been the last time she had seen him.

She hoped never to see him or his despicable father again.

"Corrie, Corrie," she whispered. "Where are you? Do you remember me?" Wrapping her arms around her waist, she rocked back and forth, a keening cry of pain rising in her throat.

"Princess Annis?"

She froze at the sound of Killian's voice. What was he doing outside her door? And then she remembered. She had asked Marri to let him be her bodyguard. How could she have forgotten?

"Is everything all right, Princess? Do you need anything?"

She tried to assure him all was well, but she couldn't speak past the lump in her throat.

Killian knocked on the door, but there was no answer. At the sound of her tears, he tried the latch. The door opened at his touch. He hesitated a moment, then stepped inside and closed the door behind him.

She sat in front of the fireplace, her head bowed. The sound of her tears tore at his heart. She was weeping for her child. With no thought but to comfort her, he knelt before her. "Annis?"

She looked up at him. Her eyes, usually as deep and blue as the

Brynn Sea, were now red and swollen; her cheeks damp with tears. She had changed into a long pink robe.

When he held out his arms, she fell into them, her whole body shaking with the force of her sobs.

He didn't tell her not to cry. Didn't promise her that everything would be all right. He simply held her, his hand lightly stroking her back, until, with a last sniff, she lay quiet in his embrace.

Killian sighed as she fell silent. He didn't know anything about her except that she was the queen's sister and her child had been kidnapped by its father. And yet, at that moment, he knew he would protect her with his sword.

And, if necessary, with his life.

CHAPTER 9

As was her habit when she was deeply troubled, Seleena worked in her garden. Turning the soil, feeling its life in her hands, soothed her soul, as did the beauty of the flowers that bloomed in a riot of color around her, the fragrant scents of sage and peppermint and lavender that perfumed the air.

Her son had been missing for four days now.

Four long days. Three endless, sleepless nights. When she closed her eyes, she was certain she could hear Steffon crying for her, knew in the depths of her heart that he was missing her as she so desperately missed him. Were his kidnappers treating him well? Was he getting enough to eat? Was he warm enough?

Sometimes, at night, she sat on the floor in his room, staring at the crib her magic had conjured. She had sewn the sheets herself, crocheted the blankets that covered him, knit the booties that warmed his tiny feet. She had drawn pictures on the wall—a red-haired witch sitting on a toadstool to represent herself, a smiling black dragon for Quinn. A soft blue rug covered the floor; the ceiling was painted with stars and moons that glowed in the dark. Would her baby ever see this room again? Would she ever see her baby again?

She knew Quinn was as worried as she was. Sometimes, when

feeling helpless became too much for him, he went out into the night. Even knowing it was useless, he had searched every town on both sides of the Brynn Sea, hoping for some sign of their son or the witches who had taken him.

In many ways, the last four days had been harder on Quinn than on her. His preternatural powers were of little help. He had nothing to occupy his hands or his mind. He was a man of action and there was nothing to be done but wait. And hope.

She kept busy by scrubbing floors and washing windows that were already spotless, cooking meals they hardly touched. She had made a poultice for one of the villagers, mended a child's broken leg, located a lost nanny goat, and spent hours in her garden, raking, pruning, weeding, planting.

Sitting back on her heels, she watched Freyja chase a bright orange butterfly across the yard, smiled faintly when the winged creature alighted briefly on the cat's nose before sailing over the garden wall.

She had just started weeding the next plot of ground when Nardik materialized beside her. "Any news?" she asked anxiously.

"None of the wizards I contacted knew the whereabouts of the witch we seek. But one of them said the witch, Melinna, might have information. He said the last he heard, Melinna was living on Ceta Five's outer ring. There's only one town on the planet, so she shouldn't be too hard to find."

Seleena's face paled. Ceta Five was a barbaric, sparsely populated planet inhabited by a race of people rumored to be cannibals. "What is she doing there?"

Nardik shook his head. "I have no idea." He glanced over his shoulder as Quinn stepped out the back door. "I assume you overheard what I said?"

Quinn nodded. Vampire hearing was a wonderful thing. He could hear conversations in houses at the other end of town if he was so inclined.

"Are you familiar with Ceta Five?" Nardik asked.

Quinn nodded. Jagg had sent him there a time or two, once to track down a pirate who owed him a debt, once to kill a man who had tried to usurp Jagg's power. The planet was like a jungle, the plants, animals, and people as likely as not to kill you out of hand.

Seleena took a deep breath. "How soon do we leave?"

A faint smile twitched the wizard's lips. "I knew you would want to leave as soon as possible. Which is why I have Dixx waiting."

"I take it you're going with us," Quinn muttered, then chided himself for his continued jealousy. Seleena had no feelings save friendship for the wizard, in spite of their past. And if Nardik still cared for Seleena, well, who could blame him? "Indeed."

* * *

Seleena gripped the arms of her seat as the pilot lifted off. It wasn't the flight she was afraid of, but the thought of meeting a dark witch on a planet that few people dared visit.

Quinn covered her hand with his and gave it a squeeze. "We'll be all right."

She nodded but she couldn't hide the apprehension in her eyes.

It was a long flight. She tried to sleep, but sleep eluded her. Nardik dozed in one of the seats across from theirs. Quinn stared out the window, his free hand idly stroking the dragon tattoo, something he had taken to doing whenever he was tense or worried.

A new day was dawning by the time they reached Ceta Five.

"Wait as long as it's safe," Nardik told Dixx as the pilot set the Airship down on a narrow strip of land bordered on both side by lush growth. A town could be seen off in the distance.

"Don't worry, I won't abandon you here," Dixx said. "You've got my word on that. If I have to leave, I'll be back."

Every instinct Quinn possessed went on high alert as soon as he stepped out of the craft. The scent of death was in every breath he took. It hung heavy in the air, a palpable presence. He sensed eyes watching them as Seleena exited the Airship.

Seleena felt it, too. He saw it in the tense set of her shoulders, the wary expression in her eyes.

"Stay close," Quinn said, drawing her near his side. "Whatever's lurking in those bushes isn't human." It was a predator. Being one himself, he had no trouble recognizing a hunter, mortal or beast.

He had barely spoken the words when a low growl sounded from the bushes beside him and a large cat-like animal with rows of jagged yellow teeth jumped out of the underbrush. Lifting its head, it roared a challenge, then sprang forward.

With preternatural speed, Quinn thrust Seleena behind him, then lunged forward to meet the charge, his arms locking around the animal's throat. The cat's claws raked Quinn's left shoulder and the dragon let out a roar of its own as Quinn broke the cat's neck, then tossed the body aside.

Quinn stood there, head down, breathing hard, all too aware of Nardik's narrow-eyed gaze.

He flinched when Seleena laid her hand on his arm. "You're bleeding." Biting down on the corner of her lip, she peeled his shirt away from his shoulder.

Quinn glanced at his arm. The ragged edges of his torn skin were already knitting together. Surprisingly, the tattoo remained untouched. He frowned as the dragon lapped up the last few drops of blood, winked at him, then closed its eyes.

Seleena looked up at Quinn, her gaze searching his. "Are you sure you're all right?"

"I'm fine."

"Hideous creature," she murmured, glancing at the dead animal.

Quinn shrugged as he pulled on his shirt. The cat was a mottled gray, easily the size of a small horse, with four-inch claws and teeth as sharp as razors. But he had seen worse. "Let's go."

* * *

The town loomed ahead, the buildings made predominately of dark wood. Houses, markets, clothing stores, fortune tellers, bars, and miscellaneous other establishments sprawled across several miles, with no rhyme or reason for their placement.

What looked like a large farm could be seen at the far end of the town. As the wind shifted, Quinn caught the distinct smell of horses and cattle, sheep and goats. And chickens. Lots of chickens.

"How do we find Melinna's house?" Seleena asked as they strolled down a wide street lined with enormous trees draped in yellow moss. "There are addresses, but no names."

"It'll go faster if we split up," Nardik said. "You take that side and I'll take the other. You'll know the place when you find it."

Seleena nodded. Crossing the street, she put everything from her mind but the need to find Steffon. Calling upon her powers, she searched for the signature of dark magic. Opening his preternatural senses, Quinn trailed a yard or so behind her.

"Do you think these people are really cannibals?" she asked.

Quinn shook his head. "If they were eating people, they wouldn't be raising sheep and cattle. I think it's just a rumor they started to keep people away from here. It's a beautiful planet."

"If you don't mind big cat-like creatures trying to eat you."

Quinn chuckled. "Well, there is that."

It really was a beautiful place. Flowers of bright pink and orange and lavender dotted the distant hills; the sky was a deep blue-gray. Trees were everywhere, some flowering, others draped in moss of varying shades of gray and gold.

He thought it odd that there were no people to be seen. No old men sitting on the front porches, no kids playing in the yards, no women chatting together on the street.

They had covered about three blocks when he caught the whiff of dark magic. Seconds later, Seleena came to a halt in front of a large house. Thick blue-black smoke curled from the chimney. A brown and white goat grazed in the yard.

"This is it." She glanced across the street to see Nardik striding toward them.

"This is it," she said again.

The wizard nodded curtly.

"So, do we just knock on the door?" Quinn asked. "Or break the damn thing down?"

Nardik bowed, then made a sweeping gesture with his hand. "Be my guest."

"Well, we've got to do something," Seleena said. "We can't just stand here and…" Her words trailed off as the front door opened.

A woman clad in a long green robe stepped out onto the narrow veranda. She was tall and thin, with a shock of short, dark gray hair and eyes as green as the cat's that had attacked Quinn. "You are not welcome here. Be gone!"

Nardik took several steps forward. "We are looking for Alexxa."

The witch's eyes narrowed. "Why are you seeking her?"

"I assure you we mean her no harm. She has information we are in need of."

Head cocked to one side, the witch waved her hand back and forth.

Quinn frowned, wondering what she was doing, then cursed softly as he felt her power sweep over him. It was like being hit by tiny bolts of lightning.

"Vampire," she hissed.

Quinn's gaze met hers. "Witch. Now that we've got that straight, can you help us?"

The witch glared at him. "Impudent creature of darkness."

He recoiled as he felt the witch's lightning scorch his skin. Summoning his own power, he sent it back to her, smirked when, with a gasp, she reeled back a few steps.

Nardik cursed softly.

Seleena gasped.

And the witch laughed. "Well-played, vampire. Well-played. I am Melinna. You are welcome in my home. Come in."

Quinn flinched when he crossed the threshold. Melinna might have invited him inside, but the wards around her house were strong enough to be felt, invitation or not. He paused inside the doorway. Melinna was supposed to a black witch. To that end, he had expected her house to be a reflection of her dark magic. Instead, the rooms were light and airy, the furniture covered in a brightly-colored print. Paintings of angels and unicorns adorned the walls. White lace curtains framed the windows. A large black bird with beady black eyes rested on a perch in one corner of the room. It squawked and flapped its wings as they entered the room.

Coming up behind him, Seleena whispered, "The bird is her familiar. Like Freyja is mine."

Quinn nodded, thinking he would pit his dragon against anything the witch could throw at him.

Melinna made a gesture that encompassed them all. "Please, sit."

Seleena and Nardik settled themselves on the sofa.

Quinn remained standing near the door. He found the combined power of the three witches to be a little unsettling. Melinna smiled at him, as if she knew exactly what he was feeling.

Nardik cleared his throat. "Can you help us?"

"Perhaps. Why are you searching for Alexxa?" she asked, taking the chair across from the sofa.

Nardik and Seleena exchanged glances.

Nardik shrugged. "We were told she is the only one who has been to Callidori and returned to tell the tale. We need to know how to get there, and what to expect when we arrive."

Melinna shook her head, her brow furrowing. "Why do you want to go to Callidori?"

"We are looking for the wizard, Wyrick."

"Wyrick!" The name hissed past her lips.

"You know him?" Seleena asked.

Melinna snorted. "Aye. Too well."

Quinn waited for Melinna to elaborate. Instead, she offered them refreshment. Seleena said she would like a cup of tea. Nardik asked for coffee, black. Quinn asked for a glass of red wine.

He glanced at Nardik, one brow arched, when the witch left the room. "Do we dare drink anything she offers us?"

"I may be old," Melinna called from the kitchen. "But I am not yet deaf."

Quinn shook his head in amusement. He had expected the dark witch to be some cranky old crone, but he found Melinna to be quite a likeable old soul.

After handing out the drinks, Melinna settled herself in a big, old easy chair. "So, you believe Wyrick is on Callidori?"

"Yes, according to our best lead," Nardik replied. "And the witch, Alexxa, is the only one who knows the way."

A wave of Melinna's hand produced a sheet of paper. She offered it to Quinn with a wink. "This is Alexxa's last known address. I have never been to Callidori, but I am told it is a dark planet in every sense of the word."

"Who told you that?"

"Alexxa, of course," she said, her face crinkling in a grin. "We are sisters."

* * *

"Sisters." Quinn shook his head as they left Melinna's house. "How do we know she isn't sending us into a trap?"

"I don't think *you* have anything to worry about," Seleena said, her voice laced with a hint of jealousy. "She seemed awfully fond of you."

"Must be my natural vampire charm," Quinn said, grinning.

Nardik snorted, then tried to cover it with a cough.

"Where are we going now?" Seleena asked.

Quinn handed her the sheet of paper Melinna had given him.

Seleena glanced at it, brows arching when she saw the address.

"Would you mind sharing?" Nardik asked with some asperity.

Seleena passed the directions to the wizard.

"Ironntown," Nardik murmured as he scanned the address. "She has been on Brynn Tor the whole time."

Quinn shook his head. "What the hell is she doing in Ironntown?" It was a dismal place, with little to recommend it. To his knowledge, the only people who lived there were those who had no family, no resources, and no hope. He seemed to remember Seleena telling him awhile back that Marri, on the run from the brother who was trying to kill her, had met Gryff in Ironntown. A lucky encounter for both of them, he thought.

A bit of Nardik's magic carried the three of them back to the place where they were to meet Dixx.

But there was no sign of the pilot, or of the Airship, either on the ground or in the air.

"He promised to come back." Seleena moved closer to Quinn. The last thing she wanted was to be stranded out here after dark. She shivered as she heard a rustling in the underbrush. Was it another of those monstrous cat-like creatures? Or something even worse?

Beside her, she heard Nardik murmuring under his breath, knew he was weaving a protective spell around them.

Quinn sniffed the air. "Dixx isn't coming."

Seleena looked at him. "How can you be so sure?"

"He's dead." There was no mistaking the smell of bloodshed and death.

"What?" She glanced around, but saw nothing to confirm Quinn's words.

"Trust me."

"Where is the Airship?" Nardik wondered aloud.

"I'm guessing whoever killed him took it and hid it somewhere," Quinn said. "Or they destroyed it."

Seleena took Quinn's arm. "What do we do now?"

Night had fallen an hour ago. Low cloud cover hid the moon and stars. Something—a bird, perhaps—let out a screech the likes of which she had never heard. It sent chills down her spine and made her stomach churn.

Quinn listened to the animals stirring just a few yards away. From the scent, he knew at least one of them was like the beast that had attacked him earlier. "I suggest we go back to Melinna's and ask her to put us up for the night."

Seleena wasn't about to argue. She was certain that Nardik and Quinn could protect her, and themselves, but the thought of spending the night in the open, surrounded by carnivores and bugs the size of bats was not at all appealing.

"Are we agreed that returning to Melinna's is our best option?" Nardik asked.

"Yes," Seleena exclaimed. "Get us out of here!"

CHAPTER 10

If Melinna was surprised to find them back on her front porch, it didn't show on her face. Opening the door wide, the witch waved them inside. As it had before, the bird squawked and flapped its wings as they crossed the threshold.

A quick glance told Quinn the witch had been expecting them. Food and drink awaited them on the coffee table in the living room.

"Help yourselves," Melinna invited. Her brows arched in surprise when Quinn filled a plate with meat and cheese. "How is this possible?" she asked.

"A little of Seleena's magic," he replied.

Melinna frowned. "You no longer need blood?"

Quinn grunted softly. "I'm afraid there isn't enough magic in the universe—white or black—to change that."

"Still, from what I know of vampires, it is quite remarkable."

"I can't argue with that."

"I have prepared places for you to sleep," Melinna said. "When you are ready."

* * *

Careful not to disturb Seleena, Quinn slipped out of bed. Melinna's dinner had filled his belly, but it hadn't satisfied his hunger.

He paused when he reached the living room. Unlike her other two guests, Melinna was still awake. She sat on the floor in front of the fireplace, gazing into the depths of a small black cauldron. The bird perched on her shoulder.

"Vampire, come sit with me."

Quinn expanded his senses. Detecting no danger, he sat cross-legged beside her. "What are you looking for in there?"

"Wyrick's location."

"I get the feeling you're not too fond of him."

She snorted. "If he were here, I would rip his black heart from his chest."

"What's between you two?"

"A century and a half ago, a friend gave me a rare gift. Wyrick took it from me."

Talk about carrying a grudge, Quinn thought. But then, he would have hunted Serepta to the ends of the earth to exact vengeance, whether it had taken years or centuries. "What did he take?"

"It was a talisman infused with unusual properties, something that could only be used once. Wyrick wanted it and when I refused to give it to him, he stole it from me."

A hundred and fifty years ago, Quinn mused. In spite of her gray hair, Melinna didn't look like she had been around that long. Just how old was she? And what kind of gift, exactly, had her friend given her? If he asked, would the witch confide in him?

He felt her watching him. Turning his head, he met her gaze, felt the force of it slam into him. In spite of her grandmotherly appearance, she possessed a hell of a magical wallop.

"You have a tattoo." It wasn't a question, but a statement of fact.

Quinn nodded.

"Though you wear it, it was not meant for you, was it?"

He laughed softly. "The tattoo was intended to serve the witch who conjured it, but she made one little mistake. Now it's mine."

"Who was this careless witch?"

Quinn tensed as the dragon stirred.

"Was her name by chance Serepta?" Melinna's voice was little more than a whisper, but barely controlled anger radiated from her like Hel's own fire. She rose to her feet, her eyes blazing with hatred.

Quinn sucked in a breath when the dragon sank its teeth into his flesh. "You've known all along," he said, his voice flat. "You killed Dixx, didn't you? That's how you knew we'd come back here."

"Clever vampire."

Quinn scrambled to his feet as the witch began to chant, her voice echoing off the walls like rolling thunder. Dark magic gathered around her, growing stronger, more intense. It crawled along his arms, raised the hairs at the base of his neck, churned like acid in the pit of his stomach as he became the focus of all that destructive power.

The bird took flight as Melinna rose in the air, her feet inches off the ground, her arms stretched out at her sides.

Quinn stumbled backward. He ripped off his shirt as he felt the dragon take on physical form and slither down his arm.

Melinna unleashed the spell with a quick wave of her wand, let out a startled cry as the dragon, now eight feet tall and angry, put his body between her and Quinn. She screamed when the curse, meant for Quinn, ricocheted off the dragon's scales and struck her in the chest, just over her heart.

Eyes wide with disbelief, she spiraled slowing to the floor, then staggered backward, blood pouring from the gaping hole in her chest, leaking from her mouth as she tumbled into the fireplace. She screamed as her hair and clothing immediately caught fire, uttered a cry for help as she made a desperate attempt to crawl out of the flames.

A puff of the dragon's breath incinerated her body, leaving only a few ashes to mingle with those in the hearth. As the witch disintegrated, her familiar disappeared.

Muttering, "Thanks, Dragon," Quinn groped his way to the sofa and sat down. Breathing heavily, he stared at what was left of the witch.

A moment later, Nardik and Seleena ran into the room, only to come to a sliding stop when they saw the dragon curled in front of the hearth like an overgrown cat.

Seleena wrinkled her nose. "What is that awful smell?"

Quinn pointed at the fireplace. "Roast witch."

Eyes wide, she stared at the dragon. "Did he…?"

"Yeah. Seems Melinna had a grudge against me."

"A grudge?" She darted past Nardik and the dragon to sit beside Quinn.

The wizard remained in the doorway, arms folded over his chest, brow furrowed.

"How could she have a grudge against you?" Seleena asked. "The two of you just met."

Quinn dragged a hand over his jaw. There were a lot of things he would rather do than mention Serepta's name and stir up the past.

"Quinn?"

He blew out a sigh of resignation. "She asked about the tattoo and when I told her it was conjured by a witch, she asked if it was Serepta." At the mention of her name, the dragon growled softly. "Melinna didn't say, but I got the feeling that she and your daughter used to be pretty close. Anyway, when I said Serepta had conjured the dragon but now it was mine, Melinna got angry and started conjuring a spell of her. When she unleashed it, the dragon stepped between us and the curse ricocheted off his chest and hit the witch. She fell into the fire and the dragon finished her off."

Seleena shuddered as she imagined Melinna being incinerated by the dragon's breath.

"One must always be careful when weaving deadly enchantments," Nardik remarked with a chuckle. "You never know when they will backfire."

CHAPTER 11

Seleena sighed as Quinn's arm curled around her waist. The dragon again resided on his shoulder, eyes closed, tail wrapped around his bicep. Nardik had returned to bed hours ago, but she couldn't sleep. Quinn had swept up Melinna's ashes and thrown them outside to be scattered by the wind, but every time she closed her eyes, vivid images of the witch going up in flames danced before her.

With all that had happened, the thought of spending the night in Melinna's house was unsettling, to say the least, but they had nowhere else to go. As for Quinn, staying awake all night was no hardship for her vampire.

Earlier, Nardik had come to the conclusion that Melinna had cast a sleeping spell on Seleena and himself to keep them from coming to Quinn's aid. When the witch died, the spell had been broken.

Seleena had asked Quinn to tell her everything Melinna had told him. She had been pondering it ever since. "Do you think Serepta was the 'close friend' she mentioned?"

He swore softly as the dragon bit him. "I'm sure of it."

"What do you suppose Ser…" Seleena caught herself before she mentioned Serepta's name again. "What do you think my daughter gave Melinna that Wyrick wanted so badly?"

"Beats me. Some kind of talisman that could only be used once," she said, no doubt for some nefarious purpose."

"Do you think she killed Dixx?"

"I'm sure of it. I can't think of anyone else who would have any reason to kill him. She must have gone after him as soon as we went to bed."

Seleena shook her head. "She never intended for us to leave here alive, did she?"

"No. I think Melinna planned to kill all of us as soon as she heard Wyrick's name. Once we were out of the way, I'm thinking she would have gone to Brynn Tor, joined up with her sister, and tried to take Wyrick out."

Seleena pondered that for several moments before asking, "How are we ever going to get back home now?"

"I've been thinking about that. I'm going out to look for our missing Airship. If it's in one piece, I can fly us out of here tomorrow morning."

"You're going now? Tonight?"

"You worried about me?" he asked with a wry grin.

"I guess not." If the dragon could take out a dark witch, one of those hideous cat-like creatures probably wouldn't be a problem. "But be careful anyway."

"Always." He kissed the tip of her nose. "It shouldn't take me long, Red. You don't have to wait up."

But he knew she would.

* * *

The sights and sounds of the night enveloped Quinn as soon as he stepped out the door. He loved the darkness, loved the night. It hadn't always been so. In the beginning, he had hated what he was and everything about it, but with the passage of time, he had come to accept his new life. And then to embrace it.

The darkness had become his friend, his accomplice. It hid him from his enemies and his prey. It surrounded him, strengthened him in ways he didn't understand. For a moment, he stood motionless in the deep shadows, eyes closed as the night's essence slowly seeped into him.

His head snapped up as a low growl drifted to him on the wind, and with it, the scent of predator.

Quinn smiled, muscles flexing, fangs descending, as the big cat padded stealthily toward him. "Come on, kitty," he called softly. "I need to feed." Human blood would have been better, but he was too hungry to be picky.

The big cat paused, ears pricked forward, at the sound of his voice.

Gathering his power, Quinn mesmerized the cat. He didn't want this one dead. He needed to feed and he had never cared for drinking the blood of dead things, human or animal.

Easing his hunger didn't take long. When he was done, he released the animal from his thrall, then dissolved into mist and floated out of the cat's reach.

Resuming his own form some distance away, Quinn transported himself to the place where they had left the Airship. Walking in ever-widening circles, he found it in a large clearing in the midst of a stand of tall timber. He caught a whiff of Melinna's magic as he neared the craft, but whatever spell she had concocted to shield or protect the ship had apparently died with her.

He walked around the Aircraft, checking for damages, but found none.

Nodding, he returned to the witch's house.

Tomorrow, they would head for home.

* * *

"Are you sure you can fly this thing?" Nardik asked, making himself comfortable himself in one of the passenger seats.

"If you're worried, I've got no problem leaving you behind," Quinn muttered as he checked the instrument panel and started the engine.

With a "humph" of disdain, the wizard folded his arms over his chest.

"Where did you learn to fly?" Seleena asked, settling into the co-pilot's seat.

"From Jagg." The man had taught him a thing or two that didn't involve murder, treachery, deceit, or blackmail.

"Do you think the address Melinna gave us is really her sister's?" she asked.

Quinn shrugged. "I don't know, but I'll be surprised if it is." They had been far too trusting of the witch, he mused as the Airship lifted off, and it had almost cost them their lives. "Like I said before, I think once she found out Wyrick might be on Callidori, she planned to get rid of us, pick up her sister, and light out after him. Might have been an interesting confrontation, watching the two of them slug it out."

"What if Alexxa isn't in Ironntown?"

"No sense worrying about it until we get there." He ran his hands over the control panel, entering the coordinates for Brynn Tor. He hadn't flown an Airship since he worked for Jagg, and never one quite like this, but the controls were similar and it took only minutes to get a feel for the craft.

He slid a glance at Seleena. She was a white knuckle flyer. He covered her hand with his, then winked at her. "Relax, Red. I know what I'm doing. We'll be home in no time at all."

CHAPTER 12

Annis glanced surreptitiously at Killian, her insides curling with pleasure at the mere sight of him. Through all her worry and angst over Corrie's whereabouts, he had been a great comfort. When she was overcome with sorrow, his mere presence was soothing, somehow. When she felt depressed, he told her silly jokes to make her smile. When she felt listless, he insisted she get out of the castle. He accompanied her on walks through the gardens, took her swimming when the weather was warm enough, rode at her side when she wanted to go riding.

At Marri's suggestion, Killian taught her how to use a bow and arrow. To Annis' surprise, she was quite a good shot, perhaps because she pictured the monsters who had taken her daughter as the target.

Today, they were fishing at the river. At least Killian was fishing. Annis sat on the grass, watching him, admiring the way his linen shirt stretched across his broad shoulders, his muscular thighs, the sharp lines of his profile, the ease with which he cast the line, the way his eyes constantly scanned their surroundings. He was always on guard, no matter where they were or what they were doing.

She flushed when he turned his head and caught her staring, although he was surely used to it by now.

He jerked his chin toward her fishing pole. "You've a bite, Princess."

"What? Oh!" She had been so engrossed in admiring him she hadn't even noticed.

"Easy now," he said as she reeled it in. "Don't jerk the line."

Lower lip clamped between her teeth, she concentrated on landing the fish, let out a hoot of surprise when she saw how big it was.

"Biggest catch of the day," Killian remarked as he took the fish off the line and dropped it into the bucket.

She grimaced as he put a fat pink worm on her hook and tossed the line back in the water.

"What's the matter?" he asked.

"Do you…do you think it hurts them?"

Killian frowned, then lifted one brow. "The worms?" He bit back a grin. "Are you feeling sorry for the bait?"

"And the fish," she admitted sheepishly. Fishing had been his idea and as much as she like being with him, she didn't think she wanted to do it again. She had always been too soft-hearted for her own good. It had always grieved her to see anything in pain.

Thinking Annis had to be kidding, Killian started to laugh, then frowned when he realized she was serious. "We don't have to fish, if you'd rather not."

"Don't let me stop you."

"Annis…"

Something in the tone of his voice made her stomach flutter with anticipation. She blinked up at him when he took the pole from her hand and laid it beside his.

Seconds stretched between them as his gaze met hers.

She licked lips gone suddenly dry when he reached for her hand.

"Annis." He didn't seem to be able to say anything but her name. But she knew what he wanted, because she wanted it, too, even though it was wrong. So very wrong. She was married to another man, a horrible man, but then again, maybe the marriage had been nothing but a farce, as had Rajj's oft-professed love for her.

She didn't protest when Killian enfolded her in his arms, holding her close, closer, until they were only a breath apart. At his nearness, warmth flooded her senses and with it, the feeling that she was exactly where she belonged, exactly where she was meant to be.

"Killian." She yearned toward him. She wanted him, she thought, needed him the way a flower needed sunlight, a fish needed water. How could she be thinking of making love to him when Corrie was missing, she thought with a stab of guilt. She had no idea where her daughter was, if she was alive or...or not. And yet here she stood, longing for Killian to make love to her. What kind of horrible mother was she, to be thinking of such a thing at a time like this?

Killian frowned as he watched the play of emotions across her face. "Do you want me to go?"

She shook her head. Right or wrong, she thought, sighing, that was the last thing she wanted.

His gaze searched hers. "Tell me," he whispered. "Tell me what you want."

"Kiss me," she murmured.

"Annis!"

Her eyelids fluttered down as his arms tightened around her. His lips brushed hers, tentatively at first, then with greater urgency. Somehow, they were lying on the grass, bodies pressed intimately together, arms and legs entwined. Having never known any man but Rajj, she had thought his kisses were wonderful. She knew now they were merely adequate when compared with Killian's, just as she knew that Rajj had used his magic to compel her to love him, to think she was happy.

What she felt with Killian was a different kind of magic, she thought, as her fingers delved into his hair, a kind that couldn't be compelled.

She shivered with pleasure as he caressed her, moaned softly as he kissed her again and yet again. His tongue traced her lips, stirring feelings and emotions she had never known with Rajj, could never have known with Rajj, because none of it had been real.

Killian realized they were no longer alone before she did.

Annis opened her eyes, feeling bereft, when he lurched to his feet. Felt her cheeks flame with embarrassment when she saw one of the Queen's mounted guards watching them avidly, a smirk on his face.

Scrambling to her feet, Annis smoothed her skirt, ran her fingers through her hair.

"What is it, Gynn?" Killian asked brusquely.

"The Queen sent me to find you. Nardik has returned to the castle."

Annis took a step forward, one hand pressed to her heart. "Does he have news of my daughter?"

"I do not know, Princess." Gynn inclined his head in her direction, then reined his horse around and rode back the way he had come.

"Killian, hurry!" Body trembling with urgency, Annis quickly gathered her shoes and cloak.

Minutes later they were riding hard for Brynn Castle.

* * *

Annis' heart was pounding like a blacksmith's hammer when she ran into the Great Hall. She glanced quickly around the room, knew a sharp stab of disappointment when she saw Nardik standing beside the stone hearth. Marri sat on a high-backed chair before the fireplace. There was no sign of Corrie.

"Annie, there you are," Marri said, patting the place beside her. "Come, sit with me."

Annis took the chair her sister indicated but she had eyes only for Nardik. "Did you bring news of my daughter?"

"We found someone who may know how to find the witch who took her," the wizard said.

"Then what are you doing here?"

He lifted one brow. "Getting a change of clothing. Spending a little time with my wife. Gathering a few things that may be useful in our search."

"Of course," Annis said, lowering her voice. "I'm sorry."

"No need to apologize, Princess. I know how worried you are. Quinn, Seleena and I will be leaving in the morning to see if the lead we obtained on Ceta Five is valid." He bowed in Marri's direction. "If you will excuse me, Majesty?"

"Of course."

"They're never going to find her, are they?" Annis lamented when they were alone. "Wyrick's magic is too strong."

Marri took her sister's hand in hers. "You mustn't lose hope, Annie. Wyrick may be powerful, but I've never known Nardik to fail at anything he set his hand to. He found you. I know he'll find Corrie, too. Now, then," she said, her tone brisk, "What's this I hear about you and Killian?"

CHAPTER 13

Seleena sat in her rocker, idly stroking Freyja's head, more discouraged than she had ever been in her life. The trip to Ceta Five had yielded nothing save an address that might or might not be valid. Her son and Annis' daughter were still missing. What if they never found either child? Was it Wyrick's intent to eventually see Steffon and Corrie wed in order to raise a new generation of dark witches? She shuddered at the thought of her son following the same path Serepta had taken.

"Oh, Freyja, I would almost rather see him dead than have that happen." She clapped her hand over her mouth. What was she saying? She couldn't give up hope. It was all she had left.

A wave of her hand brought a fire to life in the hearth. Staring into the flames, she remembered Quinn's fears that their union might produce something dark and evil. She had assured him that would never happen. But what if she had been mistaken? What if there was something horribly wrong with her? She could be possessed of some demon spirit without even knowing it. Tears welled in her eyes. What if that was the reason Serepta had so readily embraced the Dark Arts? What if the same inclination toward evil lay dormant in her son?

Sensing Seleena's distress, Freyja lifted a paw and stroked her mistress's cheek. *Do not blame yourself. There is nothing dark within you, or within Quinn.*

Seleena gazed into the cat's yellow eyes. "How can you be so sure?"

"So sure of what?"

Seleena glanced over her shoulder at the sound of her husband's voice.

"So sure of what?" he asked again.

"Nothing."

Quinn dropped down on his haunches in front of her. Taking her hand in his, he let his mind brush hers, felt his insides twist when he read her thoughts and the cat's reply. After setting Freyja on the floor, he drew Seleena down onto his lap.

"Don't go blaming yourself for things that aren't your fault, Red," he murmured, running his fingers through her hair. "You're the kindest, gentlest, sweetest woman I've ever known."

"I love you, too." She smiled inwardly, grateful that, whatever the future held, she wouldn't have to face it alone.

Cupping her face in his palms, Quinn kissed her lightly, and then more deeply. The touch of his lips on hers chased everything from her mind - every fear, every worry, every doubt. For this moment, there was only Quinn, his voice whispering that he loved her, promising that everything would be all right as he stretched out in front of the fire and drew her down beside him. She melted like hot candle wax in his arms, returning caress for caress, reveling in the strength of his arms, the heat of his kisses, the sweet abrasion of skin against skin, the weight of his body on hers…

Later, Quinn cradled Seleena in his arms as she drifted off to sleep. It never failed to amaze him that she was his wife, that she loved him unconditionally. That she had given him a son. Holding her close, he vowed once again that he would not rest until he had found their son and placed him in his mother's arms.

* * *

Apparently believing that evil was best confronted in the light of day, Nardik arrived at Seleena's house early the next morning.

Quinn tamped down his annoyance as he opened the door. As usual, the wizard was clad in black from head to foot. They had two things in common, he mused as Nardik crossed the threshold—their mutual love for Seleena, and a penchant for black attire.

He grinned when Seleena joined them a moment later. Clad in pale blue, she looked like a patch of azure sky caught between two thunderclouds.

"Ready?" Nardik asked.

Quinn nodded. "You got the address, wizard?"

"Yes."

A brief incantation took them to the location in Ironntown. The house, situated on a narrow side street, had nothing to recommend it. One of the upstairs windows was missing, the chimney was aslant, the grass behind the broken-down wooden fence was brown. A tree, barren of foliage, stood forlornly in one corner. A scrawny gray-and-white cat sent them a baleful glance, then darted under the porch.

"It looks deserted," Seleena remarked.

"Intentionally so I would think," Nardik said. "But it reeks of magic."

"Why am I not surprised?" Quinn asked. "Do you think Alexxa is as loveable as her sister?"

The wizard slid a glance in Quinn's direction, what might have been a grin playing briefly across his face.

"Well, what are we waiting for?" Seleena asked. "I'm fairly certain she isn't going to come out and tell us what we want to know."

"I'm pretty sure she isn't going to tell us if we knock on the door, either," Quinn said dryly. "Nardik, you're supposed to know everything. Got any brilliant ideas?"

"Perhaps you could go inside and work a little of that vampire charm you were boasting about the other day."

Unable to help herself, Seleena burst out laughing. The scowl Quinn sent her way only made it worse. Taking a deep, calming breath, she said, "That's enough, you two. We need to make a decision."

"She is right, as always," the wizard said. "We cannot just stand out here staring at the house all day. Let us knock on the door and see what transpires."

Seleena shook her head. "I think Quinn should go in alone."

He stared at her. "Why?"

"Well, Alexxa might be powerful, but I think she would feel more at ease talking to one man instead of to the three of us. Especially when two of us are witches."

Nardik looked thoughtful for the space of a heartbeat, and then he nodded. "Perhaps you are right."

"Okay by me," Quinn decided, anxious to be doing something, anything.

Seleena laid her hand on his arm. "Be careful."

"Always."

"We will not be far away," Nardik said.

Quinn nodded, but he couldn't help wondering if he could trust the wizard. If he was out of the way, there would be no one standing between Nardik and Seleena except Nardik's wife, an obstacle easily disposed of one way or another.

Approaching the rickety stairs leading up to the sagging front porch, Quinn thrust the disquieting thought away as he knocked on the door. He needed to keep a clear head while confronting Melinna's sister. If she did, indeed, live here.

When there was no answer, he knocked a second time. He was about to knock a third time when the door opened a crack, revealing a bright green eye, a sharp nose, and a hank of spiked white hair.

"Who are you?" the witch asked, her voice as scratchy as dry leaves in winter. "What do you want?" She narrowed her eyes, nostrils flaring. "Vampire!"

At first glance, the sisters appeared to be as different as day and night. Alexxa was short and plumb where Melinna had been tall and thin. From what he could see through the crack in the door, the interior of Alexxa's house was dark and dreary, where Melinna's had been light and airy. But they both had the same sharp green eyes.

Wondering why everyone felt the need to point that out, Quinn nodded. "I need your help."

"You are not welcome here."

"That's fine. Just tell me how to get to Callidori and I'll be gone so fast you'll think I was never here."

Her gaze flicked over him. "What business have you on Callidori?"

"I'm looking for Wyrick."

"Wyrick!" She spat the name. "Why are you looking for that ill-begotten son of a toad?" Apparently, neither Melinna or her sister had a kind word for the wizard.

"He kidnapped the Queen's niece and my son. I was hoping you could take me there."

Suspicion flared in her eyes. "Who told you I know the way?"

"A friend of mine."

"And does this friend have a name?"

"The white wizard, Nardik."

The witch glanced past Quinn, her gaze darting up and down the street. "Is he out there?" she asked anxiously.

"He traveled here with me, yes."

"Well, he was mistaken." She took a quick step back, one hand on the door.

Quinn stuck his foot in the doorway, felt the burn of the threshold's power crawl over his skin. "I'm not leaving until you tell me what I want to know."

"Indeed?" The witch pulled a long, crooked wand from inside her robe.

"I wouldn't do that," Quinn warned. "The last witch who pointed one of those things at me went up in flames."

Alexxa sneered at him, then raised her arm.

Quinn ripped off his shirt. "Now, dragon!"

The witch recoiled when the dragon took physical shape and leapt from Quinn's arm to stand between them, eight feet of tightly leashed power.

Quinn stroked the dragon's shoulder. "I suggest you tell me what I want to know before you become a living torch."

* * *

Seleena stopped pacing the alley where they had taken refuge when Quinn's voice sounded in her mind.

Seeing the expression on her face, Nardik asked, "What is it?"

"Quinn wants us."

"Did he say why?"

"What difference does it make?" she exclaimed, hurrying toward the sidewalk. "Come on!"

They found Quinn standing shirtless on the witch's front porch. The dragon sat beside him, forked tail slowly swishing back and forth, ebony eyes focused on Alexxa. The witch stood in the doorway, her expression surly, her wary gaze fixed on the dragon.

Seleena glanced at Nardik. "What do you think happened?"

"I am guessing she refused to tell him what we want to know."

Seleena climbed the stairs, careful not to get too close to the dragon. "Is everything all right?"

Quinn slid her a sideways glance. "It will be."

"Does she know how to get to Callidori?"

"Indeed she does. She was just about to give me directions."

Seleena glanced at the witch, then back at Quinn. "Can we believe anything she says?"

"I think so," he said with a wink. "Since she's going with us."

"Is that a good idea?" Nardik asked, looking dubious.

Quinn shrugged. "If she's lying, she'll be toast."

"Ah. When do we leave?"

"As soon as we find another ride."

"I will take care of that." Nardik jerked his chin toward Alexxa. "Keep an eye on the witch."

"Where do you think he's going, Red?" Quinn asked, never taking his eyes off Alexxa, or the wand still in her hand.

Seleena shook her head. "I have no idea, unless he knows of a space port nearby."

Alexxa glared at Quinn, her whole body quivering with the force of her hatred. "I will kill you for this. All of you."

"You can try. But so far, the score is dragon two, witches zip."

"Who conjured that tattoo for you?"

"I don't see as how that's any of your business."

Alexxa folded her arms over her breasts. "Who *are* you?"

"Nobody."

She snorted.

"I've been a lot of things. Hunter. Assassin. Vampire. Statue."

"Statue!"

Quinn nodded. "If it wasn't for this lovely lady at my side, I'd still be locked in stone."

Alexxa's narrow gaze shifted to Seleena. "You must be a powerful witch."

"I get by."

"You're Seleena, aren't you?" Alexxa nodded, as though pleased that she had finally identified the other witch. "Of course, friend of Nardik and the Queen. Serepta's mother." The witch took a hasty step back when the dragon let out a roar. "What's wrong with him?"

Quinn lifted one shoulder. "He didn't like Seleena's daughter much."

The dragon hissed when Nardik materialized on the steps.

"Did you find a pilot?" Seleena asked.

"Yes, there is a space port not far from here. He will be ready to go by the time we arrive."

Quinn jerked his chin at Alexxa. "How do we get her there without a fight?" The dragon was a nice threat in the flesh, but they couldn't take eight feet of dragon onboard.

"Leave that to me." Nardik produced his wand, spoke a few words, and the witch went to sleep.

Quinn caught her and her wand before she hit the floor, then held out his left arm. "Dragon?" He shook his head in wonder as the dragon grew smaller, smaller, then ran up his arm and melted back into his skin. "Amazing," he muttered.

"Indeed," Nardik said, and there was just the hint of envy in his voice.

Chapter 14

Annis sat on the floor in her chamber, her fingers entwined with Killian's, who sat on the rug beside her. It was considered scandalous for her to entertain a man in her private quarters, especially a man who was neither royalty nor kin, but she didn't care. After all, it wasn't like she was an untouched maiden whose virtue needed protecting, she thought, frowning. She was a grown woman with a child who had been kidnapped, and Killian was her bodyguard.

"You seem lost in thought," he said, his thumb gently stroking her palm.

"I guess I was. Sorry."

"Anything I can do to help?"

"Kiss me?"

With his hand cupping her nape, he leaned forward and kissed her lightly.

She moaned softly, wishing she dared take him to her bed. But there were so many things standing in their way, not the least of which was the fact that she was still a married woman, as far as she knew. For a time, she had wondered if the ceremony had been real, but on reflection, she had decided Wyrick wouldn't want any shadow of doubt over his grandson's parentage. She frowned, wondering if Marri could annul the marriage or simply declare it invalid.

When Killian started to move away, she wrapped her arms around him, needing to be closer, needing to feel his strength, his support.

"It's late, Princess. I should go."

"Just a few more minutes."

"As many as you wish." He kissed her again, more deeply than before. Time and again, he had been tempted to ask her to run away with him, somewhere far from the castle, someplace where they would not be Princess and servant, but just a man and a woman, free to love and live their lives as they pleased. But he knew she would never leave, not until she knew her daughter's fate, nor would he think of asking her. It grieved him to see the torment in her eyes, to know she was hurting deep inside and there was nothing he could do to ease the pain, no words he could say to make things better.

"Killian." She caressed his cheek, ran her fingertips over his lower lips. "I think I'm falling in love with you."

"Honey, I've been in love with you since the day I pulled you out of the river."

"Really?" She searched his gaze, felt a rush of excitement when she saw the truth in his eyes. This was what love looked like, she thought, not the coolness she had seen in Rajj's eyes, but Killian's expression of tenderness and concern.

"Really." Drawing her into his arms, he held her close, his hand lightly stroking her back.

Annis closed her eyes, a part of her bubbling over with happiness even as another part of her ached for her daughter.

She rested her cheek against Killian's chest, grateful for someone to lean on when she needed support, to comfort her when she needed solace.

* * *

"Love!" Marri exclaimed. "You can't be in love with him. You're married to another man." As soon as the words left her mouth, she realized how foolish they sounded. Love gave no thought to right or wrong, made no distinction between peasant or king.

Settling back on the couch in her private chambers, she softened her tone. "Granted, your husband is rotten to the core and will surely be executed if he's ever caught, but until then…" Marri shook her head. "Are you sure?"

"Desperately sure," Annis said firmly. "Besides, who are you to tell me who to love or who to marry? Gryff isn't royalty. Not even close to it."

Marri huffed a sigh. There was no arguing with her sister on that point. Gryff had been working in a seedy tavern in Ironntown when she met him. She had been on the run from her brother, the king, who had wanted her dead; Gryff had been hiding from Serepta's wrath.

"Even if you catch Rajj, you'll never execute him," Annis said. "Wyrick will never let that happen and I'm not sure anyone, even Nardik, can stand up to him."

Frowning, Marri said, "I wonder what kind of sorcery makes Wyrick so powerful."

"He kills people," Annis said, so softly her voice was barely audible. "He tortures them in ways you can't imagine and their suffering made him stronger." She paused a moment, reluctant to say the rest.

"Go on."

"Sometimes he…he drank their blood before he killed them."

"Is he both witch *and* vampire?"

Annis shook her head. "He sacrificed animals, too."

"And you saw him do all these despicable things?"

Annis nodded. "Men, women, and even children died at his hands." She still had nightmares about the atrocities she had witnessed inside the citadel. Sometimes she woke with the screams of the dying ringing in her ears.

"And Rajj?" Marri asked. "Did he also participate?"

"I don't know. If he did, it was never in my presence."

"Where did Wyrick get the people he killed?"

"He hired hunters to raid prisons on distant planets. They took those who were sentenced to death. I asked Rajj once why his father wanted criminals. He said the power that lived inside evil men and women was stronger."

"And the children?" Marri asked incredulously. "Did he think they were evil, too?"

"No, but Rajj said there was also strength in purity."

Marri glanced at her baby, sleeping in her cradle beside her. How could anyone steal a life that had barely begun? Surely, if there was a Hel, Wyrick would spend eternity in the deepest, darkest pit.

Needing to change the subject, she said, "About Killian, does he have feelings for you, as well?"

"Yes."

"You know you can't wed until your marriage to Rajj is nullified."

"I know," Annis said glumly, and then brightened. "Isn't there some loophole we can use? I mean, I was under a magical spell when I said yes. Isn't that grounds for an annulment? If that won't work, maybe you can you use your queenly powers to invalidate the marriage."

"I'll have Nardik look into all those options when he returns, I promise."

Beaming, Annis threw her arms around Marri. "You're the best sister in the whole galaxy!"

Later, alone in her chambers, Marri clasped her hands, unable to conceive of the carnage Annis had described. How had her little sister, who had once taken holy vows and lived sheltered behind convent walls, survived seeing such atrocities? Marri, herself, could scarcely imagine such evil.

She shook her head, wishing to dispel the images Annis had conjured—Wyrick, drinking blood, murdering innocent children to increase his magical abilities. What if, as Annis feared, Wyrick could not be stopped? What if even Nardik's formidable powers weren't strong enough to put an end to the dark wizard's malevolent designs?

CHAPTER 15

Quinn glanced out the side window of the space craft, one hand idly stroking the tattoo on his shoulder. He couldn't help wondering why, if the dragon was so powerful, more witches didn't just conjure one for themselves. Curious, he put the question to Seleena.

"I've given it a lot of thought," she admitted. "You remember I told you Ser..." She stopped herself before saying Serepta's name. "She must have used a wrong word when she conjured the tattoo. Even a wrong inflection in her voice could have changed the meaning of the incantation."

Quinn nodded.

"I've seen similar inked figures—dragons and the like—that possessed powerful magic, but never one that took on physical form. She could have infused the spell with something else, although I have no idea what it might have been. Then again, merely the wrong word could have altered the spell without her being aware of it."

"I guess now we'll never know."

"What are you going to do with her wand? Nardik asked.

Quinn shrugged. "You want it?"

"We should destroy it."

Quinn pulled it out of his pants' pocket and offered it to the wizard. "Be my guest."

Instead of taking it, Nardik muttered an incantation and the wand disintegrated into a pile of wood chips at Quinn's feet.

"Well, that was easy enough." Quinn glanced at Alexxa, still bound by Nardik's sleeping spell. "What are we going to do with her?"

"Leave her on Callidori once we have accomplished our mission?" the wizard suggested.

Quinn nodded. "Sounds good to me." He glanced out the window again, wondering what they would find when they arrived at their destination. Was Steffon there? If not, how would they ever find him?

* * *

Nardik released Alexxa from his sleeping spell when the ship approached Callidori. Quinn had expected the planet to be warded against intruders, but they landed at the space port without incident.

As previously agreed, Nardik paid the pilot half his fee when they landed, with the assurance that the second half would be forthcoming when they returned to Brynn Tor.

After they disembarked, Quinn turned in a slow circle, his vampire senses probing their surroundings. He wasn't sure what he had expected from a planet mainly inhabited by dark witches, but this definitely wasn't it. It looked like any other modern city, he thought, as they left the space port behind.

Thriving shops and restaurants lined both sides of the main street. The people he saw on the street seemed to be ordinary mortals going about their business as usual. Most of them smiled and nodded as they passed by. He detected no hint of magic in the town, dark or otherwise.

Well-tended homes were located beyond the town. Children too young for school played in fenced front yards. From somewhere in the distance, he heard the distinct chiming of a church bell.

Seleena glanced around, then looked at Alexxa. "Are you sure this is the place?"

"Of course."

Quinn shook his head. Something wasn't right. He was about to question Alexxa when he caught his son's familiar scent. Though faint, there was no doubt it was Steffon. "This way," he said.

Seleena hurried to keep up. "Is Steffon here?" she asked anxiously

"I think so."

Quinn glanced over his shoulder to make sure Nardik and Alexxa were still behind them. He frowned when the wizard shook his head. "What is it?"

"Something is not right," Nardik said, his hooded gaze sweeping right and left. "I cannot quite put my finger on it."

"Yeah," Quinn said. "I feel it, too." He stopped abruptly when they reached the end of the residential area. A single, one-story house stood on a fenced plot of ground perhaps half a mile in the distance. Painted gray with white trim, there was nothing remarkable about the place, except its location away from all the others.

"What's wrong?" Seleena asked.

Quinn nodded toward the house. "Steffon's scent is coming from there." Grasping Seleena's hand, he crossed the street.

"What should we do now?" she asked.

"I'm not sure." Lifting his head, he took a deep breath. As Nardik had said, something wasn't right. He had no sense of evil, no hint of dark magic. Concentrating on the house, he listened for the sound of beating hearts, the scent of blood, but there was nothing, just Steffon's scent. Surely they hadn't abandoned the boy here?

Coming up beside him, Nardik said, "Wyrick is not here."

"Yeah, I figured that," Quinn said, dryly. "I'm going inside."

"Not alone, you're not," Seleena chided, grasping his hand more tightly.

"All right, Red. Nardik, you stay out here with the witch. Don't let her out of your sight."

Nardik folded his arms over his chest, obviously annoyed at being told what to do, but he let it pass without comment.

Quinn opened the gate in the fence. Three steps led to a small, covered porch. Seleena rang the bell.

When there was no answer, Quinn pounded his fist on the door. "I don't think anyone is inside," he said. "But Wyrick was here recently."

Seleena chanted a few words and the door swung open, revealing a large living room, fully furnished. Still holding Quinn's hand, she stepped into entryway, only to come to an abrupt halt when Quinn couldn't follow.

"I can't cross the threshold," he said, dropping her hand. "There's no one inside, but the house hasn't been abandoned, so be careful. There's no telling what traps they might have left behind."

With a nod, Seleena cautiously made her way through the house, room by room. All were clean and tidy. Though the house was empty, she had the feeling that the inhabitants had left only recently and fully intended to return. She found food in the cupboards, clothes in the closets, a chess board in play on the table in the dining room.

And her son's blanket on a chair in the last bedroom.

Picking it up, she held it to her face, breathing in his sweet scent as tears filled her eyes. Where was he? Had they taken him with them? Or...She refused to consider anything else.

Still clutching the blanket, she returned to the porch. "He's not here."

Quinn swore under his breath; then, overcome with rage and frustration, he flew down the stairs, his hands curling over Alexxa's shoulders, his fingers digging into her flesh. "Where is my son?"

She glowered at him. "How should I know?"

"You *will* tell me," he snarled, "or you'll meet the same fate as your sister."

Alexxa thrust out her chin. "Go ahead. Burn me up!" she dared him. "Then you'll never find the brat."

"She's right," Seleena said, laying a restraining hand on his shoulder. "We need her alive."

"This isn't Callidori, is it?" Quinn asked through clenched teeth.

Alexxa's insane cackle filled the air. "No. And without me, you'll never find it. Or your son."

Quinn glared at Alexxa. Took several deep breaths. And tried to read her mind, but he couldn't penetrate whatever wall she had magicked into place. And then, letting his eyes go red, he smiled, revealing his fangs.

"You have two choices," he told her, biting off each word. "You can tell me what I want to know, or I can turn you into a vampire, in which case I will be your sire. If you don't know what that entails, I'll tell you. It means I'll be able to read your every thought, compel you to do anything I wish. And once I have the information I need, I will let my dragon destroy you."

"I don't believe you."

"No?" He jerked her body close to his and buried his fangs in the side of her neck. She shrieked as his fangs pierced her skin. "Let me go!"

He took only a single swallow, just enough to prove he meant what he said.

She squirmed in his arms, helpless against his strength. "Let me go, and I'll tell you."

Lifting his head, Quinn wiped the blood from his mouth with the back of his hand. "That's better. Now, is this Callidori, or isn't it?"

Alexxa ran her fingertips over the bloody holes in her neck. "No," she replied sullenly. "It's Dracca."

"That wasn't so hard, was it?" He took several deep breaths, willing the bloodlust to fade from his eyes.

A bit of the wizard's magic transported the three of them back to the space port.

On the way to the Airship, Alexxa made a break for it, but before she could complete her incantation and vanish, Seleena hit her with an immobilizing spell, which left Alexxa conscious but unable to move.

Inside the craft, with Quinn's threat hanging over her head, Alexxa gave the pilot the coordinates to Callidori, and then Nardik again put the witch under a sleeping spell.

Seleena took her seat, the blanket still clutched to her breast, her cheeks stained with her tears. "So close," she murmured. "So close."

Quinn put his arm around her shoulders as the Airship lifted off. "We'll find him. I promise," he said fervently.

And prayed it was a vow he could keep.

Chapter 16

Nardik released Alexxa from his spell when the Airship neared Callidori. Quinn had no doubt they had arrived at the right place this time. Under his renewed threat to turn her into a vampire, she grudgingly spoke the words necessary to get past the protective enchantment that veiled the planet.

As agreed, Nardik paid the pilot half his fee when they landed, the other half to be paid when they returned to Brynn Tor.

"Well, we're here," Quinn said as they made their way toward the city. "All we have to do now if find Wyrick, rescue the Steffon and Corrie, and head for home. Sounds easy enough."

Callidori was a small planet, as was everything he saw growing. Trees, plants, flowers, all looked stunted, their colors pale and, in some cases, like nothing he had ever seen before. The land was mostly flat, though a few small brown hills could be seen in the distance.

They passed several residences on the outskirts of town. The houses were made of wood and green brick. Some were rectangular, others were round, a few appeared to be mostly underground, with only roofs and chimneys showing. Quinn noticed an old man watching them through a second-story window, a woman peering at them from behind lace curtains.

He paused at as they reached the town proper. Head lifted, eyes closed, he opened his preternatural senses, searching for his son. There were a number of people in the house, but the scent of Steffon's blood stood out from the others. He breathed it in for a moment before saying, "He's in there."

Hope fluttered in Seleena's heart. "Are you sure?" If Quinn was wrong, if their son wasn't really here, they might never find him.

Quinn nodded. "I'm sure."

"Is he all right?"

"As far as I can tell. What do we do now? We can't just storm the place and hope for the best."

"True," Nardik said. "But there is little point in trying to hide our presence. I am sure Wyrick knows we are here."

"Let's go scout around a little," Quinn suggested.

Nodding in assent, Seleena and Nardik followed him down the main street, with Alexxa between them.

The whole town exuded an aura of black magic. It hung over the place like a malevolent dark cloud. It raised the hairs along Quinn's arms, made his stomach muscles clench. The dragon felt it, too. He stirred restlessly, his tail lashing back and forth. "Not yet," Quinn murmured, stroking the dragon's back through his shirt. "Not yet."

They passed a number of men and women as they strolled down the street. Most of them were witches who cast sideways glances in their directions, their expressions ranging from mildly curious to openly hostile. A few of the inhabitants were humans going about their daily lives, wandering in and out of shops, stopping to chat with friends, idling on street corners. Witch or mortal, male or female, they regarded the strangers with thinly-veiled suspicion.

"Odd," Seleena whispered."

"What's odd?" Quinn asked.

She made a vague gesture with her hand. "There are no children."

"Maybe they're in school," he said, though there was no school in sight.

"Maybe."

"You don't think Wyrick kidnapped them all, do you?"

"He has no need for mortal children," Nardik said. "Unless..."

"Unless what?" Quinn asked.

"Some dark witches sacrifice young children to gain power."

Quinn swore under his breath. And he'd thought Jagg was evil. Shit, the trader couldn't hold a candle to Wyrick.

The houses grew fewer as they traveled onward.

"Steffon's in there," Quinn said, pointing to a two-story house located on a hill at the end of the street. This dwelling was larger than any of the others they had seen thus far. Black smoke rose from the chimney. There were no windows visible on the main floor.

Seleena shivered. "I can feel Wyrick's magic, even from here."

Nardik took a deep breath. "I believe the whole coven is inside."

"And Annis' daughter?" Seleena asked. "Is she in there, too?"

"I think so," Quinn said. "I can hear the heartbeats of more than one child. They're faster than those of the adults."

"You're all dead," Alexxa predicted gleefully. "The three of you together aren't as powerful as Wyrick."

"Maybe, maybe not," Quinn retorted. "But if we go down, I'm taking you with us."

* * *

They spent a long while watching the house while they considered their options. Trying to sneak up on a coven of witches seemed doomed to fail. Threats would get them nowhere. They had nothing to use for leverage, nothing to trade.

In the end, Nardik suggested they just knock on the door.

"What if they conjure a spell to convey themselves elsewhere?" Seleena asked anxiously. "If that happens, we'll never be able to find them again."

Brow furrowed, Quinn raked his fingers through his hair. "We need to pique their interest, offer them something they've never seen before."

"The dragon," Nardik said.

"Right. Wyrick knows I'm hiding something. What if I offer to show him the tattoo in exchange for seeing my son?"

"What if he hits you with a death spell instead?" Seleena asked. "What if he …?"

"Red, we can stand here and think of 'what if's' all day long, or we can take a chance and do something unexpected."

"You're putting a lot of faith in the dragon," she argued. "What if he hides from Wyrick the way he did the last time?"

"He won't."

"You don't know that!"

"He hasn't failed me yet," he said with a wink. "No reason to doubt him now. Besides, the last time he disappeared turned out to be a good thing. I'm betting the dragon and the three of us can defeat anything Wyrick throws our way. Are you with me?"

She smiled at him, her expression softening as she laid her hand on his arm. "Since the day we met."

"That's my girl. Once we get inside, I'll go after Steffon. Nardik, your job is to find Corrie." He jerked his chin in Alexxa's direction. "And keep a sharp eye on the witch. We don't need her interfering."

"What do you want me to do?" Seleena asked.

"You're our backup. Stay out here and be ready for anything. I'm not sure how this will go down."

"Quinn…"

He covered her mouth with his in a long hungry kiss. "For luck," he said with a wink. "Don't worry."

Seleena murmured a protection spell as he strode down the street, hoping against hope that it was strong enough to repel Wyrick's dark magic, that Quinn's confidence in the dragon wasn't misplaced, that her son and Corrie were safe and out of danger.

Quinn murmured, "Don't let me down, Dragon," as he approached the front door of Wyrick's lair. He felt unseen eyes watching him from the second story, felt the whisper of dark magic slide over his skin like invisible fingers. He smiled inwardly. Seleena had his back, he thought, as the spell that had been directed at him from the upstairs window was rendered harmless by her interference.

Shaking off his anxiety, Quinn pounded his fist on the door. "Wyrick! I know you're there. Open the damn door. I've got something to show you."

There was a ripple in the air. The heavy door swung open. And Wyrick stood there, looking much the same as the last time Quinn had seen him—a diminutive, white-haired man clad in a long black robe.

The wizard looked him up and down, his dark eyes filled with contempt. "Either you have more nerve than I gave you credit for, vampire, or you are quite insane."

"I want to see my son." Quinn held up a hand when the wizard started to speak. "Don't bother lying to me. I know he's in there. His blood is my blood. You can't hide him from me."

Wyrick snorted. "As I said, I do not know if you are truly brave, or just stupid."

Quinn tensed as he felt Wyrick summoning his magic. "Wait! Don't you want to see what I brought you?"

Wyrick glanced pointedly at Quinn's empty hands. "What could you possibly offer that would be of interest to me?"

"The same thing you were so curious about the last time we were face-to-face."

Wyrick's gaze flicked to Quinn's left shoulder.

Quinn nodded. "Your instincts were right. Bring me my son and I'll show you something you've never seen before."

Wyrick regarded him for several moments. Quinn could almost see the wheels turning as the wizard weighed the chance to satisfy his curiosity against killing Quinn out of hand.

Curiosity won.

"Lanna," Wyrick called over his shoulder. "Bring me the boy."

Quinn went suddenly still, nostrils flaring as he caught Steffon's warm, baby scent. He looked beyond Wyrick, his gaze focusing on the witch walking toward the front door, a child wrapped in a white blanket cradled in her arms. "Steffon."

"I have fulfilled my half of the bargain," Wyrick said, eyes narrowing. "The child is unharmed, as you can see. Now, fulfill your part."

"As you wish." Quinn slowly removed his shirt, his gaze never leaving the wizard's face.

Wyrick took a step forward. He frowned when he saw the tattoo. "That is your big reveal?" He snorted disdainfully. "I have seen tattoos before."

"But none quite like this one. Now, dragon."

Wyrick recoiled as the dragon slithered down Quinn's arm, growing larger and larger still as its feet touched the floor. "What the Hel?" Delving into his robe, the wizard produced his wand with a flourish. Murmuring an incantation, he pointed it at Quinn.

"Oh, bad decision," Quinn chided, taking several steps back. "Very bad indeed. Now, Dragon!"

As he had before, the dragon darted between Quinn and the wizard's spell.

Crimson fire erupted from the dragon's mouth, dancing over Wyrick's body from head to heel until he was engulfed by the flames. He screamed as his hands beat at the flames in a desperate effort to save himself but to no avail.

The witch, Lanna, let out a startled cry as an unseen entity snatched the baby from her arms.

The wizard let out a last, terrible scream as the flames grew hotter, more intense. There was a *whoosh* of dragon's breath and Wyrick's body disintegrated into a pile of ashes.

With a wave of her hand, Lanna vanished from sight.

Quinn glanced around. "Seleena?"

"I'm here." She materialized beside him, their son in her arms.

"Didn't I tell you to stay outside?"

"You needed me here."

Quinn's gaze rested on the child sleeping in her arms. "Is he all right?"

She nodded, tears of joy sparkling in her eyes. "They didn't hurt him."

Relief washed through Quinn. "Where's Nardik and Alexxa?"

"I don't know."

"Take Steffon back to the ship. I'm going inside." When he was certain Seleena was safely away, Quinn glanced at Wyrick's ashes, wondering if he would be able to cross the threshold. Sometimes, when death had been committed in a house or the owner had been killed, the threshold lost its power. Was that also true for the homes of witches and wizards?

Quinn took a tentative step forward, felt the faint shimmer of magical energy as he crossed the threshold. Detouring around Wyrick's cooling ashes, he hurried down the dimly-lit hallway, the dragon at his heels.

A glance into the rooms they passed showed all were empty of life. Some had obviously been deserted quickly—candles left burning, a half-eaten meal on a table, a chair over-turned in haste.

Muttering, "Where the Hel did the rest of the coven go?" Quinn continued on down the corridor until he came to a stairway leading down to the next level. "What do you think, dragon?"

The beast made a soft, snuffling sound.

"Yeah, I was afraid of that."

With the dragon following close behind him, Quinn descended

the stairs cautiously, all his senses alert. He paused in front of the door at the end of the short hallway. There were people behind it—Nardik was one of them.

With a whispered, "Stay close, dragon," Quinn put his hand on the latch.

From inside the room, a deep voice called, "If you open that door, the child dies."

Shit! Quinn thought for a moment, then grinned. *Dragon, wait thirty seconds then break down the door. Got it?*

The dragon hissed in reply.

"I hope that's a yes," Quinn said dryly. Dissolving into mist, he slid under the crack between the door and the floor.

A tall, blond man held a baby against his chest, a wand in his free hand.

Nardik stood three feet away, his gaze fixed on his opponent, his own wand at the ready.

Stalemate.

Neither man seemed aware of the gray mist hovering near the ceiling.

Quinn counted the seconds in his head. When he reached twenty-nine, he materialized beside the blond.

At thirty, the dragon broke down the door.

Quinn grabbed the baby and tossed it to Nardik, then grasped the blond by the shoulders and sank his fangs into the man's throat.

The blood was very bitter, but very filling.

"You about done there?" Nardik asked as Quinn drained the life out of the witch.

Wiping the blood from his lips, Quinn let the dry husk fall to the floor. "Never let a good meal go to waste."

Nardik lifted one brow.

Was he amused, Quinn wondered, or repulsed? "Was that Annis' husband?"

"I believe so. Where is Seleena?"

"Waiting for us at the Airship, with Steffon." Quinn glanced around the room. "Where's Alexxa?"

Looking sheepish, Nardik muttered, "She got away."

"What? How the Hel did that happen?"

"There was a flurry of magic between Rajj and myself when I stepped into this room. In the confusion, she managed to slip out the door."

Quinn cursed under his breath. "Do you think she'll give us any trouble down the road?"

"If she is wise, she will stay out of my way."

"And mine." Looking at the dragon, Quinn held out his left arm. "Good job," he murmured, as the dragon shrank to rat-size, scurried to its customary place on his left shoulder, and melted into his skin.

Nardik smiled down at the pretty, curly-haired baby grasping his finger. "Corrie, I believe our work here is done."

* * *

Quinn felt the sting of tears in his eyes when he climbed on board and saw his son sleeping peacefully in Seleena's arms. It had all been worth it, he thought, as he settled into the seat beside her. All the pain, all the worry and anguish of heart and soul, none of it mattered now that they were all together again.

Seleena smiled at him, tears shining brightly in her own eyes as she clasped his hand in hers. There were no words to convey her feelings, she thought, not words enough in the entire universe to express her gratitude or her love.

"I don't need the words," Quinn said, squeezing her hand. "I love you, too. You're the bravest woman I've ever known."

Nardik boarded the ship a few minutes later. He nodded in Seleena's direction as he took the seat across the aisle.

Moments later, they were in the air, bound for home.

CHAPTER 17

Annis couldn't sit still, could scarcely contain her excitement. Ever since Nardik had sent word that the children were both safe and sound and were on their way home, she had been unable to relax or think of anything else. Corrie was safe! Soon, she would hold her precious daughter in her arms again. The thought made her so light-headed, she thought she might faint right there in front of everyone!

Oblivious to the others gathered in the Great Hall, she threw herself into Killian's arms when he entered the room. "Did you hear the good news?"

All too aware that he was in the presence of the Queen and her consort, not to mention several servants and a couple of court visitors, Killian gently disengaged himself from her embrace. "Just now," he said. "I'm so happy for you, Princess."

She frowned at him when he backed up several steps, putting a discreet distance between them. "What's wrong?"

Killian glanced around the room, hoping she would understand how unseemly it had been for her to throw herself at him when they weren't alone.

Comprehension dawned as Annis followed his gaze. The servants looked shocked. Her mother appeared bewildered. Gryff looked amused, while Marri seemed merely resigned.

Annis breathed a sigh of relief when the doors to the Great Hall burst open and Nardik strode into view, a blanket-wrapped bundle in his arms, thereby giving the others in the room something else to think about. Seleena trailed behind the wizard. Steffon slept in her arms, his head resting on her shoulder. Quinn brought up the rear.

Annis ran toward Nardik, her arms outstretched. Joy blossomed in her heart as he placed her daughter in her arms. "Bless you, all of you!" She ran her fingertips over Corrie's cheeks, then placed a kiss on her brow.

Looking up, Annis smiled at the three people who had risked their lives to find her daughter. "How can I ever repay you?" she asked, her voice thick with tears of gratitude.

"The look on your face is thanks enough, Princess," Nardik assured her.

Seleena and Quinn nodded in agreement, then followed Nardik across the room.

The wizard sketched a bow in Marri's direction, then went to stand beside Amerris.

Quinn also bowed to their Queen. Unable to curtsey properly with Steffon in her arms, Seleena bowed her head respectfully.

"We are forever in your debt," Marri said. "If there is ever anything you want, anything you need, you have only to ask and it's yours."

"That's most kind of you, your Majesty," Seleena said, smiling at the baby cradled in her arms. "But we have everything we need."

Marri looked at Quinn. "Have you any requests?"

He shook his head. "Like she said, we have everything we need."

Marri nodded. "The offer stands, nevertheless."

Gryff leaned forward. "One day, when you have the time, I'd like to hear about that dragon on your shoulder."

"Someday, I'll show it to you," Quinn promised, slipping his arm around Seleena's waist. "But not today. If you'll excuse us, we've been away from home far too long."

Gryff nodded his understanding. "Of course. Go with our thanks, both of you." He took Marri's hand and gave it a squeeze as Quinn and Seleena left the room.

After dismissing their visitors and the servants, Marri looked at

Nardik. "I would like to know what happened while you were searching for Corrie. Are there likely to be repercussions?"

"None that I can foresee."

"Were there deaths?"

He made a vague gesture with his hand. "It was necessary to...ah...dispose of a few rebellious witches."

Marri glanced at Annis, who had taken a chair in the corner, her attention riveted on her daughter. Killian stood at her side, his gaze fixed on Annis' face.

"What of Wyrick and his coven?" Gryff asked.

"Wyrick and his son are both dead," Nardik said quietly. "The other witches fled. I do not foresee any trouble coming from any of them."

"But it's possible?" Marri asked.

"As well you know, Majesty," Nardik answered with a rare grin, "anything is possible."

Marri's lips twitched in amusement. Truly an understatement. Her husband was a shapeshifter. Nardik was a wizard with extraordinary powers. Quinn was a vampire. Truly, anything was possible.

* * *

Annis stood at her chamber window, gazing at Brynn Tor's twin moons. Corrie was safely home, asleep in her cradle, apparently none the worse for her ordeal.

Rajj was dead, as was his father.

She tried to feel sorrow, sympathy. But all she felt was an overwhelming sense of relief that neither Rajj nor Wyrick would ever be able to hurt her or Corrie or anyone else again.

She was free, Annis mused, free of Rajj's enchantment. Free to marry again. She felt herself smiling as she thought of being Killian's wife, sharing his bed, having his children.

Killian. Even though it was late and she was in her nightgown, she went to the door, intending to call him, only to find that he wasn't standing guard in the corridor.

Frowning, she glanced up and down the long, narrow hallway, but he was nowhere to be seen.

He had been there every night these past weeks, she thought as she closed and locked the door. Why was he not there now?

* * *

When Killian was still absent in the morning, Annis went to Marri in search of answers. She found her sister in her private quarters, having breakfast with Rory while her infant daughter slept in her cradle.

Marri looked up as Annis entered the room. "Good morrow," she said, smiling. "Will you join me for a cup of chocolate and toast?"

"No, thank you. I've eaten. I was wondering…that is…um, did you reassign Killian to some other duty?"

Marri nodded. "With Corrie's return and the danger past, I didn't think you needed a bodyguard anymore. Are you sure you won't have something to eat? I can ring for Darrla."

Annis shook her head. "Where's Killian now?"

"Training with the other knights, I believe. How's Corrie?"

"I want him back."

"Annis, sit down."

Scowling, Annis did as she was told. "I want him back," she said again, more forcefully. "I need him."

"What you *need* is to think of your reputation," Marri chided gently. "The servants are already spreading gossip about the way you threw yourself into his arms yesterday."

"I don't care what they think. I don't care what anyone thinks."

"But I do. You're my sister, Princess of Brynn Tor, and you need to behave appropriately in public." Marri regarded Annis for a moment. "You're not still thinking of marrying him, are you?"

"What if I am? I know he wants me…"

"I have no doubt that he wants you," Marri said, choosing her words with care. "But are you sure he has marriage in mind?" She held up her hand when she saw the argument rising in her sister's eyes. "I'm sure he cares for you, Annie, but are you certain he wants to marry into the royal family with all that it entails? This life isn't for everyone, and it will be more difficult for him, not having been born to it."

"Gryff is doing all right," Annis said sullenly.

"Yes, he is, but it didn't come easily to him. And he still chafes at the responsibility from time to time."

"You just don't want me to marry him because you don't think he's a suitable match. Well, Gryff wasn't such a great match, either, until you made him a lord and awarded him several tracts of land in the North Country."

Marri sipped her chocolate. "It was no more than he deserved. He saved my life and the lives of others more than once."

"That's not why you rewarded him."

Annis was right, Marri admitted with a sigh. She had done it so she could marry Gryff. "Just promise me you won't rush into anything. Or do anything foolish, like running off together. If you want to marry Killian, and he wants to marry you, then you have my blessing. For propriety's sake, I ask that you wait at least six months. You're a recent widow, after all. Since few outside of Brynn Castle know the full extent of Rajj's treachery, to most it would appear unseemly for you to marry so quickly."

Six months! It seemed a lifetime, but now that she thought about it, Annis knew Marri was right. Any court gossip directed at her behavior now might stain Corrie's reputation in the future.

"The time will go fast," Marri assured her.

Annis nodded dubiously.

"Remember who you are. Your wedding will be an occasion of state. We have much to do while you're waiting, assuming Killian wants this marriage as much as you do. Announcements will have to be sent to heads of state. We'll have to decide on a menu. We need to find a suitable position for Killian."

Jumping to her feet, Annis threw her arms around Marri's neck. "I said it before and I'll say it again. You're the best sister in the whole galaxy."

"I'm glad you think so, but the man in question hasn't yet asked for your hand."

CHAPTER 18

For the second time in his life, Killian found himself standing before his Queen.

"I'll come right to the point," Marri said. "Annis is in love with you. I know she was married before but she's still very young. I need to know how you feel about her before things go any further. Or too far, if you take my meaning."

Killian felt a wave of heat climb up the back of his neck and stain his cheeks. "Your Majesty, I..."

"You may speak freely. Anything you say will remain between the two of us."

Killian cleared his throat. "I love Annis with all my heart. I know nothing can ever come of my feelings for her, but I swear to you that I haven't defiled her in any way. I would never..."

"You misunderstand me. Annis wishes to marry you."

"Marriage?" Stunned, Killian blinked at her. "Annis wants to marry *me*?"

"You seem surprised."

"That doesn't begin to cover it," he said.

:"Do you love my sister?"

"Yes, Majesty, more than my own life."

"Do you wish to marry her?"

He nodded, unable to speak, unable to believe he was being offered something he had never, in a thousand lifetimes, thought possible.

"Then I'll leave the rest to you."

Killian bowed, then turned and left the room, a spring in his step Marri had never seen before.

Sitting back, she closed her eyes, remembering how desperately she had yearned to be Gryff's wife. They had been through Hel and back before they could be together, but it had been worth every pain, every sacrifice. Sometimes the road to love was strewn with rocks and thorns, she mused with a wry smile, but when that love was real, it always seemed to find a way to turn the thorns into roses.

* * *

Mind reeling, Killian left the Great Hall. He had the Queen's permission to marry Annis, something he would never have foreseen. Doubts crowded his mind as he made his way up the stairs to Annis' chambers. She was of royal blood. He came from peasant stock. It had taken years of arduous effort to work his way into service in Brynn Castle, to prove he was good enough, strong enough, loyal enough to wear the King's colors. But to be part of the royal family...he shook his head. It was a miracle.

He paused outside Annis' door, hoping the Queen wasn't playing some cruel trick on him and that Annis truly wished to be his wife. He took a deep breath, and then another, before knocking.

Killian took a step back as the door flew open and Annis launched herself into his arms.

"I'm glad to see you, too," he murmured.

"Where have you been?"

"I had an audience with the Queen."

"With Marri?" Feeling suddenly sick to her stomach, Annis wrapped her arms around her waist. Had Marri changed her mind about allowing her and Killian to wed? Was she sending him away? Had he come to tell her goodbye? "What did she want?"

"Nothing bad. Maybe we should go inside," he suggested as one of the castle maids came up the stairs.

Annis nodded woodenly. If it wasn't bad news, why did they have to go inside? She walked to the window and looked out, flinched when he shut the door.

"Annis?"

She turned slowly to face him, only to blink in astonishment when she saw he was down on one knee. When he held out his hand, she walked toward him, felt her insides quiver when his fingers closed over hers.

"I love you, Annis," he declared. "Will you do me the honor of being my wife?"

She tried to speak but her mouth was suddenly dry, her vision blurred by tears of joy. He loved her. She read the truth in the depths of his eyes. Honest brown eyes that would never deceive her. There was no dark magic in this man. None at all.

"Annis?"

"Of course I'll marry you."

The words were scarcely out of her mouth when he sprang to his feet, wrapped her in his arms, and twirled her around the floor.

Save for her daughter's birth, it was the happiest moment of her life.

* * *

Annis sighed as Killian kissed her cheek. Marri had been so wrong, she thought glumly. The time did *not* go by fast. True, there was much to do and every day was filled with wedding preparations of one kind or another, and still the hours seemed to crawl by. She felt as if she had been waiting for five years instead of five months. In a few weeks, Marri would announce their engagement, and they would wed the following month.

In the interim, by Marri's degree, Killian had been given command of the Queen's army. She had also granted him title to a grand estate located on a large parcel of verdant land adjacent to Brynn Castle. It was a lovely old place set among towering pines. Annis had visited there once, years ago, and fallen in love with the house, with its beautifully frescoed ceilings and stained glass windows.

Marri had forbidden Annis to be alone there with Killian until they were wed.

"It's a beautiful night," Killian murmured. "And there's a beautiful woman at my side. What more could any man ask?"

Annis smiled up at him as they strolled hand-in-hand through the castle gardens. Killian was as different from Rajj as summer from winter. There was no guile in her beloved's eyes, no deceit in his voice. She knew, with every fiber of her being, that he truly loved her, as she loved him.

She chafed at having to wait another two months to become his wife. Even though she understood Marri's reasons for making them wait, the waiting grew harder with every passing day. What made it even worse was pretending to be in mourning for a husband she had never loved, a man who had kidnapped her daughter, then left Annis for dead in the bowels of the citadel.

But the worst part about not being Killian's wife was being unable to share his nights. And his bed. Sometimes she thought she might go mad with wanting him.

"Annis?"

"I wish we could just run away and get married tonight."

Drawing her into his arms, he said, "I know, sweeting. I know." He kissed her again, his hand sliding up and down her back, pulling her closer as he deepened the kiss.

She leaned into him, her body aching with need as she slid her hands under his shirt. She was sorely tempted to sneak him into her room, might have done so if the lights strung through the trees in the garden hadn't started flickering.

Annis grinned inwardly, knowing it was Marri's not-so-subtle way of telling them that it was time for Killian to go home.

He groaned softly, as reluctant as she to say good night. "Until tomorrow," he murmured.

"Tomorrow," she repeated wistfully.

One last kiss and he was out the garden gate.

Annis sighed as she returned to her chambers.

Two more months until they could go home together and be a family. It seemed like forever.

* * *

And, suddenly, the day of the wedding was upon her.

Annis woke with butterflies in her stomach and a smile on her face. By tonight, she would be Killian's wife, free to hold him and touch him and love him as much and as often as she wished.

Annis was too nervous to eat, but her mother and Marri urged her to do so.

After a quick breakfast, the three of them went into Annis' room to get ready for the ceremony, which would take place in the Winter Grove Chapel, which wasn't a chapel at all, but an ancient church hewn from glistening marble and onyx.

Amerris held Corrie, patting the baby's back as she watched her two daughters.

Annis sat in front of her dressing table while Marri brushed her hair until it snapped and crackled. "Up?" she asked. "Or down?"

"Down," Annis said, smiling at her sister in the mirror. "Killian likes it that way, you know."

Marri smiled back, a silent prayer of thanksgiving rising in her heart. Annis was home again, apparently none the worse for her ordeal at Rajj's hands, and happier than Marri had ever seen her. Her cheeks were pink, her eyes bright with hope for the future.

Annis' wedding gown was made of yards and yards of pale pink silk and lace that fell to the floor in graceful folds. The bodice was square, the skirt sprinkled with crystals that twinkled in the lamplight. Matching crystals adorned her hair. A silver locket, wedding gift from her betrothed, nestled in the hollow of her throat.

"You look positively radiant," Marri said as she set the floor-length veil in place.

Annis beamed at her. "I feel beautiful. And oh, so lucky."

"If you ask me," Amerris said, "it's Killian who's lucky." She placed Corrie in her crib, kissed her forehead, then turned and gave her youngest daughter a hug. "I wish you every happiness, child."

"As do I," Marri said, wrapping her arms around her mother and sister. "We all have much to be thankful for this day."

There was a knock at the door and then Gryff poked his head in. "Hey, bride, are you ready yet?" he asked with a wicked grin. "The groom's getting impatient."

* * *

The beautiful old church adjacent to the castle was filled with people, most of whom Annis had never met. Heads of state, clerics, dignitaries visiting from other planets, and the like. All dressed in their best. All hoping their presence would be noted and remembered by the Queen against the time they might need a private audience, a favor, a pardon.

Moonlight peeked through the stained glass windows, casting rainbow shadows on the floor and the ancient walls. The soft glow of a hundred candles filled the room with a pale golden light. Bouquets of white flowers and green ferns adorned the altar, a white runner covered the center aisle.

Marri sat in the front pew, along with Amerris and Nardik, Quinn and Seleena.

But Annis had eyes only for Killian. Clad in a fine black jacket, crisp white shirt, black trousers and boots, he stood in front of the altar, hands clasped in front of him, looking every bit as nervous as she felt. His hair was slicked back, save for one wayward lock that fell across his brow.

Gryff walked her down the aisle, kissed her lightly on the cheek, and then solemnly placed her hand in Killian's.

Annis' heart skipped a beat as Killian's fingers closed around hers. At his touch, her nerves dissolved like morning dew. She scarcely heard the words the priest said until he asked, "Do you, Killian, take this woman to be your lawful wife according to the rites and laws of Brynn Tor?"

She held her breath as she waited for Killian's answer.

"I do."

"And do you, Annis, take this man to be your lawful husband according to the rites and laws of Brynn Tor?"

"I do!"

"Then, by the authority granted to me, I now pronounce you husband and wife."

Butterflies took flight in Annis' stomach as Killian drew her gently into his arms. "I will love you every day of my life for as long as I live," he said fervently, and sealed his pledge with his first husbandly kiss.

Sitting in the front pew, Marri took Gryff's hand and gave it a squeeze. "And just like the Queen and her handsome consort," she murmured, wiping a tear from her eye, "they all lived happily ever after."

Chapter 19

Quinn stood outside, letting the cool night air envelop him. Crickets and tree frogs serenaded the night. A faint breeze stirred the leaves of the trees. He had been vaguely troubled for the last few weeks, though he could not say why. But for this moment, as he gazed up at Brynn Tor's twin moons, he felt utterly at peace. Seleena was waiting for him in their bed. Their son slept in his cradle, and all was right with the world.

Earlier, they had attended Annis' wedding. The bride had been beautiful, the groom obviously ill-at-ease in the company of so many high-ranking men and women. Quinn didn't know if it had been the press of so many bodies, the stink of so much cooked food, the scent of so much blood, or the beating of so many hearts, but it had filled with him a growing restlessness.

The dragon had sensed his agitation. Quinn had felt the whip of its tail. Seleena, bless the woman, had also been aware of his distress. Taking him aside, she had suggested they leave when the first toast to the happy couple was over.

He had felt better when they were back home, but now, he was again plagued by the same sense of unease that had never been far from his mind. He told himself he was imagining trouble where there was none.

His love for Seleena and his son grew stronger, deeper, every day.

Steffon was thriving, a happy, healthy child more given to laughter than tears.

There had been peace in the land for the last seven months. Save for Alexxa, they had vanquished all their enemies. Still, it troubled him that the witch had so easily given Nardik the slip back on Callidori. Even more troubling was the fact that she lived on Brynn Tor. Had she returned to her home in Ironntown? He told himself the witch would not be so foolish as to come back here looking for revenge, not when it meant contending with the dragon.

And yet, he had killed her sister, scattered Wyrick's coven, threatened her life. People had sought vengeance for far less.

He lifted a hand to the tattoo on his shoulder, wondering, as he had in the past, exactly how powerful the dragon was. Sometimes he had the feeling that the creature was an actual, living, thinking being and not just some magical hologram capable of inflicting death and destruction.

Quinn? Seleena's voice whispered in the back of his mind, soft and sexy and filled with promise. *It grows late and my arms grow lonely without you.*

A thought took him to her side.

"What troubles you?" she asked as he slid into bed beside her.

"Nothing for you to fret about, Red," he assured her as he drew her into his embrace. Her body molded to his, a living flame in his arms, stirring his passion and his hunger. And his never-ending need for this woman and no other.

He moaned softly as she caressed him, her touch igniting his desire even as it soothed his hunger.

He rose over her, lost in the love he read in her eyes. His worries about the future would keep until tomorrow.

Tonight, he wanted only the warmth of his woman's body against his, her arms tight around him, her love enfolding him this night and every night for as long as he lived.

Epilogue

The dragon stirred when it was certain its host was asleep. It slithered down the vampire's arm, growing in size and shape as its feet touched the floor.

The witch's cat hissed and darted under the bed, then stared out at him through unblinking yellow eyes.

Amused by the furry little creature, the dragon left the house by the back door.

Outside, he rose to his full twelve-foot height. It felt good to stretch his legs and his wings. He lifted his head, breathing in the cool night air, drinking in the sights, and the smells born to him on the breeze. Lesser creatures scurried out of his path as he strolled through the gardens.

The dragon glanced back at the house. His host, the woman, and the child, all slept peacefully, unaware that he took on physical form every night in order to guard their home and their lives. Unaware of the danger heading this way. He could smell it, taste it on his tongue.

It tasted like death.

Taking to the skies, he soared over the sleeping village, ever alert to the slightest movement below, to any hint of danger.

When he was certain all was well, he returned to the yard. His charges slept on, ignorant of the fact that it hadn't been a spell gone wrong that bound him to the man Quinn, and his family.

No, the dragon thought, folding his wings, it had been his own choice to accept Quinn as his master. Though the evil witch, Serepta, had conjured him from ink, the blood of a young dragon, and her own dark magic, she had also imbued with him with greater power than she realized.

It made him the master of his own fate, granted him the ability to decide who he would serve. And who he would destroy.

Someday, he would tell Quinn.

And it would change everything.

ABOUT THE AUTHOR

Amanda Ashley is one of those rare birds—a California native. She's lived in Southern California her whole life and loves it. She married her high school sweetheart, and they have three sons, all handsome enough to be cover models!

Amanda never intended to be a published author. It just happened. She has always loved to read, though—Mary Stewart, Louis L'Amour, Zane Gray. And then she discovered romance novels. One night, when her husband was at work, and her kids were in bed, and there was nothing on TV, she sat down and started writing a book of her own. And she's been writing ever since.

Amanda also writes historical romances as Madeline Baker. She has published over 90 books and novellas, many of which have appeared on various bestseller lists, including the New York Times and USA Today.

www.amandaashley.net
www.madelinebaker.net

www.ingramcontent.com/pod-product-compliance
Lightning Source LLC
Chambersburg PA
CBHW070434120726
47910CB00003B/780